COST OF ATTAINMENT

RULES DUOLOGY

ALEX LANE

To my wonderful husband, thank you for pushing me to the finish line.

1 CLARA

Three days. They'd been back for three days. They'd been out of Noxvalis for a week. And still, none of it felt real. Clara felt the world pass by in a blur.

She stood at attention. She answered the questions Command presented. No, there hadn't been 10 vials. Only 9. No, they hadn't had an opportunity to stop Carver from being taken. Yes, she had seen the experiments. Yes, they were atrocious. Yes, Quorath had every reason to fear what Noxvalis was capable of. No, she hadn't seen the king. Yes, she had failed on the private assignment they had given her. She, of course, presented her deepest apologies, though her heart wasn't in it.

She could tell they didn't believe her. Her heart ached, but not from their disappointment.

She was halfway through the questioning on the third day, and she was drawing on all her training to stay focused. "I have reason to believe Noxvalis presents a greater threat than the vials would indicate. Their biological experiments are terrifying, to be sure, but they have the items they need to dirty bomb all of Quorath."

Every person in the seats for Command leaned forward, "And this is the first time you are mentioning it, Operative Harris?"

"My apologies," Marsh lowered her eyes in deference, "I wanted to ensure we answered all of your questions on our first assignment before I addressed another problem."

Clara could have sworn the woman rolled her eyes. "Continue, Operative Harris." She said firmly.

"The last shipment came in two days before Clara and Carver arrived. I had heard rumors they were creating dirty bombs, but I thought it would be impossible for them to get that much of a radioactive substance. I also heard rumors they bombed a few towns a couple days from Noxvalis. I didn't believe those rumors to be true."

"But?" The woman prodded, clearly annoyed by Marsh's run around on information.

"We passed through those towns on our way back to base. They were ghost towns. It looks as though people packed up and left. It's possible some of them were warned, but for the rest...families don't leave photos of their children on the mantle by choice."

Collectively, Command seemed to shrink away from them, desperate to put a few extra inches of air between them and the Operatives standing before them. Clara turned suddenly, staring at Marsh as though she didn't recognize her. Not once during their trip did Marsh mention anything to her about this theory. The entire trip, she made it immensely clear she wanted nothing to do with Clara. But this? This was information Clara had a right to know!

"The only form of radioactive material they would be able to obtain and stabilize has a half-life of 74 days. It isn't long enough to remain a risk. By the time we passed through, the effects would have been nonexistent." Marsh clarified.

"If what you say is true, what are the effects of this type of dirty bomb? Wouldn't you have found bodies in the towns, Operative Harris?"

"They have enough materials to bomb all of Quorath. The first effect is shrapnel. Bombs exploding in every town will cause mass panic. And the effects of the radiation? Burns and weakness at best, acute radiation poisoning and death at worst. They will weaken us, allowing Noxvalis to swoop in and decimate us. I can't imagine Noxvalis wants us to know how close they've gotten to us. I'm certain they removed the bodies either to burn or for their own experimentation."

"Hmm. How confident are you in this information? You did say it was information you collected from rumors." Aside from the one woman, all of Command sat perfectly still. Clara barely breathed, anxious that anything she did would make this situation reflect poorly on her as well. This was Marsh's problem to deal with.

Marsh lifted her chin, "I was right about the vials. I am right about this. I would stake my life on it."

"In a war, it may come to that. You are both dismissed, for now. You may resume a normal life on base until further summoned."

Clara turned to leave, but Marsh didn't budge. "I'm not kidding about the bombs. I know which lab their materials are stored in. We have to do something, or they will wipe us out."

"Your concerns are heard, Operative Harris. Please follow your orders. If you are needed, we will summon you."

Marsh's fists clenched, and Clara waited for another outburst. Instead, her shoulders slumped, and she turned to follow Clara.

As soon as the Command doors closed behind them, Clara turned on Marsh. "What the hell was that? You knew those towns were abandoned by radiation? Don't you think this was information I had a right to know?"

"I'm not doing this with you." Marsh chuckled mirthlessly. She began walking down the Raven hallway, but Clara grabbed her wrist and spun her back. Marsh broke her hold and stared her down. "I suggest you return to your sector."

"What else do you know you aren't telling us?" Clara searched Marsh's eyes, not sure what she was looking for.

"I watched you leave your partner to die. Do you really think you're the person I'm going to trust with anything I know? Go to hell, Clara." Marsh spat her name like it was bitter in her mouth.

Clara felt the words like a knife in her chest. The guilt she carried for days came back in a rush of pain, and she had to remind herself to breathe. Marsh continued walking away, down the hall to the Raven sector. Into the sector Carver belonged to. But he wasn't here to follow her.

2 CLARA

Over the past week, Clara had slept only when exhaustion had dragged her under. And every time she succumbed to it, she regretted the choice. Tonight was no different. She woke up, drenched in sweat, Carver's name ringing through her head.

She forced herself out of bed and into her training clothes.

She braided her hair back, avoiding even a glance in her mirror as she finished readying herself. She wasn't prepared to see her reflection and confirm she was the monster she feared she was becoming. The insides of her cheeks were raw, and she probed the spots with her tongue as she focused on braiding her hair.

She closed her eyes, taking a deep breath in and out. Carver's face flashed across the inside of her eyelids. The determination as he lifted the gun. His braced stance. He hadn't hesitated. Bang. She ran. Her chest tightened, so she counted her breaths. It didn't release.

Shaking the images from her head, she stepped out of her room and walked to the dining hall. The din was comfortably familiar, but she found no relief in being back. Her skin crawled through the noise. She grabbed a tray and pushed it down the line, filling it enough to satisfy her before training.

Then she automatically walked to the table she and Reese usually sat at. It was a force of habit. Reese wasn't there yet, and Clara began eating in silence. She wished she could say she had missed her friend, but right now all she wanted was to be alone.

Her request was granted for less than five minutes before Reese slid in across from her. The usual energy that radiated off her was dulled by her concern for Clara. She didn't say anything for a few minutes, and Clara could feel the unspoken words hanging like a weight between them.

Finally, they suffocated her. "I'm back," she tried to smile, but the words fell flat.

She kept her left hand under the table, pressing her thumb nail under her middle finger nail. She thought the pain would lessen the pain in her heart. She pretended it worked. She wasn't running from the table.

Reese nodded. "And…" she didn't continue.

"And the girl we met in Noxvalis came back with me."

Reese ate a bite with no response, and Clara knew Reese wouldn't push her. "He didn't come back with us." She finally admitted. The words felt like a poison drenching her lungs. How could she have left him? But she did. She had.

Reese nodded, adding no words to the conversation. No sympathy, no hugs. She just sat there, granting Clara's unspoken request for silence.

"I know it was my fault." Clara was still drowning in the silence. It was what she thought she wanted, but her own thoughts were scarier than anything anyone else could say. Reese was the closest person she had to a friend, and she had to tell someone. If she didn't, she would truly drown. She would sink beneath the waves of her thoughts and never pull herself out. *Maybe it would be better.*

"Clara, you're always this hard on yourself. You need to give yourself grace. You're an amazing operative. I'm sure this wasn't your fault." Reese sympathized immediately. She was always the optimist.

"No, you don't understand." Clara's voice almost broke, but she controlled it. Inhale. Exhale. This was her fault; she could, and would, take full responsibility.

"You've always blamed yourself for things entirely out of your control." Reese continued to make excuses for her. She really was a good friend, even if she wasn't being honest about Clara's true character.

"Reese. It *was* my fault." Clara shut her eyes tightly. She couldn't be more blunt. She had to make her understand. Someone else needed to see the monster she was.

"Okay, I'll play along," Reese finally acquiesced, "Why was it your fault?"

Clara took a deep breath in as she began her story, "We had an assignment. Together. But they gave us separate papers. My orders were to leave him to his own devices after I retrieved the vials. If he didn't make it, that wasn't up to me."

"What?" Reese's jaw dropped. "They wanted you to sacrifice him? That's so messed up."

Clara shook her head, "If I had followed their orders I think I could have lived with myself. Like if that was the only way. Because I didn't have a choice, right? Carver," she swallowed back the pain at saying his name, "Carver didn't realize I was brought onto the mission to go in and kill everyone in our way."

Reese held up a hand, "You're literally an assassin. What did he think you were there for?"

Clara exhaled, "I don't know. He said he was going to go in without me. That he didn't need me. He was trying to cut me out of the assignment." She bit her lower lip, prodding the split, prepared for the moment her friend realized what a terrible person she is, "I decided to do some recon work on my own. It worked really well. I actually managed to steal a keycard from a guard who thought I was a drunk Calyndor girl."

"Damn, girl, pop off." Reese grinned.

Clara shook her head, not smiling in return. "I was so proud of myself. So excited to show him my contribution to the mission. So excited to finally prove myself to him. It was so dumb. So damn stupid."

"What happened?" Reese gently prodded.

"He wasn't there when I got back to the bookstore we were staying in. You see, the girl we were staying with had immediately developed a crush on Carver." Clara flinched inwardly at his name in her mouth.

"And that's the girl you brought back with you?" Reese quickly caught on.

"Yes. So I came back to the house with a plan for how we could succeed. He wasn't there. I went looking for him and found him in a bar with her."

"Nooooo." Reese grimaced.

"Kissing her," Clara added.

Reese's jaw dropped, "You're kidding. She stole your man like that?"

Clara rolled her eyes, "He wasn't my man. I made it very clear I didn't want him to be my man."

Reese slammed her hand on the table, and Clara flinched. "Bullshit, Clara. You've been in love with him for the last three years."

Clara blinked away the tears that filled her eyes. "That's not true." She sniffed, bringing herself back into the moment. "Anyway, I decided I could fulfill the assignment without him. He wanted to cut me out, and I knew I could pull it off."

"So you went in alone." Reese supplied. Clara couldn't look at Reese now.

"Yes. At first, everything went well. I didn't see anyone. The labs were abandoned in the middle of the night. But, Reese, the things I saw." She shuddered involuntarily. "They had babies in capsules of fluid, splicing their genes with other things, changing these children into creatures."

Reese grimaced.

"It was awful. I don't think I'll ever get those images out of my mind. And the people there? When we saw them displayed for the festival, the people jeered. They laugh and jeer at the creatures, calling them abominations and making them perform for the crowd. But they were all people once." She closed her eyes against the memories.

"I can't even imagine having to watch that." Reese softened her voice.

Clara blinked away the memories, returning to her story. "Anyway, the lab was empty, except for one man who came into the room with all the creatures. I did what had to be done." Reese nodded, no disgust found in her features. They were Vipers, after all. They always did what had to be done.

"Then I found the lab with all of the vials. It was labeled exactly as Command had written it would be. There weren't 10 vials, though. I only found 9. I put them into a bag after wrapping them in towels. I didn't encounter anyone else. I made it to the end of the hallway, to the door I could leave from after the guard change. Then the alarms went off.

Soldiers began pouring in from the hallway I had come from. But thankfully, the hallway was tight enough that they could only fit one after the other. I honestly can't remember exactly what happened. I just know I kept fighting. When the doors behind me opened, I thought I was done for."

"What happened??" Reese leaned forward, her fingers grasping the edge of the table as Clara continued.

"Carver." Saying his name again didn't hurt as badly. "He had a pistol and started shooting at the guards, screaming for me to run. It was enough of a distraction. I ran into the forest and quickly made it to a back alleyway where I shed my blood-covered clothes so I wouldn't stand out. Then I went back to the bookstore."

Reese tilted her head, her eyebrows narrowing, "So you succeeded. You got the vials. And you brought them here."

"He didn't come back. I don't know if they captured or killed him." Clara's voice was barely a whisper. "It's all my fault he's not here, too. If we had gone in together, we could have both made it out."

"You don't know that, Clara." Reese shook her head.

Clara's posture crumpled anyway. "But I do. I have to live with his blood on my hands."

Reese didn't have a response for that. She continued to sit there with Clara, both falling into a painful silence. Clara didn't blame her. What could she say?

3 CLARA

Clara wore herself out in the training room, training straight through dinner. Reese came in to check on her, but even she didn't bother trying to drag Clara out. When Clara could barely move, she finally decided it was time to head to bed. She showered quickly, struggling to lift her arms from the hours-long session she put them through.

There was pleasure in the pain. Her body still listened to her, even if it was sore and weak from the traveling and lack of consistency the last couple of weeks. She climbed into her bed, pulling the covers over her head and falling asleep.

Unfortunately, it wasn't a dreamless sleep. Only a few hours later, she sat straight up, sweat dripping down her body, her breaths coming in gasps. She blinked quickly, attempting to dispel the images. Surely Carver was dead. They hadn't turned him into a…monstrosity. She had to believe they killed him. She couldn't live with herself if it were anything else.

She paced her room until the clock showed 0600, a time she deemed appropriate to be found in the training room. Any earlier, and there was always the chance of her being reported unstable to Command. She was disciplined if she was there at 0600.

She *felt* unstable, but if she was labeled that, they would restrict her movement. And she had always used movement as a cure for the neuroticism that plagued her. She'd have to talk to that hellish psychiatrist Command had brought in a few years prior.

Reese found her shortly before breakfast. "I had a feeling you'd be here again."

Clara barely nodded, focusing on her posture as she lifted a set of weights. "You need to come to breakfast."

"Why?" Clara responded, grunting through the weight.

"It doesn't benefit anyone if you run yourself into the ground. You have to keep going." Reese answered casually, arms crossed over her chest as she leaned against the doorframe.

"Why?"

"It's not time for you to die yet."

Clara rolled her eyes, breathing heavily, "At least if I die, I don't have to worry about getting other operatives killed."

"Oh, whatever. You can't die yet. You're my friend, and I happen to like you alive. Besides, you can still do some good."

"I don't believe you. Didn't you hear my story yesterday?" Clara dropped the weights in frustration, turning her full attention to Reese. "I'm a danger to everyone around me. You shouldn't even be friends with me. I'm a monster."

Reese shrugged, "Everyone makes mistakes. The question is, can you learn from those mistakes and do better next time?"

"I fucking killed someone!!!" Clara shouted, all of the pent-up anger releasing in her tone.

"You're literally an assassin," Reese answered evenly, unmoved by Clara's outburst. "You kill people as a career. Weird life choice if you're this sensitive about it."

Clara deflated, "I got my best friend killed."

"Ouch, I thought that was me."

"Ha ha," Clara answered mirthlessly.

"Carver chose to sacrifice himself for you. Make his sacrifice worth something." Reese shook her head, "I can't imagine he would be too happy knowing you're not sleeping or eating. He might feel like his death wasn't worth much. He considered his life worth yours; it's time you do the same."

Reese left, leaving Clara's head spinning. Was she right? Had Carver valued her life that much? She closed her eyes, seeing him standing there, gun pointed awkwardly. *"Run, Clara, run!"* His voice echoed through her head.

Once the memory became too painful, she headed to the dining hall. She grabbed a tray, avoiding eye contact with any of the operatives around her as she walked through the line. Then she joined Reese at their table.

Reese smiled at her, "See? Doesn't it feel better to be in the land of the living?"

"No." Clara answered, eating quickly.

"Well, at least you're eating, I guess." Reese's chatter didn't continue, though Clara didn't notice. She was far too focused on eating and keeping her food down to care what anyone else was doing.

Once she was done, she stood without commenting. "See you for lunch." Reese stated.

"Don't push it." Clara picked up her tray, reluctantly adding, "I'll be here for dinner."

Reese smiled and clapped her hands, prompting a slight smile from Clara, "Excellent, I consider this progress!"

"Is this all because I skipped dinner last night?"

"And because you've been here for three days and haven't deigned to check in with me even once. I got worried. I thought you might be unable to walk or something." Reese pouted.

"Command had us in for questioning."

"For three days? Huh, that's interesting. You'll have to fill me in on that tonight." Reese picked up her own tray. "We'll manage to break this depression off you somehow."

"If only it was that easy." Clara muttered as she dumped her tray and added it to the stack.

She walked quickly to her room to get her hand wraps before her next self-assigned training. A few operatives cleared out of her way, eyeing her nervously. She wondered what had been said about her while she was gone, and since she'd returned.

The other operatives had always given her some amount of berth. Her success on assignments remained unparalleled, and her ruthlessness during challenges their first year here had caused many operatives to permanently avoid her. She preferred it this way. Yet she'd never seen them shrink to the opposite side of the hallway when she passed.

She shook off the weirdness, grabbed her hand wraps and headed back to the training room. She slowly wrapped her hands, legs wide as she stretched them. She counted her breaths, attempting to clear her mind.

Once she was in front of the bag, she went through her practiced routine. She punched, kicked, and shifted her weight, keeping her body lithe but strong. The blows stung her knuckles, but she relished the pain. She was so focused, she didn't hear the training room door open as the newest class of Vipers filed in.

She kept her gaze honed on the bag, tuning them out. She forgot that graduation from basics was the week they were gone. Yay. Her favorite. A new segment of kids who had no idea what the real world held from them.

"Operative Richards!" She straightened when her name was called, turning to face the trainer. It was Misty Ashton. She had been one of Clara's trainers. They had caught up briefly before Clara's last assignment, but Clara hadn't shared anything related to the actual assignment. She still wouldn't. Clara nodded at her respectfully. Misty respected Clara for the assignments she continued to take on. During Clara's first year, she was still sent on assignments. But when she got pregnant in Clara's second year, Misty took on a permanent position as a trainer.

She nodded to Misty, "Operative Ashton."

Misty held a hand out to Clara as the class watched, "This is one of our best Vipers. I'm sure you've heard the rumors about 'the Eclipse'?" Her voice dropped into a conspiratorial tone.

The class gasped, looking at Clara wide eyed. She knew the class was only three years younger than her, but Clara felt like there was a lifetime between them. As she looked at their faces, she saw the innocence she couldn't remember having anymore.

Clara smiled tightly, knowing she would have a few words for Misty later on for this. She knew Misty would just ignore her. "Operative Richards, or 'Eclipse', what words of wisdom would you give for our newest class?" Misty asked expectantly.

The class gazed at her, expectation in their eyes. They were so desperate for her to say something, for her to be a voice of encouragement as they worked towards what she was. But how could she want anyone else to become a monster? "However awful you think the war is, however awful you think it will be to kill someone, it is so much worse. There is no hope here. The sooner you learn that, the better."

Eyes widened, and jaws dropped. Misty grimaced, "Operative Richards just returned from a long assignment. We'll ask her again once she has a few more days to recover. Now, today we will practice..."

Clara stormed out of the room, letting the door slam behind her.

In the hallway, she bent over, putting her hands on her knees. She breathed deeply, trying not to let the panic climb her throat. It started slowly, the spiraling anxiety in her belly. Then it clamped her chest, until it wrapped around her esophagus. She slid to the ground, unable to care if anyone saw her as she buried her face in her knees.

She reminded herself to breathe slowly. In and out, in and out. She pinched her wrists, digging her fingers in, begging the pain to ground her, but it wasn't enough. Eventually, Clara allowed herself to truly remember him. Since she had come back, Command had buried her in questions and she hadn't been willing to let herself think back to what actually happened. To Carver. She told Reese what happened, but explaining the events was different than remembering him.

She hadn't thought about his smiles. About the festival when he kissed her in an alley, her hands pinned above her head, her gut twisting as she looked at him. Desperate. Then, what felt like a betrayal with Marsh.

Marsh. She needed to know what else Marsh knew about Noxvalis.

If Marsh had kept the information about the bombs quiet, what else was she keeping hidden?

With a directive in mind, Clara shook the heaviness off and stood to her feet. She walked quickly down the path towards Command, determination in every step. Marsh may not like her, but Clara needed her information.

The bell rang for lunch, making Clara's destination easy. She walked through the halls, assuming without thinking it through that the Raven's sector would mirror the Viper's. It did. She marched into the dining hall, eyes scanning the room. It felt so much like the Vipers. People were getting food, talking, and smiling. The color of their clothing was lighter than the Viper's. Instead of a sea of black, the room was filled with grays and browns—only the occasional pop of black.

Her eyes finally landed on Marsh. She had expected Marsh to be sitting alone, still figuring out how to behave back in the sector after so much time away from it. But no, she was sitting at a table surrounded by other Ravens. They were all talking and laughing; Marsh was the center of attention. Clara snarled.

She walked to her, standing across the table from her.

"We need to talk." Her voice was firm enough to cut through the din, and the table silenced with the authority in her tone.

"No, we don't." Marsh's voice stayed sugar sweet, her smile still pasted for her onlookers.

Clara scoffed, "Bold choice. But you know we do."

"I don't know any such thing." Marsh continued her sugar-sweet charade. A few of the Ravens at the table fidgeted with their food, not taking their eyes off the exchange.

Clara exhaled heavily, "Marsh, get your shit together and come talk to me. Or are Ravens so pathetic they can't handle a fucking conversation?" The other Ravens at the table looked at her with wide eyes. A few of them tilted their heads toward her, as if impressed by her guts.

Marsh clenched her jaw, but didn't let her smile drop. "Fine."

"I'm soooo glad you aren't afraid of a conversation," she smiled, waving to the rest of the Ravens as she led the way to the hallway.

Marsh remained silent behind her until they were far enough from the dining hall that they wouldn't be overheard. She crossed her arms over her chest, glaring at Clara, "I had hoped with our differences in sector we could finally get the space we needed from each other. It's far too soon for me to be willing to interact with you." Her words were careful.

"Great. What else do you know about Noxvalis?"

"I know many things. None of which do I wish to share with you."

Clara opened her arms defensively, holding up her hands, "It's not like I want to be here. I need to know."

Marsh tightened her hold on her arms, "Why, Clara? Why do you need to know? So you can botch the next assignment just like you did this one?"

"I retrieved the vials," Clara responded, careful to keep her tone from becoming defensive. The only thing worse than talking to Marsh was letting Marsh have something over her while they were talking.

"You didn't, though." Marsh smirked, "You retrieved nine vials. Meaning Noxvalis still has one. So. You failed. Big whoop. It's time you learn to accept that. Little girl, grow up. "

Clara took a breath, slowly exhaling before she responded, "That's aside from the point. What else does Command need to know about Noxvalis?"

"I told them everything relevant for the time being." Marsh didn't budge.

"Then you are hiding information?"

Marsh rolled her eyes, "Hiding is such a condemning word. I am, hmm, withholding information until the time is right to share it with Command. What I know doesn't benefit them now. No need to waste both of our time."

Scoffing, Clara answered, "What a diplomatic way of avoiding the truth. You're hiding information!" She threw up her hands, "What? Did your time in Noxvalis so corrupt you that you now play for both sides? What do you gain by not telling them?"

This finally hit a nerve, and Marsh's eyes flashed in anger. "I don't have anywhere else to go. You want to know why I'm "hiding" information? Because I've been gone so long, Command has forgotten what made me valuable. What's to stop them from deciding I no longer have a purpose here and kicking me out? I would have nowhere to go. As long as I remain useful, I'm safe. That doesn't make me a double agent."

Clara refused to admit Marsh had a point. If she stopped long enough, she would admit there was logic in Marsh's response; however, the perfectionism that raged within Clara told her Marsh needed to be fully transparent. "Why not give it all to them? Wouldn't that prove your value enough?"

Marsh responded quickly, "People's memories are short. I'd be valuable for a moment, and worthless in the next. You can think whatever the hell you want about me. But I have faithfully served Quorath, and I will continue to do so. I'm just careful to ensure Quorath also serves me."

"Be careful what you choose to withhold, Marsh." Clara shook her head, "You may think you're protecting yourself, but you could end up on the wrong side of things if your information proves as valuable as you seem to think it is."

"Thanks for the warning. Touching you care. We're done here." Marsh walked back towards the dining hall, turning once she was in the doorway, "Oh, and don't ever come back here. If you were someone I wished to socialize with, I wouldn't have made it so abundantly clear I absolutely hate you." She continued walking, sticking her middle finger in the air to emphasize her point.

4 CLARA

As much as she didn't want to, Clara kept her word and met Reese for dinner. This time, their table was swarmed by people nodding or smiling at Clara as they walked by. Anxiety crawled up her spine. They hated her earlier to love her now? "You could at least smile back, you know." Reese chided, waving at some of the bypassers.

"Why would I smile back? I don't know why they're smiling."

"They're smiling because you retrieved the vials. Your mission is considered one of the most successful for our kingdom to date. You handicapped the newest creation from Noxvalis. And," her eyes took on a mischievous twinkle, "They just heard the news."

"Command released information on our–my–assignment?" She choked over the word "our", quickly replacing it. Reese let her concerned look linger for only a moment before she moved on.

"Yes. Most of us were informed today. You missed lunch, so you weren't here for the announcement." That explains why the attitude shifted so dramatically.

Clara nodded with tight lips as two more operatives passed and smiled at her. "I was busy."

"You were training?" Reese said, more like a statement than a question.

"Actually, no. I went to talk to Marsh."

"Ew, gross. Why would you ever do that? We hate her." Reese tossed her braids over her shoulder.

Clara let out a soft chuckle, and Reese grinned in triumph. "Just because we hate her doesn't mean she isn't valuable."

"Sureee. That's how that works. Anyway, why'd you go to talk to our enemy?" Reese speared a green bean, sticking it in her mouth.

"You can't tell anyone what I'm about to share with you." Reese drew her fingers across her lips, making the motion to lock them shut. "I really shouldn't even be telling you."

"Now that you've started, you're committed to finishing. I won't tell anyone. In all of our years, when have I ever shared something you told me?"

Clara thought back over their friendship, "When have I ever shared personal information outside of assignments?"

Reese tapped her lips with her fork as she stared into space, finally bringing her gaze back to Clara. "Outside of your history with," she paused awkwardly, "him," she continued, "I don't think you've ever shared anything. And you only shared about him because I literally forced you to. You were so depressing to be around when you first got here. I had to know what the reason was."

"You're not helping your point." Clara reminded.

"What was my point? Oh, yeah. You need to tell me why you intentionally sought out Marsh. See, you don't have to worry about me sharing a secret at all. Chances are I won't remember it anyway!" Reese giggled.

"Okay, fine." Clara inhaled, trying to squelch her frustration with Reese's cheerfulness. She reminded herself that Carver was a wound only she (and Marsh somehow? unfortunately?) carried. It wasn't Reese's to bear.

"Yay!" Reese practically squealed.

"Keep your voice down if I'm going to tell you!" Reese shrank playfully, thoroughly chastened. "When we were before Command, they questioned us for three days over the events of the assignment." Reese nodded; that part wasn't a secret. "Our stories corroborated, nothing seemed to shock Command until the very end. When we were dismissed, Marsh informed them that Noxvalis had all the materials necessary to begin assembling bombs. Radioactive bombs."

Reese's eyes widened, but she didn't interrupt as Clara continued, "Command didn't seem to have any idea that was possible. Their sole focus had been the vials. Marsh just spit out the information like an 'oh, by the way.' So I found her today to see what else she knew from her time in Noxvalis that she wasn't sharing."

"And?" Reese leaned forward conspiratorily.

Clara shook her head, the frustration she felt becoming a heavy weight. "She wouldn't share anything."

"Do you think Command will send another operative to retrieve those?"

Clara didn't answer for a moment, her brain needing an opportunity to catch up. She had so thoroughly closed the door to Noxvalis that it hadn't even occurred to her that Quorath would need someone to go back. Someone familiar with Noxvalis. Her heart started racing. Would she even want to go back? She didn't let herself answer that question, instead responding to Reese, "I don't know. I haven't heard anything. I'm assuming you haven't either?"

"Nope. No new assignments since you've been back, either. Do you think they would send you back?" Reese hesitated over the question, but she asked it anyway.

"I don't know," Clara answered honestly. "But there's no one better suited to the assignment, so if they send anyone, it would be me." Reese raised an eyebrow at her. Defensively, Clara explained, "I'm familiar with Noxvalis. I already know the layout. I know what happened last time and what to avoid this time. It's more than anyone else knows."

"Except Marsh." Reese grimaced.

"She just returned from years undercover. There's no way in hell Command will send her out again that quickly. Besides, it's not exactly like she's given them a reason to trust her."

Reese shrugged, "For your sake, I hope you're right."

After dinner, Clara made her way to the training room again. This time, she ran until her pounding thoughts aligned with the thud of her footsteps. She ran until sweat dripped down her brow, and exhaustion clouded her vision. Anxiety filled her chest as she considered going to bed. The nightmares would come again. Her legs itched, a new sensation for her. It made her feel like her skin was crawling with the things she couldn't say, and couldn't bear to think.

She stretched slowly, procrastinating her return. If she could change things, she would.

She realized that now.

She thought once the sector recognized her as someone important, it would be enough. But the ache in her chest...the only person she wanted to recognize her as important never would. And it was her fault.

The anger burned hot, bringing tears with it. Self-hatred welled within her. She had been told to leave him. She always knew it was a possibility he wouldn't return, but the way things played out remained her fault. He was a better person than she ever would be.

For the first time since she returned, she let herself cry.

5 CLARA

For once, Clara didn't remember her dreams, but when she woke up, she still didn't feel rested. She yawned, forcing herself out of bed the moment her eyes opened. If she stayed beneath the covers, she'd wallow. Wallowing wouldn't help anyone. Reese's lecture played through her mind. One person wanted her to stay alive. Was that enough?

She made the bed perfectly, subconsciously stepping into her practiced routine. The books were perfectly stacked on her dresser. She ran her fingers over their spines. She hadn't been able to open them since she returned. She could only imagine how disappointed her father would have been in her choices. She couldn't bear to see his writing.

She hadn't even told her mother what had happened. When she got back, they gave her a letter her mother sent. It was a few days behind, but her mother was letting her know she had moved in with her parents, Clara's grandparents, and was selling the house.

Clara was so numb, she hadn't even considered that the place she and Carver met would no longer be hers. She was glad her mother had someone. She couldn't be there for her.

Before she became too entranced in her thoughts, she noticed the envelope on the floor. She bit her lower lip as she picked it up.

. . .

"Clara Richards -

You have been summoned to Command. Join us in the war room at 0900 for your new assignment.

Command."

Her heart raced, both from anxiety and excitement. She certainly hadn't expected to be summoned this quickly. She dressed carefully, braiding back her hair precisely. This had to be about Noxvalis. Surely, Command had decided to address what Marsh had said. She was going back.

That thought finally solidified in her mind, clearing everything else out. She left her room and headed to the dining hall. Emotions would have to wait. She couldn't be paralyzed. She had to be the assassin Ferris had trained. Brutal and harsh. Determined and focused.

After she went through the line, she sat across from Reese.

She ate half of her food before she realized Reese hadn't said a single word yet. Taking a sip of her coffee, she commented, "You're uncharacteristically quiet."

Reese pursed her lips, "Okay," she finally said sheepishly, "If I share something with you, will you promise not to be mad at me? It's not my fault."

"You didn't," Clara started nervously, but Reese interrupted with a nervous laugh.

"No, no, I didn't share your secret. Of course, I didn't do that. Have a little faith in me, Clara."

"With the way you started, you had me concerned. I don't think there's anything else you could share that would make me angry."

"I received a summons from Command." Reese searched Clara's

eyes, waiting for her response. When she didn't respond for a minute, she added, "Are you upset?"

"I'm confused." Clara tilted her head, processing the information. "What time are your summons for?"

"0900. Why? Please don't be mad at me. If this has to do with Noxvalis, I don't know anything about it."

"Reese, take a breath. I'm not mad. Even if it does have to do with Noxvalis. I'm confused because I also received a summons for 0900."

"Oh."

"Yeah. This is a first."

"The best friends together!" Reese smiled, but Clara could see the uncertainty in her expression. "Do you think it has to do with Noxvalis? Or Marsh or something?"

"You said Command implied our return from Noxvalis was a huge victory, right?" Clara asked, and Reese nodded in agreement, "I wonder if they're hoping for the same success with a second assignment. It's possible at least."

"Well, we can walk together!" Clara smiled at Reese's positive attitude.

They finished their food quickly, making their way to Command well before 0900. When they were almost to the doors, Clara muttered, "Well, if we were unsure on whether or not this has to do with Noxvalis, we don't have to be unsure anymore. It definitely does."

"What makes you so sure?"

Clara nodded at the auburn-haired girl already waiting outside the doors, "That's Marsh."

Reese's lips formed a perfect, "Oh."

Marsh glared as soon as she saw them approaching. "You've got to be kidding me."

"Don't worry, I hold the same sentiments." Clara was quick to confirm.

Reese looked between the glares, finally stepping into Marsh's line of sight, "Hi, I'm Reese!"

Marsh looked over at her dismissively before returning her eyes to Clara, "Do I look like I care?"

Reese stepped back to Clara's side, "Wow, you really weren't kidding about her. I thought you had to be exaggerating at least a little bit."

"Aw, you talk about me?" Marsh answered.

"I filled Reese in on my assignment to Noxvalis. Since you were my host there, your name came up."

They stood in silence. Reese bounced on her toes. Clara resisted the urge to yank her arm and pull her flat on her feet. It was unprofessional, but the doors hadn't opened yet. If Reese needed to bounce to stay positive about this situation, letting her was the least she could do. Finally, their patience was rewarded as the sound of the large handle turning was followed by the slight creak of the doors' massive hinges.

Clara laced her hands together behind her, facing forward with her shoulders back and her head held high. She threw a sideways glance at Reese, who had stopped bouncing, and looked professional. Good. They needed to be prepared for whatever this assignment was.

They walked in, and Clara's heart tripped as she noticed the man in the center of the room. But no, he was too broad to be Carver, and his hair was far too dark. Her heart dropped, but her posture didn't. They joined him in the middle of the room. He didn't turn to look at them.

"Operatives," this time it was a man's voice. "You have been summoned because of the information we have received regarding Noxvalis."

He tilted his head towards Marsh, who inclined hers in return. "We have confirmed the information Operative Harris relayed to us, slow as she may have been in choosing to relay it."

Marsh's face flared red, and Clara held back a smirk. Of course, Marsh wouldn't have been the only operative within the walls of Noxvalis. How foolish did Marsh think they were?

"In the wake of this new information, the need for a secondary assignment has arisen." Clara straightened. "I shouldn't have to tell you we can't allow Noxvalis to make any type of radioactive bombs. Even if they aren't lethal, dirty bombs would wreak havoc on our kingdom, which is already on edge." Clara nodded her agreement.

"That is why you have been summoned. Operatives Harris, Richards, Johnson, and Harper, you are traveling to Noxvalis. You have the rest of the day to prepare and update Johnson and Harper on your intel. I suggest you choose thoroughness, Operative Harris. Leave no stone unturned."

Marsh visibly flinched, but she tilted her head in deference. The man just observed her before turning his gaze to Clara. "Operative Richards, I suggest you detail why you failed last time and bring back better results this time."

Clara nodded, refusing to flinch the way Marsh had. The rebuke stung, but she expected it.

"You all have the same assignment. Retrieve the radioactive isotope, and return it to us."

Retrieve, not destroy. Clara heard the same phrasing that caused her concern last time. She bit the inside of her cheek to keep from interrupting.

Silence filled the room after this edict. Command remained guarded, their faces hidden as always. Marsh and Clara glanced at each other, and Marsh lifted one shoulder in a small shrug. Clara didn't fidget or let her perfect posture drop. The man in the middle, Operative Harper, folded his arms across his chest, his muscles taut. Clara tried to figure out if she knew him. But after cycling through all the members of the Vipers she could call to mind, she didn't think he was a Viper. Spider? No, he was too toned for that.

"Operative Harper is running point on this assignment. Operatives Richards and Harris, you will defer to him. Understood?"

"Yes, sir." They both nodded, even as Clara wanted to reject the instruction. Someone who hadn't been to Noxvalis couldn't lead the assignment.

The man watched them in silence, as if daring them to oppose his instruction. Reese shifted her weight to one foot, and Clara almost poked her back into position. Finally, the man spoke, "You are dismissed. Operative Harper, I suggest you discuss the materials needed with Operative Harris and let us know by 0300."

"Yes, sir," Operative Harper spoke for the first time. His voice gruff.

"You leave at 0600. Dismissed." Command finally said.

Operative Harper immediately turned on his heel, glaring at Clara as he walked past, and left the room and walked down the hallway to Ravens. She was right. He wasn't a Viper. He was another Raven. Great.

The girls didn't speak as they walked out at a normal pace. The doors were closed behind them, and Clara finally took in a full breath. She was going back to Noxvalis. "What's with the muscle?" Reese nodded down the Raven's hallway, "I didn't know you had pissed off more than one Raven."

"She seems to have a habit of making enemies with Ravens," Marsh remarked cattily.

"Get over yourself, Marsh. You made yourself my enemy."

Marsh scoffed, "Oh, is that so? As if you didn't come into my home with your bitchy attitude and bickering. Be honest. I bet you're relieved you're on this assignment. What, you're hoping for redemption? Yeah right. The only redemption you'll get is if *you* die this time."

Reese's jaw dropped, but she didn't have a chance to respond before Marsh was storming down the Raven's hallway.

"She's..." Reese searched for the right word.

"A bitch. She's a bitch. You can be honest about it. But I deserve it. I'm a bitch too."

Reese laughed, "You may be...a lot, and a little too aggressive, but bitch is pushing it."

Clara gave her a look as they started walking back towards their sector, "Okay, maybe you're a little bit of a bitch. But even you have lines you won't cross. You didn't tell her you hoped she would die. Though if you decided that's the route you want to go, I'm 100% behind you. Your call." Reese shrugged, "Hell, if you want, I'll off her myself."

"I may not like Marsh, but that doesn't mean she deserves to die. She has some good qualities." Clara thought, "I'm sure she has good qualities. She has to have at least a couple." Reese giggled at the silence that extended between them, "Okay, even if I can't think of any, that doesn't mean I want her to die."

"Did you know the guy who was in there?"

Clara shook her head, "I didn't recognize him. But he seemed to recognize me."

"Well, you are famous." Reese deepened her voice, "The Eclipse."

"Please never do that again."

"This trip should be fun. Two Ravens who hate you and me to break the tension. Basically, I'm a sacrifice. Oh, yay!"

Reese smiled, and Clara finally laughed, "It won't be that bad. We're all adults. We'll figure it out."

"Yeah, cuz adults *never* hate each other enough to kill each other." Clara just shook her head.

They didn't speak again until dinner. Clara spent the afternoon packing after one last training session. She couldn't stop moving long enough to think about what going back to Noxvalis actually meant to her.

"I assume you're packed." She stated when she sat across from Reese.

"Obviously." Reese grinned, her shoulders drawing up towards her ears, "I'm so excited!"

Clara smiled gently, "I wouldn't be. It's different than anything you could expect. It's the kind of assignment that costs something."

"I'm still excited. I haven't had an interesting assignment in months."

Clara ate a slice of her chicken, chewing quickly before the flavor had a chance to fully set in. Her appetite had been practically nonexistent lately, and if she thought too hard about what she was eating, she would probably throw it all up. So, she asked Reese, "You haven't updated me on the guy you were seeing. What happened to him?"

Reese shrugged, "Ended up being only a couple of nights' fling. He was cute, it was fun, neither of us actually wanted to get to know each other." Reese nodded towards a group a few tables over. "He's the blond at that table." She shook her head, "I also don't know what I was thinking, dating a blond. They don't have the right kind of energy for me."

Clara laughed, "Right kind of energy for you?"

"You know, I'm bubbling and cute," she put her hands under her chin, "I try to see the best in the world. If I'm thinking seriously, I need someone who balances that. Not someone who wants to pretend the entire world is made of cotton candy."

"Wow, um, okay, there is so much I could question in that statement. But, instead, I'll ask this. Something serious? I thought you weren't looking for anything serious."

Reese stared into the distance, "I didn't think I was either. But this fling just didn't...for lack of better words, and don't you dare have your mind in the gutter, hit the same way. I think I'm ready for something real. I think I'm ready to stop seeing guy after guy, and find someone who truly wants to know me."

"That's awesome, Reese. I really hope you find him."

"Yeah," she sighed, "Me too. It's a lot harder to have hope when you set your expectations high."

6 CLARA

Clara rose well before 0600, double and triple checking her bag had everything she needed. She was convinced something was missing. If this assignment were anything like the last, she wouldn't need to bring much. Still, she packed as many weapons as she could fit. She checked each and every knife on her body. She folded an extra set of clothes and braided her hair back tightly.

When she was done, she still had 30 minutes before she needed to be in front of Command. She took a deep breath, closing her eyes. When she opened them, she walked slowly until she was in front of the mirror. She ran her fingers over her braid and finally met her eyes in the mirror.

The circles under her eyes were darker than ever, and more hollow than she'd even seen. Her cheeks had sunk in a little. She turned in the mirror, noting all the places where it seemed she had lost weight. She had tried to keep up with meals, but she knew that in the last week, she hadn't had more than a handful. The six days of the trip back and three days before Command, she didn't think she had eaten at all.

She bit her lip as she continued to stare at herself. "I hate you," she whispered, watching the words form on her reflection. She smiled, fake, cold, and bitter, "But this is your chance. Your chance to mess it all up again. At least this time," she widened her smile, "You can make sure *you're* the one who dies."

She stared at herself for a few more minutes, letting the weight of Carver's death weigh on her. She thought about how he had tried to protect her, how all of her frustrations with him were because of his misplaced valiance. And her? She was the one who was actually a monster. He had every reason to hate her. She made sure of it. Still, he sacrificed himself...for her.

She took a deep breath in and exhaled heavily, releasing every thought of him that was trying to stick around. She needed to be focused. She had other people to protect. She had other people who needed her head in the game. She had to do better this time. There wasn't another choice.

She threw her bag over her shoulder, walking to Command. Reese joined her in the hallway, and Clara had to take a few more breaths, so she didn't snap at Reese for being so bubbly. It wasn't even 0600 yet!

"What was the train ride like? Did you get sick with the movement?"

"No."

"What did you think of the male operative they're sending with us? That will be interesting, right? He seems at least a few years older than us. Ooo, I wonder if he's a trainer. Do you think that's why he was picked for this?"

"I have no idea, Reese."

"Do you think Marsh will try to kill you on the train today?"

They were almost to the end of the hallway. Clara could bear it for a couple more minutes. "If she actually wanted to kill me, she would have done so already."

"Okay, but like, she could just accidentally kill you on this trip. Would Command even question it? Don't worry, though, I'll protect you."

Once they reached the doors, Reese silenced. She didn't bounce, she didn't chatter, she just froze.

Clara almost didn't notice; she was so caught up in her own thoughts. But after a couple minutes, she asked, "You okay?"

Reese shook her head frantically, her small braids flying across her face. "I've never done this."

"You've been on plenty of assignments." Clara answered dismissively, "It's just the pre-assignment jitters. Everyone gets those. Even I get them."

"It's not that. Clara, I've never been on an assignment of this caliber."

Again, Clara dismissed her, "Reese, no one goes on assignments of this caliber. Carver and I were the first trip sent to Noxvalis to do what we did. Assignments of this caliber will probably become the new norm now."

"You're not listening," Reese snapped. Clara's eyes widened, "I can't do this. I've never been involved in an assignment off base."

Clara tilted her head, "What do you mean you've never been off base for an assignment?"

"I've never left the base. All of my assignments have been internal."

"What?" Clara sputtered, "Like you've been killing other operatives?"

"No, no. Spying on them. That's all. Mostly..." Reese trailed off, but then shrugged like it wasn't a big deal, "You wouldn't believe the kinds of secrets men will spill when your legs are open."

"That's the assignment they gave you?"

Reese ignored the question entirely, "I haven't left base since before training. I can't help but think they're sending me because I'm expendable."

"You're not expendable, Reese. Not to me." Clara patted her shoulder, unsure what other method of comforting would be appropriate. "And I've done this before, so I'll make sure you stay safe."

"Just hope she does a better job of that with you than she did with Carver!" Marsh interjected in a singsong voice as she joined their group, the other Raven behind her.

He nodded at Reese, but glared at Clara once again.

"What's your problem?" Clara asked, but the doors to Command opened.

They filed in, awaiting their final commands. "We're relieved to see you are capable of following instructions, Operative Richards." Command began with a jab, "Operative Harper has the papers for all of you. Last time, Operative Richards was able to enter because of the festival. There is no festival this time, so you will be breaking into the kingdom." It was a woman speaking to them this time. Clara could've sworn the voice was familiar, but of course, she'd never know.

Marsh coughed, and Command looked at her sharply before continuing, "Operative Harris led us to believe there is no outside way into the kingdom. Our other contact has proven her report false. Operative Harper has the map to direct you to the entry point. Does everyone understand?"

"Yes, ma'am," they responded in unison.

"Excellent. Imperfection will not be tolerated on this assignment. Do not make the mistake of believing your lives are worth more than those of our citizens here. You are doing this for them. Retrieve the radioactive pieces and return. As long as one of you makes it back with the pieces, this mission will be considered a success. The train is outside. All additional materials you need for this assignment have already been loaded." The woman let the words sink in before she ended with, "Dismissed."

Clara squeezed her hands into fists as they walked towards the train. This was her way out. She could honor Carver's death by sacrificing herself to save someone else. Maybe, she could even sacrifice herself for Marsh. Wouldn't that be the perfect way to honor him? Sacrificing herself for the girl he liked more than her.

They boarded in silence. Reese's eyes darted around nervously, but Clara was proud of how she held herself together. Marsh climbed on top of one of the crates, crossing her legs and leaning against the train wall. Operative Harper stood in the back corner, arms still crossed over his chest. He wore brown today, his clothing blending into the shadows of the train car.

Clara sat across from them, near the entrance of the train. Reese sat carefully beside her, glancing between the other two parties. The train door closed, and still no one said anything. This continued for a while, until Reese finally broke the silence.

"Sooooo," she drew the word out. Marsh stared her down, and Operative Harper deigned to give her his attention, "How does this work? How do we work together if we can't even have a conversation?" She chuckled nervously.

Operative Harper stepped forward, bracing his knees as he stood in the middle of the train car. Clara remembered his words the day before being deep, but the intonation of his voice still surprised her. He had a slight drawl across his words as he answered, "We won't be."

"What does that mean?"

Marsh rolled her eyes. "Nathaniel, don't scare the poor girl." She pouted at Reese. Reese returned the favor by showing Marsh her middle finger.

"It's Nate. I only work with people I can trust. You," he pointed at Reese, "I haven't decided if I can trust or not. You're friends with," he snarled, "her. And that's a mark against you."

Clara jumped to her feet, "Okay, what the hell do you have against me? I don't even know you!"

"You are Clara Richards. Joined the military at age 18. Assigned to Vipers. Received the name 'Eclipse.' Haven't turned down a single assignment. Succeeded in every torture operation."

"Great, you know all about me," sarcasm dripped from her tone, "I still don't know you, and none of what you listed is a good reason for you to hate me. You should be grateful I'm on this assignment. By your own account, I am the assassin you need."

"Don't interrupt." He didn't raise his voice, but the look he gave her caused her to shiver involuntarily. Marsh smirked. "Carver Vaughan's ex-girlfriend." Clara's jaw dropped. "Murderer of the boy I mentored." He stated.

He let the words sink in before he continued. "While your achievements may be vast and worthwhile to someone, they aren't worth shit to me. In addition to the list I provided, you are rash, impudent, headstrong, prideful, arrogant, and insecure. Not a team player. Command hoped pairing you with Carver would change that. It didn't. You're a danger to all of us."

Clara opened her mouth to respond, but she couldn't think of any rebuttal. He was right. She was a danger to anyone who worked with her. Reese stood up next to her, "I think that's an unfair assessment of her." She said slowly, Nate raised his eyebrows, motioning for her to continue. "Clara is extremely loyal. She has been there for me every day since we started in Vipers together. Anything she did the last time she was in Noxvalis was for the sake of the *assignment*."

Clara's heart contracted. Reese's faith in her was touching, but entirely misplaced. Nate hadn't said a single thing that was untrue. Reese didn't stop there, though. "She is a huge asset to this team. Everyone on this train, aside from me, had a relationship with Carver." Reese looked at Marsh, Nate, and finally looked at Clara. "Clara has the ability to put the assignment first, no matter what the cost is. And yes, this past assignment cost something. It cost her something. But that isn't a reason to reject the skillset she provides."

"Are you done?" Nate's question came out with a growl, and Reese held her hands up defensively.

"Yes, I'm done."

"Do I need to remind you of the order of command here?"

"Not at all." Reese tilted her head towards him, "Command placed you in charge. Ultimately, I will defer to your judgment and carry out your instructions. However, being submitted to your leadership doesn't mean I can't explain an objection I have. You're the leader, but we're still a team. Teams usually work best together."

"Hpmh." He grunted. "I will take your objections into consideration." He eyed Clara.

Clara sat back down, feeling small beneath his gaze. She wanted to speak up and say he was right, Reese was wrong, but something inside her said she needed to be a part of this mission. She needed to prove she could be a team player. She needed to succeed this time.

7 CARVER

Pain. His whole world was pain. Blinding, searing, breathtaking pain. He couldn't tell the difference between waking and sleeping anymore. Days passed without any realization, and his only thoughts were to beg for a release. But no matter how much pain he was in, his body wouldn't let him die.

It fought to keep him alive, and he cursed it with every bit of awareness he had left.

Finally, finally, the pain receded enough that he became more aware. The lab around him became a normal view, and the panic he remembered feeling at the worst of the pain subsided. White outfitted people rushing around him, needles poking into his skin. Some delivered a small measure of relief, but others only intensified his agony.

When he slept, he chased the same figure in his dreams, never able to catch her. The dark-haired, blue-eyed girl who haunted him. She ran through the woods, laughed with him, smiled at him, yet in some dreams she hated him. His heart would break. He was supposed to know her–love her even. Every morning when he woke up, he tried to recall the girl's face. But every morning when he woke up, he couldn't remember who she was.

8 CLARA

"Now that we have allegiances out of the way," Nate had moved a crate to the center of the train car and was sitting on the edge, "It's time we start planning for the retrieval."

Marsh nodded, "Once we're inside Noxvalis, we should be able to stay at the Midnight Quill. I told my neighbors I was shutting down for a bit to visit some friends I made from Calyndor."

"Smart." Marsh grinned at Nate's approval. "We'll take the long way around the kingdom. Can't be near enough for the archers to spot us. That will add at least a couple days to what you traveled last time," he paused, "Clara."

She leaned forward to join the conversation. "What is our timeline for completion?"

He shrugged, "This was a spontaneous assignment. We wouldn't even be going if this information had been given to Command when it was first discovered."

Marsh flared red, "That's–"

Nate held up a hand, "Not looking for an objection here, Marsh. Look," he sighed deeply, "Let's be honest about this. This assignment is, at best, a suicide mission. You heard their final edict. If even one of us returns, they will consider it a success. We're here because we are no longer considered useful."

"Why would you be sent on a suicide mission?" Reese asked, "Aren't you like one of the trainers or something? Right? You said you were Carver's mentor. You've gotta be valuable to them."

He smiled sadly, "I'm aging out. I refuse to leave, and the younger, stronger operatives are desperate to take my place. I'm not useful the way I was when I was younger." He chuckled, "I'm old now."

"You don't look old to me." Reese answered bluntly, "I mean, I would even go as far as to say you're in your prime."

Marsh laughed. Clara spoke, "What about the rest of us? You said this was a suicide mission because we're no longer valuable. You explained why you aren't; I know why I'm not. But Marsh? Reese?" Clara looked at her friend with concern in her eyes, hoping this wouldn't be something that would cause her world to crumble.

"Well, Marsh is an obvious one," Nate said.

"Do explain. I think I've proven myself quite valuable to Command." Marsh interjected.

"You hid information. They can't trust you anymore. It doesn't matter what you learned in Noxvalis if you aren't willing to share it. At worst, you're working for someone else. At best, you're withholding information for your own personal gain. Neither option serves Command."

Marsh swallowed hard. His eyes narrowed on Reese, "But you, Reese, I don't know why you're here. You're the only part of this that doesn't make sense. You don't have a reputation, and you're still young."

"Ha," she exhaled. "I don't have a reputation? That's funny."

Clara shifted beside her, trying to see what was going on in her mind. Nate looked surprised as Reese continued, "I have a reputation. And not the kind you want, like Clara's." Clara flinched, but was more concerned with where Reese was headed than what was said about her own reputation, "I've always been a bit of a flirt. A bit extroverted. The type of girl men want to trust. I didn't realize that would be exploited when I became an operative."

"You don't have to share anything you don't want to," Clara whispered.

Reese looked at her with gratitude in her eyes, "No, I want to share." She took a deep breath, "Assassins often collect far more information than expected. My job was to ascertain the loyalties of the new recruits after their first couple of assignments. I was supposed to see what they knew, what they had learned they weren't supposed to know. And, if they were going to break after their first kill."

Marsh's jaw dropped just enough that her lips formed a slight "o," as Reese continued, "My job was to seduce them. I then reported my findings to Command. If it became clear they would be a threat to our sector, it was my job to handle them." She dropped her gaze to the train car floor, fidgeting with her boot laces.

Clara was too shocked to say anything as the silence fell over the car. Nate was the one who finally spoke, "You found out something they didn't want you to know, either."

Reese met his gaze, "That, and I wanted out."

"Dangerous request." Nate shook his head.

"Perhaps. But I did it for them for three years. I was tired of seducing men only to kill them if I discovered they weren't loyal enough. Can you imagine that being your life? Sleeping with people to discard or kill them?"

Clara shook her head, "I'm so sorry, Reese," she whispered.

Reese shrugged, "I told them I wanted out a couple of days before Clara returned. They didn't give me an answer. This assignment was the first communication I received from Command after my conversation with them. All that work I did for them, and for what? Like you said, Nate, it's a suicide mission."

"Maybe not," Clara spoke up carefully, "Marsh and I at least know what we're walking into. If we plan it correctly, maybe half of us can make it out. I'll volunteer to be one of those who doesn't."

Nate raised his eyebrows, "Clara Richards offering to sacrifice herself? That doesn't sound right to me."

"Piss off, Nate." She blurted without considering he was their mission leader, and quickly continued, "I messed up on the last assignment. Don't you think I know that? I hate myself for what happened to Carver, and if I could fix it, I would. But I can't. So let me make amends in whatever way I can."

"Hmph," Nate grunted.

"If we're going to survive this, we're going to need her." Marsh admitted, "I hate her too, believe me. However, I would like to survive this. If we cut her out of the assignment, we sign our own death warrants."

"I won't make any promises. But, for now, I will try to include everyone in this train car on our mission. Clara, I don't trust you." She nodded at Nate's comment, "But for the sake of this mission, I am choosing to see if we can work together."

"So, where do we start?" Reese asked.

9 CLARA

Hours later, they were finally pulling up to their second stop. It was the same town she and Carver stopped in, and she remembered the diner favorably. Their first stop had been brief, just long enough for everyone to unload and relieve themselves. "There's a diner with rooms here. There's also a bar across the street that's disgusting. I recommend staying away from that."

She and Reese jumped off together, leaving Marsh and Nate to follow behind. "Reese, I had no idea." She said once they were out of earshot.

"I know." Reese's voice was soft.

"I'm so sorry. I should have asked more about your assignments, about your life."

"Caring more about me would have been nice, Clara. Until now, it would have been irrelevant anyway. Like, it would've been nice to know you care, but I wouldn't have been able to tell you anything. So you would have cared about me, only for me to lie to you. That wasn't the friendship I wanted either."

"I'm really sorry. I don't know how I can make up for being the shit friend I've been the past few years, but if I can, I would like to." Clara felt the words resonate in her. She hadn't handled things with Carver correctly, but anything she could do to handle things with people better now, she would try. She might hate herself, but as long as she was alive, maybe she could help people who deserved it. Like Reese.

Reese smiled, "You don't have to 'make up' for anything. What's done is done. We move forward, and you have the opportunity to be the friend you weren't."

"Deal."

Clara led them to the diner, memories of Carver flashing through her mind. She remembered the way he leaned against the train car during their trip. She recalled their interaction the last time she was here. He had gotten the last room and teased her for it. Her stubbornness had led her to the absolutely disgusting bar. He had cared enough to get her a room in the diner.

"You look sad." Reese remarked, "How are you doing with this trip?"

"I've only been here once. Those memories aren't ones I want to dwell on long." She shook her head, wiping the memories away. She needed to focus.

"One room please," she said to the older woman behind the counter.

The woman slid them a key with a shrewd look, which Clara promptly ignored. "Your diner is so cute! I love a quaint establishment," Reese smiled at the woman. She grunted, shook her head, and turned away from them.

Clara took a seat at one of the dining tables, with Reese sitting across from her. "I'm assuming you're fine bunking together?" She asked.

"It makes more sense than having two separate rooms for the time we're here," Reese responded amiably.

"I wonder what Marsh and Nate will do."

"I doubt it'll be each other, if that's what you're thinking." Reese giggled.

Clara snorted, "I couldn't imagine them together. He's soooo," she trailed off, trying to put it into words.

"So what? Aggressive about right and wrong? Blunt and honest? Focused and determined? Truthfully, I find him…refreshing."

Clara snorted, "Refreshing isn't the word I used. Oh, and thank you."

Reese looked up from the menu. "For what?"

"For defending me to Nate. You knew he was right, but you still defended me so he would give me a shot."

Reese shook her head, "Clara, he's not right. You made mistakes, but we've all made mistakes. You're a good operative, and he should recognize that." Clara bit her lip, "You need to believe me. This world needs you. Our kingdom needs you. This assignment is a chance to prove just how much. But this time, you need to trust the people around you enough to actually work with them."

Nate and Marsh walked in, each grabbing keys before joining them at the table. Marsh sat on Clara's right, with Nate on Clara's left. "I told him we should eat somewhere that you're not. I'm tolerating way more of your presence than I wanted to just by being trapped on the train." Marsh said insolently.

"And I told Marsh we have to learn to work together as a team," Nate replied with his deep rasp.

"Thank you, I think," Clara answered quietly. "I do want to be part of this team."

"I know."

They ordered when the waitress came by, and fell into silence. They had run through their entrance to Noxvalis over and over again on the train car, and Nate said tomorrow they would plot their entry to the labs. There wasn't much else to discuss.

"What made you become operatives?" Reese asked with a sip of her drink. Clara was wrong. According to Reese, there was always something to talk about. But with the silence at the table, she didn't think anyone was going to answer.

Finally, Nate spoke up. "I was a troubled kid. My parents kept threatening that the only choice for me would be the military." He paused, sipping his dark amber drink, "But when I graduated high school, barely, I might add, I decided the military was the path I wanted to take. I signed up, and never looked back. The discipline was good for me. It was the right choice."

"Have you ever thought about leaving?" Reese asked.

"No. The Ravens are my home. I've never found anything, or anyone, I guess, that's worth leaving for. I've learned how much deception the world holds, and I enjoy bringing some of those secrets to light."

"Marsh, what about you? What made you join?"

"I have no idea."

"You could at least be civil with Reese," Clara muttered.

Marsh glared at her, "I wasn't being uncivil, Clara. I genuinely don't know why I joined. I can't remember anymore. Maybe I joined because I thought I could serve the greater good. Maybe I joined because it was the path of least resistance. Maybe I joined because I was bored. I. Don't. Know."

The waiter stopped by the table with their plates of food. The conversation paused as he set the plates down in front of each of them.

"Why do you stay if you don't know why you joined?" Clara asked after the waiter stepped away.

She took a bite of her food, savoring the well-flavored chicken.

Marsh took a couple of bites of her food before she answered. "Why does anyone do anything? I guess I stay because I have nowhere else to go."

"No family?" Reese asked, looking at Marsh sadly.

"I had family, but I haven't been in contact with them since Noxvalis. They didn't know I was sent, and they begged me not to join the operative leagues. They thought my chances of survival were better as a foot soldier than an operative. I disagreed. I was in Noxvalis for so long, and writing them would only endanger them and my position, so I didn't."

Reese didn't respond. Clara did, "I get that. My mom was so disappointed when I joined the military."

"Why?" Marsh asked, the venom that was usually in her tone when speaking to Clara was no longer there.

"My dad was in the military. As was…" she cleared her throat, "Carver's dad. That's how we knew each other, actually. He and his mom moved in with us after his dad died. My dad was killed a few weeks later." She swallowed, staring at her plate.

The chicken and green beans swam in her vision. She blinked hard, trying to force back the tears. She couldn't say anything else about why she joined. The other reason she joined the military was now dead. *If I hadn't joined, he might still be alive.*

Reese saved her, "I joined because I wanted to make a difference. I grew up in a family full of civil servants. People who served every chance they got, in every area they could. I wanted to make a difference. I know what I did was "valuable", but I don't think they'd be proud of my contribution." She said the last sentence quietly, and Clara tried to give her a comforting smile now that her vision was back to normal.

"I think that's enough team bonding." Nate scarfed down the rest of his food, "I would like a good night of sleep before another day on that train, so that's it for me. I suggest you all turn in early as well."

He left the three of them sitting there. Reese caught Clara's eye and nodded towards Marsh. Clara raised her shoulders in question. Reese nodded towards Marsh again and mouthed "fix it." Clara inhaled deeply.

"Marsh," she began.

"Immediately, no. Whatever you're about to say, just don't."

"I know we had a rough start, but I would like to start over." She quickly added, "If we can." Clara's gut twisted even as she said the words. She actually hated Marsh, but she hated herself more. And if she could learn to live with Marsh, maybe she could learn to live with herself, too.

Marsh sat back in surprise. "Start over? You got Carver killed. We can't just gloss over that like it didn't happen. You are everything Nate said on the train and more. Nate may be able to move forward with you, but I was there when it happened. I watched everything he said about you happen in real time. You haven't changed. And you can't just pretend that away."

Marsh pushed herself back from the table and stormed off.

"Well," Reese said gently, "You tried."

10 CLARA

Clara woke up before Reese the next morning. Silently, she slipped out of bed and started her stretching routine. She knew how badly the train ride locked her muscles, and she was desperately trying to keep the soreness from setting in.

Reese yawned loudly as she sat up in bed. "What are you doing?"

"Stretching, want to join me?"

"Not particularly," Reese replied as she lay back down. "I would like to go back to sleep. But that's not really on the agenda for today."

"No, it's not." Clara agreed, "You'll tolerate the train better today if you stretch first."

"It's way too early for you to use logic with me."

"What about bribery?" Clara teased, "If you get up and stretch with me, I'll show you where to get the best breakfast burritos." She didn't let herself think about how the last time she got those burritos, she bought one for Carver. She had better things to focus on.

Reese groaned, "Ugh, fine. I'll stretch with you."

Her feet hit the ground with a thud as she untangled herself from her blanket. She leaned over, copying Clara as they went through the motions. Arms up, then back to their toes.

"See, this isn't so bad."

"Speak for yourself. I'm not having fun." Reese replied honestly. "All the stretching I've done was for a very different muscle group."

"I don't think I want to unpack that," Clara straightened, "Time to get dressed and leave."

"You have way too much energy in the morning," Reese grabbed her bag and locked herself in the bathroom. Clara glanced around the room, replaying Nate's instructions for entering Noxvalis.

The door they would enter through was towards the back of the forest. It wouldn't be hard to walk through, but they would have to force the door open. Apparently, it was either half-buried or at the top of a ditch? The vagueness around the door's location was a little concerning. She wasn't looking forward to it, but they could do it.

The door would put them in the back of a slum alleyway. There was always a risk someone in the slums would see them, but that's where Reese and Clara would come in handy.

Nate hadn't given them specifics on the order they would enter, but Clara knew it made sense for her to go first. If there were any problems, she would dispatch them quickly. Reese might hesitate. She wanted to trust her friend, but after hearing her story, she was concerned Reese was ill-equipped for this assignment. As far as she knew, neither Marsh nor Nate had ever killed anyone. It made sense for her to be the first one.

Of course, it would be up to Nate's discretion.

She hadn't decided how to feel about him. He seemed big on rules, and once she would have agreed with him. But this previous assignment made her feel like some rules were made to cause harm, not to be useful. Some rules were meant to be broken. She didn't know if she trusted him to do what needed to be done when it came down to it.

Reese came out, dressed and ready to go. Clara quickly took her turn.

"Hey, Clara?" Reese called from outside the bathroom door.

Clara finished washing her face. "Yeah, Reese?"

"Are you scared? Nate said this was a suicide assignment, and I don't think he's wrong. I try to, like, not be afraid, but I'm not ready to die."

Clara deliberated between the two answers that filled her mind. The truth, and what Reese needed to hear. The truth was, she could not care less if she died on this assignment. She was far more afraid of surviving it. But the likelihood they all died was quite high. Reese needed to hear that it would all be okay. She needed to believe they had a shot.

Clara bounced the answers around her head, finally settling on, "No, I'm not scared, and you don't need to be either." The compromise between the truth and what Reese needed.

She pulled the door open and slung her bag over her shoulder. "Ready?"

Reese nodded, grabbing her bag. They walked down the stairs together, and Clara ordered them burritos.

"Do you think we should have gotten some for Marsh and Nate?"

Inwardly, Clara rolled her eyes. Marsh and Nate could fend for themselves. "I'm sure they're okay."

"I just thought it would be nice," Reese shrugged.

"Do you want to order more?"

Reese smiled, "It wouldn't hurt. Think of it as a peace offering."

Clara ordered four more burritos so everyone would have two. She didn't care if Nate or Marsh went hungry. Although Reese had said she didn't need to make amends, Clara still wanted to. For Reese's sake, she would play nice. Ordering burritos was a small effort towards that.

Once they had their food, they took their time walking back to the train. The sun was rising in brilliant orange and pink colors. The air was crisp, but Clara knew it was deceptive and would be much warmer by the time they began their trek into Noxvalis.

Nate was already leaning against the side of the train, but Marsh was nowhere to be seen. "We brought you food!" Reese called cheerfully once they were close enough. "Hope you like breakfast burritos!"

Nate pulled his shoulders off the train, standing straight. Reese rummaged in the bag of food Clara was holding to pull out the burritos they ordered for him. She handed them over, "Clara says they're amazing."

"Thank you," he said gruffly, and it seemed to be a strain for him to say the words.

"Of course! It was actually Clara's idea!" Reese lied, nudging Clara with her elbow.

He nodded at Clara, but didn't repeat the sentiment. She nodded back. Clara and Reese stepped into the train, taking a seat against the wall furthest from the door.

"Oh my word." Reese groaned after she took a bite, "You weren't kidding. These are amazing burritos. Like, I would go through the train ride and the fear of dying all over, if it meant I get to have this burrito again."

Clara laughed, "They're good, but I don't think they're that good."

"Oh, they most definitely are. You have to be the one to give these to Marsh. Once she eats one, she'll have no choice but to forgive you for everything." She took another bite and continued around the food in her mouth, "Seriously. These burritos are practically a miracle."

"I don't think it's going to be that easy," Clara answered in between bites.

Nate joined them in the train car, choosing to sit on the side opposite them. "The burritos are good," he said.

"I had them last time I was here." Clara explained, "I convinced Reese to stretch with me this morning by telling her I'd give her a phenomenal burrito if she stretched."

"And she did not lie. It is phenomenal. Ten out of ten would stretch again."

Marsh finally stepped into the train car, sitting on the same wall as Nate, as far from him as she could. Reese poked Clara, so she stood and took two burritos to Marsh, "We brought burritos."

Marsh eyed them, not making a single move to take them.

"They're really good," Reese added.

"What makes you think I want anything from you?" Marsh snapped.

"I don't think you want anything from me. But I thought you might want a burrito from the diner. They're really good, and we're going to be on the train for hours." Clara held them out again. Marsh crossed her arms over her chest.

"If she wants to weaken herself before the assignment, that's her choice," Nate said. "I would take another burrito." He held his hand out, and Clara gave it to him.

She held the other burrito out to Marsh again. Marsh closed her eyes and leaned back into the train car wall. Nate shrugged at Clara, "You tried," he mouthed.

She went back to sit with Reese. Reese patted her leg apologetically. If Marsh wasn't willing to accept Clara's olive branch, Clara wouldn't keep offering it. Marsh was an adult, and she could make her own decisions. If her decisions hurt other people, it really wasn't Clara's business.

The train started down the tracks, and the three of them finished their food. Nate balled his wrapper up and set it to the side, clapping his hands. Marsh lazily opened her eyes, barely deigning to look at him.

"Let's talk about our entry plan. Clara, it makes the most sense for you to go through the doorway first. If there's anyone we need to be concerned about, you can take care of them." She nodded. *At least he's smart enough to make that decision.* "I'll follow, with Marsh next, and Reese last."

He looked at Reese, "Are you comfortable dispatching threats if someone is on our tail?"

Reese glared at him, "Yes. I'm a Viper. Of course I'm comfortable with it."

Nate held up his hands, "Didn't mean to offend." He pulled out the map they had surveyed the day before. "Marsh, can you show me the route we will need to take to reach the Midnight Quill from here?"

She moved slowly towards him, and then traced her finger from the doorway to the bookstore as she leaned over the map. "Our best bet will be to stick to the alleys. Since we're coming in through the slums, we don't need to worry as much about being turned in. Most of the slums don't pay enough attention to be a problem. And if they are, Clara is certainly capable of killing them."

"Was that a compliment or an insult, Marsh?" Clara asked, "Careful," she tutted, "You're losing your edge."

Marsh flipped Clara off without taking her eyes off the map. "The part that will be the hardest for us is getting through the town square. Our outfits shouldn't stand out too much, but without a festival, people will be more wary of strangers." She sat back. "King Herring isn't stupid. He knows someone broke in before, and he got one of us. Who knows what information he gathered? Soldiers will be on high alert, and I wouldn't be surprised if they've upped the number of guards and changed the security for each of the labs."

Clara agreed, "Most likely they'll start with the lab I broke into. It's barely been a week, do you think they will have resecured the lab we need?"

Marsh pursed her lips, "King Herring moves quickly. He knows you stole from him. He knew Carver was one of us. He won't wait to secure his kingdom. I'm willing to bet he secured the labs in order of importance to him." She pointed at their destination on the map, "This lab has all of their radioactive materials. He probably upped the security here simultaneously to the lab you were in."

"What does that mean for us?" Reese asked.

"It means we'd better know exactly what the hell we're doing," Nate said.

11 CLARA

The train stopped at the abandoned towns for less than an hour before they were off again. "Last time, they dropped us off here, and the conductor and his helper disappeared entirely. We walked from here." Clara remarked.

Nate laughed, "Did they tell you what happened?"

She shook her head. He laughed again, "The conductor was extremely superstitious. When the town didn't have the movement he knew the town should have, he and his helper hid in one of the cars until you and Carver left. Once you were out of sight, they turned around."

"Wait, actually? All this time, I thought they had died or something." She nodded towards Marsh, "Plus, it wasn't until I got back that I even knew why the towns were abandoned."

Marsh didn't respond. Nate said, "I'm sure it was concerning for you to have the extra days of walking and no explanation."

Clara shrugged, "The assignment is the assignment. I don't expect things to go perfectly."

She leaned back against the wall, trying to get comfortable. Nate had informed them before their last stop that they would sleep on the train tonight. The train would drive through the night, then drop them at the last safe point.

Although the tracks weren't directly headed towards the war front, there was only so far Command was willing to send civilians. And, since Noxvalis had bombed cities closer than they ever had, Command was even more on edge. Another attack could come at any point, and they all needed to be prepared.

Reese pulled a t-shirt from her bag and folded it into a makeshift pillow. "I'm pretty sure at least one of these crates has blankets," Nate spoke up.

Blinking slowly, Reese sat up, "And you waited all this time to tell us? What kind of sadist are you?"

He stood and walked over, holding out his hand to pull her up. Reese stared at his hand before finally letting him pull her up. He tugged her to her feet in one graceful motion. He took a dagger out from the sheath at his side and used it to pry open the crates.

It took them three crates before Reese squealed, "These blankets are so soft!"

Clara smiled to herself at her friend's enthusiasm. "Clara!" She shouted, "Do you want one?"

"Yes, please."

"Reese," Marsh said sharply, "We are literally in a train car. There is absolutely no need for you to ever shout."

Nate frowned at Marsh, and Reese's enthusiasm dimmed. "Sorry," she murmured.

Nate glanced between the two of them and decided to comment, "Marsh, I know you have a history with Clara. I don't know exactly what the history is, but I can imagine. That being said, we are on this assignment together. She is being a team player and trying to make amends. You are not. You don't have to trust her; I get that trust is earned. I don't expect that of you. I do expect you to be a little more enjoyable to be around. As you said, we are trapped together in a train car. We are only going to spend more time together as this assignment progresses. So, I need you to get over yourself and give this team a shot. I get why you have issues with Clara, but Reese has been nothing but kind to you."

Reese looked up from the ground and smiled at Nate. Clara was a little surprised when he smiled back.

"Marsh, can you be a team player?"

Marsh inhaled deeply, taking her dear time responding, and Clara almost rolled her eyes.

"Yes, I can be a team player."

"Great. Because we're all going to need to work together if we want to beat the odds Command has given us."

Reese brought over two blankets, and Clara gratefully accepted one. It was big enough for her to lay it out and fold the other half over her. Since the sun had heated the train car throughout the day, it wasn't too cold even as they drove through the night.

She copied Reese and folded one of her shirts under her head. Reese fell asleep quickly, her breaths slow and deep, where she lay a couple of feet away from Clara.

Clara stared at the ceiling, trying to force herself to relax. She could handle this. She could help this team. She would make sure they survived, no matter what it cost her. She could handle whatever the cost was. She didn't have anything left she cared about.

She blinked slowly, wishing she could go back and trade her life for Carver's. He didn't deserve the fate she handed him. He deserved so much better.

She counted her breaths, in, 2, 3, 4, hold, 2, 3, 4, out, 2, 3, 4, desperately hoping it would ease the panic climbing her throat.

The train rumbled beneath her, and she closed her eyes, remembering how it felt to be on this train with Carver. She had called it torture, because it was. But not for the reasons she proclaimed. It wasn't torture because she hated him. It wasn't stifling because she wished he were dead. It was brutal because...because...her eyes flew open. It was torture because she loved him.

She felt the tears fill her eyes. She blinked through them, letting the droplets slide down her cheeks. She had always been proud to be stubborn. What had stubbornness gotten her? The death of the only man she loved. The death of her best friend.

Anxiety swirled again, and she sat up, desperate to do something, anything. She was trapped. The train walls were tightening around her. The single light flickered occasionally, and the shadows seemed to come closer and closer. She counted her breaths again. In and out. In and out.

"Hey," Nate whispered. She startled, not responding. "You okay?" He tried again.

Of course, she was okay. She was always okay. She inhaled shakily and shook her head no. He blurred in her vision as he moved to sit directly across from her. She pulled her knees in, hugging her arms around them.

He scratched the back of his neck, "Listen, I know I gave you a really hard time..."

"I deserved it," she whispered, almost imperceptibly. She sniffed, another tear streaking down her cheek. She wanted to be seen as strong. She wanted Nate to know she was competent. Even if she wasn't.

He sighed deeply. "No, you didn't. We all make mistakes, Clara. Especially in our field of work."

"Not like mine."

"You think you're so special," he shook his head with a sad smile, "You're not."

She wiped her palms across her face, effectively streaking the tears further.

"If I had a handkerchief, I'd offer it to you. Unfortunately, that's not the century we live in. I've lost a partner before, too. I blamed myself."

"Was it your fault?"

He shrugged, "Does it matter? I can replay the scenario a thousand times, wondering if I had done this or that differently, could I have saved them? But they died. Once someone is dead, the options are clear. Do you live with them in mind? Or do you let their death be the cause of yours?"

She sniffed, "I won't lie and say I trust you, Clara. I was pretty pissed about what happened to Carver. Honestly, still am a bit. It's been easy for me to blame you." He shook his head, "But sitting across from you in this train gave me time to reflect. It's not fair for me to blame you. We all do what we must to survive. It is the number one instinct we all have. I can't fault you for being a survivor. It's basic biology."

"How do you know I won't do the same thing this time?" She asked, tightening her arms around her knees.

"I don't. But the survivor instinct is one that can be overcome."

"Oh yeah? How do you overcome biology?"

"By rewriting it. You can choose to sacrifice instead of survive. The first time you survive at the cost of someone else, it rewires your brain. You look at the whole world differently. What happened isn't a mistake that's made twice. Not by someone who truly has good intentions."

12 CARVER

Carver woke up, blinking the sleep away peacefully. He took a deep breath in, and released it. There was no pain. After days of being entirely enveloped in pain, he felt...amazing. The pain had become so normal, he had forgotten what it felt like to be okay.

He sat up in bed slowly, examining his hands in front of him. One still had a needle protruding from the back of it, he snarled at it, pulling the needle out. The pinch he felt was nothing compared to what he had suffered in the days prior. The machine began screaming, but he didn't react, even as the sound reverberated through his skull.

He rolled his neck, taking stock of the rest of his body. Everything seemed to be in place.

Bright lights suddenly turned on over him, and he squinted but his eyes adjusted quickly. Two women in white outfits rushed in. "Hey," he coughed as they tried to push him back into his bed. He swallowed hard, his throat so dry there was nothing to swallow.

"Ladies, I appreciate your attention to detail, but please. Give him some water, and dim those lights. I would like to have a moment with my prize."

His prize? Carver squinted in the bright lights, waiting for them to relent. They turned the lights off, and his vision was spotty as he tried to concentrate on the voice in front of him.

"Tell me, Mr. Vaughan," the man came into focus, his gray hair a sheet around his shoulders, his lips curved into a diplomatic smile. "Do you feel well rested?"

One of the women placed a cup of water in his hand. Greedily, Carver gulped it down, coughing when it hit his throat the wrong way. The man in front of him didn't flinch. He patiently awaited an answer.

"Yes?" Carver couldn't help the question in his voice. What was happening?

"Excellent. How does your body feel now? Has the pain finally abated?"

"What do you know about my pain?"

"A great deal, Mr. Vaughan. I was here through many of the surgeries that saved your life. It was a difficult and painstaking ordeal; for you, of course, more than anyone else. We are so relieved you survived."

An acrid taste lingered on Carver's tongue as he finished the water. "Surgeries?" He squinted, "What exactly did I survive? And who are you? Where am I?" His mind scrambled to put the pieces back together, but there was nothing before the pain. Logically, he knew he had to have a before. But all he grasped as he reached for answers was a pounding headache as one more question surfaced. "Who am I?" This question was softer than the others. The knowledge he didn't know himself anymore was a frightening thing to grasp.

He knew he had to have known himself at some point, right? He existed. He was here. He had to have had a beginning.

"You are a miracle," the corner of the man's eyes crinkled as he smiled. "You survived the impossible."

"And my name?" Carver bit back the irritation filling his chest.

"Carrion."

Carrion swallowed hard. "What happened to me?"

The king's eyes crinkled, "You don't remember?"

Carrion shook his head, and the king spoke again, "Sometimes, the brain pushes away information that is too terrible for it to live with. If you don't remember, I think it is best that the past is left in the past. Your future is now, Carrion."

13 CLARA

Halfway through the next day, the train rumbled to a stop. Nate stood to his feet, stretching out his chest, "Well, team, this is where we get off. Hope you're ready for the long walk ahead of us."

Reese bounced on her toes, her bag already slung over her shoulder.

Clara slowly stood to her feet, folding the blanket into her pack with everything else. Nate nodded at her, and she nodded back.

"We should only have two days of walking from here."

"And then we're back in Noxvalis," Marsh muttered, stepping off the train as soon as the doors were opened.

Nate sighed, "I want the two of you to give more grace to Marsh. She lived here for so long, it can't be easy going back in this capacity."

"I'll try to talk to her a little more and see if I can get her to bounce out of it," Reese volunteered, following Marsh off the train. "I'm pretty good at making people like me."

Nate only shook his head. Reese and Marsh set the pace, Nate and Clara following far enough behind that she couldn't hear what Reese was saying. "Feeling any better?" Nate asked.

Clara shrugged, "Better is relative. I'm on my feet, I have a purpose in mind, I'm okay."

"You don't always have to be okay."

"For the sake of this assignment, I do." She inhaled. "So tell me this, what made you forgive me so easily?"

"Forgiving someone isn't the same as letting go of the anger. I'm still angry."

"I don't think that's true," she said softly.

"I wasn't being fair to you. You've been through hell and back. I may want to blame you, but that doesn't make it fair to blame you."

"Nate, I don't want to call you a liar, but I call bullshit. What I did," she bit her lower lip, "It was unforgivable. I know that. You know that. What changes that?"

"Unforgivable is a harsh word. I don't know," he stared off in the distance. "A couple things helped, I guess. From what I read in the report, Carver sacrificed himself for you. He thought you were worth something, and if he thought that highly of you, that's worth something to me."

"I wish he hadn't," she murmured.

"I know that too. You seem pretty determined to save everyone you can in this suicide mission. That means something to me, too."

The path slowly turned into the forest she recognized, and they stayed near the tracks. Marsh laughed at something Reese said, and Clara relaxed, hoping their team of vagabonds would be able to bond enough to survive.

Clara finally responded, "It's not like I had a choice in joining the suicide mission. I was assigned, same as you."

"Still, you're handling it well. Consider me impressed." Nate answered.

Clara chuckled dryly, "A suicide mission for the practically suicidal. It's a bit ironic. But you can take solace in the fact that I want my death to mean something. I want to be able to keep our team alive, even if I'm the cost."

"That's noble."

"It's honest."

They fell into a comfortable silence, nothing but the birds chirping and the branches snapping under their feet as they walked. The sun began to set when Nate called up ahead, "We'll keep walking until we reach the town. We should be almost there."

Softer, he asked Clara, "Did the radiation in the towns have any effect?"

"I didn't even know there was radiation. I didn't know until Marsh told Command after we were back."

"How did Carver take the emptiness in the town?"

She thought back to their perusal of the town and smiled as she remembered teasing Carver for being afraid of rats. "Pretty well. We were cautious, but it quickly became apparent there wasn't anything to fear. Actually, Carver was most afraid of rats. I was just tired, though curious as to where the people were." She looked up, pausing at the sunset. The sky exploded into hues of orange and pink. "I teased him for being skittish, and we found a house we felt safe staying in. It was nice to stay in a real bed. The next couple of nights were spent outside."

"Ah, so we have camping to look forward to."

Clara laughed. "Sure, if that's your thing. I definitely prefer to be inside."

14 CLARA

"You weren't creeped out by this town at all?" Reese scoffed as they stood at the edge of the town. Dust blew through, and the heavy silence was broken only by the occasional slamming shutter. "Ugh," Reese shuddered. "Are you sure we have to stay in one of these houses?" She looked at Nate, imploring. He rolled his eyes, and she changed her tactics to pouting, sticking her lower lip out, and widening her eyes.

"You'll be fine, Reese." He patted her on the shoulder, his hand lingering as he surveyed the town before them.

"We bypassed the town on our way back," Clara explained. "But we also didn't take the most direct route to the train tracks. This is the easiest path forward from the train."

She slung her arm around Reese's shoulder. The motion felt foreign, but Reese put her arm around Clara's waist, seeming to enjoy the affection. "You'll be fine," Clara emphasized with a smile, "After this, you'll get to camp for a couple of nights. You should really enjoy this while you can."

Reese groaned playfully.

"Suck it up," Marsh muttered, charging into the town. Nate was quick to follow.

"I thought you had made progress with her," Clara said as she stepped away from Reese and stretched her arms above her head.

Reese frowned, "I did. At least I thought I did. Maybe I am losing my touch with people."

"Nah," Clara answered quickly as she began following Marsh and Nate. "Marsh doesn't count as a person. You haven't lost anything with people." She shot Reese a glance from the side of her eye. "Besides, it seems like you're growing on at least one of the people here."

Reese laughed, "Yeah, I was shocked when you put your arm over my shoulders, but I'm certainly not complaining."

"Uh-huh," Clara prodded gently.

Reese sobered and replied quietly, "I told you, I'm not looking for anything casual. I want something real. Something worth having. I don't want to have someone for a moment and discard them in the next. If you're referencing Nate, I'll remind you that he's at least a decade older than me."

Clara squinted at her, "Is not. Five years at max. He's like 28, maybe."

"Girl, I don't know what you're on, but you don't get aged out at 28. He's at least 33."

"I think you're wrong."

"Oh yeah?" Reese's eyes sparkled with the challenge. "Let's ask him, shall we? Oh, Nate!" she called in a sing-song voice.

Marsh shook her head, not even looking behind her. Nate turned, holding his arms up in a question, but waiting for them to reach him. "Nate," Reese's voice stayed sugar sweet. "How old are you?"

"35. Is that really so important?"

Clara's eyes widened in shock. "Ha." Reese turned on Clara. "I just needed to settle an argument."

Nate sighed heavily. "Now is not the time for arguments. Especially about my age," he raised his eyebrows, "we need to find which of these buildings is the best fit for sleeping."

"We can stay in the one Carver and I did last time."

"Lead the way," Nate held out his arm.

Clara focused on remembering each of the houses and steps they took last time until she saw the white fence. Her breath caught, but she didn't change her pace. "This is it." She motioned. "The only thing I don't know is if there are enough beds. We only found two. Well, there was also a child's bed."

"You specifically remember the child's bed?" Reese questioned.

Clara shrugged, "It was vehicle themed," she murmured as she pushed through the gate.

It creaked gently, and the rest of their crew filed in behind her.

Clara's vision blurred as she approached the door, and she was grateful for the darkness obscuring her. She pushed it open, carefully counting her breaths as she stepped through the doorway. *One.* She remembered scanning the room with her flashlight, and Carver not knowing he had one too. *Two.* "This place gives me the heebie jeebies," he had said, and she had mocked him. *Three.* The baby's room, the life she would never have. *Four.* The child's room, she had teased him about sleeping in.

"Well, this is lovely," Marsh commented as Nate closed the door behind them.

Clara stepped further into the house, once again noting the framed photos on the mantle. "It's far superior to the forest." Reese answered, "I will certainly take the opportunity to sleep in a bed. The train was not all that comfortable."

"So soft," Marsh muttered, already climbing the stairs.

Clara followed her quickly, with Reese on her heels. Marsh barely paused in each doorway, taking inventory in a glance and moving forward. Clara, however, paused in the doorway of the children's room. The vehicles on the wall and the small bed reminded her of how she told Carver he was a child and should stay in the bed. "Fitting," she had said.

She felt Reese at her shoulder, but she didn't turn. "Let me guess," Reese whispered, "You made a comment to Carver about how he should stay in this room."

Once the words were spoken, it felt like the memory broke. He wasn't here. She wasn't teasing him. He was gone. Clara sniffed, trying to hold the tears at bay. She wouldn't break. She couldn't. She was strong enough to keep going. She would absolutely keep going.

"Yeah," she turned away from the room, giving Reese as much of a smile as she could manage.

"You've got to be kidding me," Marsh said from the guest room.

Clara's heart sped up. The beds. She forgot they left the beds in one room, entirely unmade.

"What's wrong?" Reese pushed ahead, standing on her tiptoes to see over Nate and Marsh's shoulders since they stood in the doorway. She dropped suddenly, sending a sympathetic look at Clara.

Marsh backed up slowly, glaring at Clara, "I just need you to answer one question."

Clara swallowed hard. Nate leaned against the doorframe, crossing his arms over his chest as he let the scene play out. Reese chewed her bottom lip, but Clara forced herself to focus on Marsh. "What question can I answer for you, Marsh?"

Marsh scratched her neck before dropping her hands at her sides. "Did you love him?"

Reese's eyes widened as Clara glanced around the room. Did she love him? "Um," she coughed, "That's not an easy question to answer."

"Sure it is, Clara," Marsh lifted one shoulder with a frown, "Did you love the man who gave his life for yours?"

Clara resisted the urge to shut her eyes. She didn't want to remember Carver in this moment. It was too much. Every moment, every interaction. The emotions he invoked in her. The intensity he made her feel. No one had access to her emotions the way he did. She had never hated anyone as much as she hated him. But love? Yes, she had never loved anyone the way she loved him.

"Yes," she whispered.

"Sorry?" Marsh cupped her ear, "Did you love Carver, Clara?"

Nate stepped away from the doorframe. "I think it's time we find beds and sleep now."

"No, she can answer the question. She owes me at least that. If she doesn't owe it to me, she owes it to the man who died in her stead.

Did you love him?!" Marsh shouted the question, her voice filling the empty space.

Clara couldn't stop the tears anymore. They filled her eyes, and with a single blink spilled over her cheeks. She answered with conviction, even as her voice was breaking, "Yes, I loved him. I have loved him since I was 15. I hate myself for what happened to him. If I could go back in time," she gasped through the sob climbing her throat, "I would give my life in an instant. But I can't!" Her voice grew in volume, "So here I am doing everything I can to make amends and honor the life he gave."

"Ha," Marsh rolled her eyes.

Nate grasped Marsh's upper arm, "That's enough, Marsh. You got your answer. The two of us are going to head downstairs to see if we can find more beds."

He squeezed Reese's shoulder with his right hand as he passed, "The two of you should take this room. We'll reconvene in the morning. Get some rest."

He directed Marsh down the hallway and down the stairs.

Clara wrapped her arms around herself, sniffing as she tried to control the sobs. Reese stepped in front of her and pulled her into a hug. "It's okay," Reese tried to comfort her.

"But, it's not. He's dead."

"You don't know that for sure yet. We don't have any evidence of his death. Regardless, you're okay," Reese moved her hand in calming circles against Clara's back.

"I don't feel okay."

Reese pulled back, keeping her hands on Clara's shoulders as she looked at her, "You're still moving forward. You're here with us, and that's enough."

15 CARRION

Carrion spent the morning letting the people in white outfits poke and prod him. King Herring, the gray-haired man, had assured him it was for his safety before he started training.

Carrion didn't really care about his safety. He felt he had stayed in bed long enough and was ready for training to begin. But at King Herring's orders, he stayed put.

His bed was surrounded by white curtains to create privacy. He couldn't see anything beyond the curtains, but the cacophony of noise drew his attention until the tests started. He tuned in and out to various conversations, none of which was of any interest to him. He didn't flinch when the needle was inserted for another test. He didn't flinch at the straps they attached to him, or growl at the machines that beeped around him. He didn't complain about the backless, oversized gown they had him wearing. He behaved as ordered by the king.

He cleared his throat when a man stepped in front of him with a small flashlight and moved it across his eyes. "What kind of tests are you performing?"

The man's eyes widened in alarm at Carrion's question. "I, um, that isn't a question I can answer for you.'

"Isn't this your job?" Carrion tilted his head at the man. "I thought you would be able to answer basic questions about your job?"

The man practically gulped. "Sir," Carrion didn't miss the tremble in the man's voice as he narrowed his eyes, "You will have to ask the king. I have been instructed only to handle this...observation. Anything beyond that, you will have to ask the king."

Carrion smiled dismissively, noting the man's use of observation as opposed to test. "Ah. So you aren't privy to the information I am seeking. I will ask His Majesty this afternoon."

The man's eyes stayed wide as he nodded, hurrying to finish his examination.

When the man stepped out, Carrion was finally alone. He closed his eyes and inhaled deeply. The air smelled sharply of astringents and a variety of chemicals. He inhaled again. Those smells combined with the less pleasant smell of people in less than desirable positions. Blood and waste filled his senses as he tried to sort through each smell. Once he was satisfied with his knowledge, he stood to his feet.

He stretched his arms out over his head, grateful that everything responded as he hoped it would. He didn't know what led him to this place, or what had occurred, but he was grateful for the care he received.

He squatted low and remained there for a few breaths, completely comfortable in the position. He stood straight, then leaned over to touch his toes.

He heard a gasp behind him. He straightened and turned to see a young woman, her face bright red, with a stack of clothes held in her hands. She didn't say anything, just continued to blush as she averted her gaze from his. Her blonde curls were pinned tightly to her scalp. He thought it looked brutal.

"Can I help you?" He asked when she didn't speak or look up at him.

"Oh, um," her blush deepened. "I brought you clothes."

She took one step forward, deposited them on the bed, and fled from the room. He frowned as the curtain settled, closing her out, and reached for the clothes. He took off the gown he had been wearing, still confused by her prompt exit. He had only been stretching.

He slowly unfolded the clothes, finding he was grateful for the tighter fit after so long in the gown. Another woman stepped into the room, her arms held behind her back with perfect posture. "Carrion," her voice was sharp, leaving no room for questions, "King Herring sent me to escort you to training." Her black hair was cut into a sharp bob at her chin. Her lips were bright red, and intensity radiated from her.

He paused, sizing her up. Her dark eyes scanned him from head to toe, and he resisted the urge to fidget. He left himself open to her scrutiny, reminding himself there was nothing this woman could do to him. He had absolutely nothing to fear. He slipped his hands into his pockets, letting his posture become more casual.

"Training? Why do I need to go to training?"

She pursed her red lips, "King's orders."

He tsked, "Not good enough. I haven't complained about the machines, the restraints, or the tests, but if I'm going to train, I need a reason." He slowed his words, "Why do I need to train?"

She exhaled sharply, "We've tested what we can internally. Blood, sight, hearing, etc. I won't run through the whole list. The king needs you to test the rest. Training is the way to ensure that your body is working...*properly* again."

Carrion mulled it over in his head. He did want to please the king. The king had helped him thus far. Besides, what else was he going to do?

He tilted his head, "After you, lady."

The corner of her lip twitched, but she didn't respond to his comment. It made him want to poke at her again. He bet he could get a reaction. She pushed the curtain back fully and started walking. Her heels clicked on the tile floors, and he quickened his pace to keep up. They walked past other rooms, if they could be called that, like his. He tried to see past them, tried to see what else was happening, but it was all he could do to keep up with her.

He kept his eye on her back, pace remaining fast, as he tried to get a glimpse of anything that was around them. He finally saw one other person behind the curtains. His pace slowed. A gaping red hole was all that was left of this man's right eye. He sat on the edge of his bed, his other eye refusing to focus on anything.

The white coats saw him as he passed, and were quick to close the curtains. He tried to find the woman, finally spotting a glimpse of black hair far ahead. He rushed to catch up to her. "If you get lost, Carrion, I will not be coming to find you." She said once he was directly behind her again.

He quickly stepped forward so he was walking next to her. "It seems unfair that you know my name but I don't know yours, lady."

Her eyes skimmed him briefly before focusing forward, "Life's a bitch."

He fell back, again following her. He didn't let her rejection of small talk bother him. They wound through massive rooms full of these identical 'curtain rooms' before reaching a massive door. She scanned her card against the keypad and then entered a code. He counted eight beeps, but couldn't see over her shoulder for the actual numbers.

The door opened, and he was quick to follow when she stepped through. As soon as the door closed behind them, silence descended. He had grown accustomed to the noise of the other room, and now the silence felt heavy. The only sound was her heels on the floor.

She didn't look behind once, expecting him to follow as she walked down hallway after twisting hallway. Finally, they arrived at another door. This doorway was smaller than the previous, but she repeated the same motion. Scan the card, type numbers, open the door.

She stepped inside, holding the door open for Carrion. He stepped into a massive training room. It extended further than the current lights did, ending in shadows over a full boxing ring. Punching bags hung from the ceiling in perfect rows, and the weight racks were full of everything from dumbbells to bars.

"Your trainer will be here shortly." She started to leave, but he spoke up.

"Is the king coming as well?"

She frowned at him, "I can't imagine the king being interested in the likes of you."

She closed the door, leaving him behind. The sound echoed in the training room. He turned in a circle, taking it all in. He wondered if he should be afraid. Was that the normal reaction to not remembering your past? Or was it better to keep moving forward? He didn't know what was normal, but he didn't feel afraid. When he woke up, he had felt concerned about his loss of memory, but already that concern had faded.

He picked up a weight, wondering if it would feel heavy after his time in bed rest. He inhaled, then exhaled as he curled it upwards. He barely felt his muscles tighten. He frowned at the weight. It was one of the heavier ones on the rack. He tried again with the same result. He set it down, about to pick up another weight, when the door opened.

"Carrion!" The voice was loud, filling the room with its echo. "I was told you would be in here."

Carrion turned and stood at attention. His arms felt natural behind his back, and he straightened automatically in anticipation of whatever would come next. "And you are?"

The man walked around him, assessing every part of him. He didn't answer the question until he was back in front of Carrion. "My name is Raze. I'm the personal trainer to the king and those he deems in need of my services."

Carrion smiled inwardly. He knew the woman was wrong. The king *had* personally visited him, and he *was* important. He nodded at Raze respectfully. "Sir," Carrion tested the word on his tongue, choosing to defer authority until he knew more about his own situation and station, "King Herring didn't give me any specific instruction as to what my training would involve. I would be interested to know what the goal is as we begin working together."

"Please, call me Raze." Carrion nodded. "I'm not at liberty to discuss the end goal of your training." Carrion almost rolled his eyes. Why was everyone so secretive about his life? What did they know that he didn't? "However, I can say my role is to push you to your limits. We will be exploring fighting techniques, weight training, and weaponry. The king would like to see how hard we can push your body. He's given us a week to discover what your limits are."

Carrion kept his posture sharp, watching the man in front of him. Raze was at least a head shorter than him, but his shoulders were almost twice as wide. "Raze, a week doesn't sound like enough time."

Raze's eyes squinted at him, "That's not the attitude I need from you, Carrion. Drop and give me 200 push-ups."

Carrion's jaw dropped, but with a look from Raze, he obeyed.

16 CLARA

Two days later, Clara could see the walls of Noxvalis in the distance. The journey had been grueling, and with their current crew, she realized how much of her first trip she had been distracted by Carver. Even in the misery of forest sleeping, he had provided something else for her to focus on.

She rolled her shoulders before circling her neck, trying to work out the kinks at the top of her back. "Okay, team," Nate called them to attention, "It's time we change direction." He held the map in front of him, squinting at the walls in the distance. He pointed to the small mark on the map, "This is where we're headed to get in. He pointed to the south side of the walls. "That's where we need to go."

They all nodded. Even Reese had fallen silent on this last leg of the journey. No one had slept well the night before, and although Marsh was beginning to cooperate, Clara wouldn't have said things were easier. They just *existed together*. That was the best she could hope for, apparently.

They started walking where Nate had pointed as he continued to speak, "Does everyone feel confident in our plan? It is vital we stay in the cover of the trees until we're ready to go through the doorway.

They shouldn't have regular patrols on the walls this far down, but I'm not willing to take any chances."

"Our best shot is to find it in the daylight, then use it after the sun sets," Marsh said.

Nate nodded, "That's what I was thinking. Clara, are you still okay to be the first one through?"

"Of course. Whatever the mission requires," she responded quickly.

"Reese?" Reese looked over her shoulder at Nate, "Are you still okay with having our backs?"

"Yes, sir!" Reese quickened her pace, and Clara kept up next to her. "I wouldn't mind having his back," Reese whispered, taking another peek behind them.

"Reese!" Clara laughed, "As you pointed out, he's over a decade older than us."

Reese smiled wistfully, "And the years have done nothing but perfect him. Have you seen that ass?"

Clara shook her head, rolling her eyes upward, "I thought you only wanted something if it was serious."

"Oh, he's serious. His take-charge attitude is hot. He's serious about every single step of this assignment."

"You know that's not what I meant."

Reese shrugged, her smile dropping, "It would be serious enough. As serious as something can be before we all die."

Clara shoved her, and Reese stumbled over a rock before righting herself. "Please don't talk like that. We won't die. If we all work together, we can do this."

Reese shoved Clara back, her smile returning. "How do you do it?"

"Hmm?" Clara carefully climbed over a fallen tree.

"You've gone on so many assignments. How are you not afraid? How do you keep going?"

"Spite," Clara answered with little thought.

"Spite?" Reese questioned.

"When someone tells me I can't do something, I become absolutely determined I can. Carver told me I wasn't capable of surviving as an operative. Actually, he pulled strings to get me appointed as a Viper because he thought I'd drop out, but that's beside the point." Reese's jaw dropped, "I always remind myself I can do whatever other people tell me I can't. It's how I keep going."

"Spite," Reese repeated. "Yeah, I have some people I would like to spite."

Clara raised an eyebrow at her, "Oh?"

Reese kept her gaze ahead, "The last guy I...you know, I actually started to like. It's what first made me consider abdicating those assignments. He was different from the other Vipers I've met. He seemed to have good qualities."

"What happened?"

Reese huffed, "I got my next assignment."

Clara grimaced. Reese continued, "I was too scared to tell Command I wouldn't do it. So I broke things off with him. He said some things I don't really want to repeat."

"Well, you may have dodged a bullet then?" Clara attempted to be the optimist, but it didn't feel right.

"I don't want to repeat it because everything he said is true. It cut. I still left, and proved him right on everything he said."

"I'm sorry, Reese."

"That was the last assignment I did for Command, of that nature. You know, I told them I wouldn't anymore. That gave me the drive to. Maybe that counts as spite?"

"I think so, and even if it doesn't, you have a great use of spite here. You can spite Command by surviving this assignment."

"Brilliant," Reese sang. "Then I will survive, for the sake of spite." She giggled.

"Everything okay up there?" Nate called.

"I'm going to survive out of spite!" Reese called back.

Clara looked over her shoulder at Nate and shrugged. "It's better than calling it a suicide mission."

Marsh rolled her eyes. "Great. Now there's two optimists."

"I'm offended that you think I'm an optimist just because I think I can survive. That's a very low bar." Clara shouted over her shoulder.

"It's my bar."

Reese started moving faster, and Clara kept up with her. "Okay, seriously though," Reese whispered, "Do you think I have a shot with Nate?"

"Reese, I am the last person on Earth you should be asking about *anything* dating-related. Believe me. Whatever I have to say, you should not be following it."

Reese pouted, "I'm only looking for a yes or no."

Clara took in her friend's expression and the begging look in her eyes. *What the hell.* "Yes, I think you have a shot."

Reese squealed, then tempered her excitement, "You know that means you're going to have to talk to Marsh again. See if you can make amends or at least keep her occupied."

Clara forced a smile, "Oh, I was so hoping for that opportunity again. I'm really missing being called a bitch!"

"She's not all bad. I talked to her for a little bit. You actually have a lot in common."

Clara groaned. "That is not what I wanted to hear. I really wanted to hear that we are nothing alike."

17 CLARA

"Okay, team. We should be approaching the door. Let's slow down and keep an eye out for any holes in the wall or other weak points. Maybe even debris stacked against the wall." Nate called them to attention.

They fell into silence, and Clara was grateful. As much as she was enjoying the time with Reese and truly getting to know her friend, she was ready to have her mind back for a bit. Reese could talk on and on, and had for the last hour.

Clara scanned the wall carefully, keeping her eyes bouncing between that and her feet. They trekked on for another hour, pausing to climb over a couple more trees that had fallen. Clara led the way, Reese behind her, and Nate taking up the rear.

"I think that's it." Clara pointed ahead of her. The vines crawling up the walls had split into a gap, pieces on the sides broken, while thinner vines had already begun regrowing across the center.

Nate stood by her side, squinting at the door. He groaned. "Hell, that's going to be a tight fit."

Reese stood beside him, staring at the door with them. She quietly responded, "That's what she said."

Clara turned to look at Reese in surprise, but Nate didn't take his eyes off the door. However, Clara noted the light pink tinge on his face. He cleared his throat. "We should take a few minutes to rest, drink, eat, whatever else you need to do." His voice trailed off momentarily. "Then regroup here as the sun is setting. That will give us the best chance for success."

Reese saluted him. Nate exhaled heavily, set his pack down, and walked into the forest away from them. Marsh eyed Reese, "You're an interesting one."

"Oh, you're talking to me now?"

Marsh held her breath before answering, "Nate said we had to be a team."

"And because Nate said, you'll listen?"

"Nate is the most respected Raven there is. He's been an operative for years, and everyone praises him. He was someone I looked up to before the assignment that landed me in Noxvalis."

"He seems like an amazing guy," Reese stared in the direction he had departed.

"He is." Marsh answered, eyeing Reese sardonically, "But he doesn't do relationships. Ever. I don't think he's ever even slept with a girl. The assignments are everything to him, and anything that doesn't complete the assignment effectively, is worthless."

"Why are you telling me this?"

"I'm telling you not to get attached. He'll be whatever he needs to be to make sure the three of us stay in line, but once this assignment is over, he won't remember you exist." Marsh shrugged, leaving her pack next to Nate's and walking into the forest in the opposite direction he headed.

Clara gave Reese what she hoped was an encouraging smile, "You do know how to pick 'em."

"You do know how to pick 'em," Reese mocked.

They both set their packs on the ground. The lack of weight was an instant relief. Clara folded her body forward, hands on her toes as she breathed in and out. "Am I allowed to ask?" Reese said tentatively.

Clara raised her head enough to respond, "Ask what?"

"What should I expect? What happened last time you were here?"

Clara blinked quickly, unprepared for the rush of emotion with the simple question. She stared at the ground, continuing to stretch. "Of course. We need to survive this. Ask whatever you need to ask."

"Is the food different here?"

Clara laughed. "You didn't need permission to ask that question." She stood up and stretched her arms across her body, pulling against the tension from carrying packs for so long.

"I know, but it's not what I really wanted to ask."

Clara chewed on her bottom lip, her tongue finding the spot she'd already cut. She hadn't even realized she'd done so. But anxiety had a way of working itself out of her body. "Ask what you want to ask, Reese. No need to play games or brush around it."

"Are you okay? Are you capable of handling this assignment well? After...Carver?" Reese's eyes were gentle, albeit imploring.

Clara inhaled deeply, trying to push past the anger that rose in her chest at the suggestion she might not be capable of this assignment. She was capable enough to do anything she was handed. She always had been, and always would be.

"I'm capable of handling this assignment," she sounded robotic, but she meant it. Clearing her throat, she tried to add more feeling to her words. "I need this. I know what this place is like. I've seen the destruction they create. We can't let them do this to our people. We can't let them win. I don't want innocents to suffer because of the monstrosity that is Noxvalis."

She looked around, ensuring neither Marsh nor Nate was near before she continued. "My additional assignment the last time I was here was to assassinate the king. That's why they sent me."

Reese's eyes widened, "That's a true suicide mission."

"No more than this is. If I had figured out how to, if I had been smarter and less reckless, I could've done it."

Reese shook her head. "Guards always surround the king. They wanted you to kill yourself. Command wanted you to be Noxvalis's problem."

"I don't think that's true."

"It is." Nate's voice behind Clara came as a surprise, but not enough for her to startle. She had forgotten he was an impressive spy.

Of course, he was able to sneak up on them. It wasn't surprising. "Over the last decade, Command has become less and less…righteous, for lack of a better word. They have sacrificed operatives and hidden information. I don't think they're all corrupt. We have some really good leaders, but there is a sect within Command that is no longer operating with Quorath's best intentions in mind."

Reese nodded in agreement. "They've taken to killing our own. As shown by my assignments."

Clara looked between them, "Then why do we stay? Why are we doing this for Command if they're no better?"

"We're not doing it for Command. We're doing it for the people of Quorath. They deserve our protection. It isn't easy to separate them from Command, but it has to be done. It also isn't true to say Quorath is no better." He sighed, running his hand through his hair as Marsh approached.

"Command may not be 'good,' but they are the lesser of two evils." Marsh motioned towards Clara, "You saw it firsthand. There isn't much worse than the experiments Noxvalis is willing to partake in. Even if Command is corrupt, they still have one foot in morality, and that's something worth fighting for."

"If we make it back," Nate started.

"When," Clara interrupted.

He shot her a look, "When we make it back," he corrected himself, "We can start talking to other operatives and make sure we have the whole picture. Then we can begin to change things. Command was never created to operate with no checks. The military is in place for that check. If we have enough evidence, we can make a change."

"We're soldiers. Why would anyone trust our involvement in politics?" Clara challenged, even as hope rose within her that maybe they could change things for the better.

"We've seen things people don't even know exist. Ignorance is bliss, but we will remove that ignorance. We'll give them a reason to trust us."

Nate scanned each of their faces. "We will survive this," he decided. His eyes made it to the sky, the sun beginning its descent.

"Okay, team. It's time." They all nodded. "Carry your packs in your hands. You won't be able to go through the door with them on our backs. Clara, you'll go through first like we planned. Marsh will push your bag through once you clear the doorway. She'll push hers through as well, then she'll follow. I'll come through next, and Reese, I'll take your bag. You'll stand at guard until all of us are through. Then it will be your turn."

"Yes, sirrrr," Reese's eyes sparkled. Clara hid her smile with a cough, and Marsh rolled her eyes.

"At least someone here understands the proper amount of respect," Nate said, giving Clara and Marsh a look.

Clara picked her pack up and walked to the edge of the forest. There was only about 10 feet between the edge of the forest and the walls. The dirt had pulled away on both sides, creating a trench. Thankfully, it had been days since it had rained, but she knew reaching the doorway comfortably would be a challenge. She carefully slid down the side of the trench on her side. It wasn't deep, maybe three to four feet.

She left her pack at the bottom and reached the door on the other side. It was just above her head. She grabbed a handful of the vines with her left hand and pulled herself up enough to have her knee on the dirt before the door. The door cracked open, then caught on the vines.

She slipped a dagger out of its sheath at her side and used it to slice through the vines covering the door. Then she leveraged the dagger between the wood and the door, finally pulling the door open.

She grunted as it swung open, causing her to slip from the ledge and catch herself with the vines. She felt her shoulder pull, and gritted her teeth. She grabbed the vines with both hands and pulled herself up. Once both knees were on the ground, she crawled through the doorway.

On the other side, she quickly stood, taking notes of everything around her. She heard the bustle of the city, but thankfully, their intel had been correct. She didn't see anyone else in the alley.

The doorway was behind a building with two different alleys on either side of the building. Those alleys were blocked off by buildings as well. Her heart raced, and she didn't like how caged she felt between the wall and the buildings. She inhaled deeply, exhaling slowly as she waited for Marsh to come through.

She crouched to the side of the doorway, ready to grab her bag, and watched everything around her. A couple of seconds passed, and then Marsh pushed her bag up. She pulled it through the doorway. Next came Marsh's bag, and Clara set the two bags to the side of the doorway. She took position standing in front of the door between the alleys, daggers ready at her sides. She didn't pull them, but stood ready to at a second's notice.

Marsh scrambled up through the doorway, breathing hard when she came to stand next to Clara. "Can't believe I'm admitting this," Marsh muttered, "But you made that look way easier than it actually was."

Clara barely glanced her way as she stayed focused on her task. "When I'm at base, I almost never stop training."

"I can tell," Marsh said with an eye roll. She knelt and pulled Nate's bag through the doorway. Clara turned sharply to the right at a rustle, but it was only a cat. It eyed her the way she eyed it, and she didn't relax as Marsh pulled Reese's pack up.

Nate followed, coming to stand behind Clara's shoulder as she continued her observation. "Anything?"

Clara nodded to the right, but the cat was already gone. "Only an orange cat."

By the time Reese was up and they pulled the doorway closed, the sun had fully set. They pulled their packs back on, and Marsh took the lead.

18 CARRION

Raze didn't give compliments. He was brutal in his position of making Carrion the best. But after five days of training with him, Carrion knew he was better for it. The first two days, his body hesitated. He remembered the previous pain clearly, and he could feel the fear of that pain returning in every action.

Raze terrified that fear out of him. He pushed Carrion harder than he knew his body was capable of. They trained all day, every day, breaking only for lunch and dinner, then back at it. Raze didn't believe in breakfast, wanting Carrion to have at least one workout that was fully fasted.

Carrion was already beginning to enjoy pushing himself. He took it all in stride, following through with each and every action. "Sharpen that movement! You act like you've never held a sword before!" Raze shouted, jabbing him in the side where his posture wasn't correct.

"I haven't," Carrion admitted, "As far as I know at least." Raze didn't respond, but didn't punish him for the comment. This was the fifth weapon he had trained with this week. Day 1 was daggers, day 2 guns, day 3 stars, day 4 bo staff, and now, day 5. So far, this was his least favorite.

The sword was heavy, and reluctant to do his bidding. Even with his strength, he could feel the weight of the weapon pulling on muscles he hadn't tested yet. He went through the motions Raze had drilled into him again. "When will this come in handy? Why would I ever choose a sword over a gun?"

Raze huffed in the back of his throat, "It's a matter of discipline. While not useful in the battle, the art of swordsmanship and the muscles used in it are something you won't learn with another weapon."

"Don't all weapons possess discipline?"

"Every form of training maintains its own level of discipline and learning. But swordsmanship is not one often taught. Because of that, it requires an additional level of determination to master its art."

Carrion accepted the explanation, continuing through the motions. After a few more passes, he felt his muscles relax into the movement. He had noticed that over the last few days of training. Something would be difficult, but after enough rounds, his body would fully accept it. He didn't know what he had been like before the accident, but he did find it strange how quickly his body accepted new movements.

With all the training, he still hadn't woken up sore. When he closed his eyes to sleep at night, he fell asleep immediately. Once or twice, a lingering thought tugged at his mind. A girl, maybe? Dark hair? But when he tried to grasp the thought, it always slipped away.

Raze walked around him, examining his posture again. "Get some water, then we will practice."

"Yes, sir." Carrion hung the sword back up on the wall and grabbed his water bottle.

"The king has decided he would like to see your progress in two days," Raze said the words monotonously, and Carrion wondered what Raze actually thought about the king's attention.

"Excellent. I'm certain I'll be ready by then."

Raze nodded, "Of course you will. With my training, you could be ready tomorrow."

Carrion didn't disagree, keeping all his comments inside. Raze's training wasn't the reason he was capable of the feats he was discovering. Raze may have encouraged him and provided the lessons, but all of the skill was his alone, and Raze couldn't take credit for that.

"Of course." Carrion agreed instead.

"Okay, sword up. Time to see if you can beat me."

19 CLARA

Clara set her pack down in the bookstore's kitchen, feeling far more relieved to see the familiar space than she had expected. "Reese, Clara, you can take the third-floor bedroom. Clara knows where it is. The armoire in the room has extra blankets and a change of sheets." A small twinge bloomed in her chest at Marsh's words, but she pushed it away. "Nate, are you good with taking the couch down here?"

"Absolutely. Anything beats sleeping in the forest."

"Excellent. Now that's out of the way, Nate?" Marsh pulled a chair from the table and slid into the seat.

Nate leaned against the wall, arms crossed over his chest. "Everyone needs to get some rest. We should have enough food so we don't need to go out tonight. Marsh, are your connections here still good?"

She nodded. "I was careful not to burn any bridges or raise suspicion when I left."

"Excellent. You'll need to loan clothing to Clara and Reese for tomorrow. Command didn't send us anything fitting for Noxvalis, another example of a suicide mission, and these black uniforms will certainly stand out. I brought a few t-shirts and pants I had from other assignments, so I should be fine for the time being."

"Understood," Marsh looked over Reese and Clara. Clara was smaller in frame than Reese and taller. Reese was stockier, though Marsh was curvy enough that it would hopefully fit. "Clara, I don't think any of my pants will work for you. But I have a couple skirts you should be able to pull off. Reese, I think you can fit in my stuff, but it might be a little tight."

"Skirts, my favorite," Clara muttered.

"Are you saying I'm fat?" Reese pressed a hand to her chest in mock offense.

"You're certainly not fat," Nate answered very matter-of-factly. He looked over the three of them. "You're not at all the same size-wise, but hopefully Marsh's stuff will work okay until we can get clothes that actually fit you."

Reese yawned, covering her mouth with her hand. "Get some rest," Nate's eyes crinkled as he looked at Reese. "Tomorrow will be a long day, so everyone should take advantage of tonight."

Clara shouldered her pack with a grunt, "Reese, I'll show you where our room is."

Reese followed her up the stairs, and Clara opened the door, expecting everything to be different. But it was all the same.

The pallet Carver slept on was still on the floor, the blankets strewn. The bed was unmade, covers wadded up, and pillows lying on the floor where she had tossed them. Clara stepped into the room slowly, scared to disturb anything. Reese put a hand on her shoulder.

Clara shook the feeling off. He was gone. This room, the pallet, wasn't a memento to him. It wouldn't bring him back. They needed to sleep, so she needed to handle this.

She set her pack in the corner, careful not to look at Reese. She didn't want Reese to see how desperately she was holding back tears. She started with the bed, stripping the sheets off, wadding all the bedding up, and setting it next to the armoire. She opened it and pulled the sheets out.

Reese silently helped her remake the bed. "The bathroom is there," Clara motioned towards the open door.

"Sounds good. I'm going to go back downstairs to get some...I'm going to run downstairs for something. I'll be back." Reese answered. Clara looked at her quizzically, but Reese was gone before she had a moment to question what she was going downstairs for.

Once the door closed behind Reese, Clara finally folded Carver's pallet. She picked up his pillow, holding it against her chest, and breathing in the scent of him that was left. The tears came quickly then, and this time she didn't stop them. She leaned against the edge of the bed, holding the pillow to her chest as she sobbed. She had gotten her best friend killed. The only man she had ever loved, and he was dead because of her stupidity.

The tears didn't last long, but they left her with a pounding headache. She looked up, surprised that Reese hadn't returned. She swiped her hands across her face aggressively, wiping the remnants of tears away as she added Carver's bedding to the pile she had made. She opened the door and peered down the stairs, hoping Reese was okay.

She slipped from the room, silently closing the door behind her. She tiptoed down the stairs, listening carefully. Hushed voices came from the kitchen. She padded her way across the floor, then pressed her back to the side of the doorway. Light flooded from the kitchen across the floor, but she stayed hidden just to the side of it.

"I think you're really pretty, Reese. Gorgeous, actually. That's not the problem." Nate's voice was the first she heard. Clara's heart thundered. She most definitely should not be present for this conversation, but she couldn't find it in herself to move.

"Oh yeah? Then what's the problem? You were definitely flirting with me earlier." Clara winced at the sass in Reese's voice and wished she could see Nate's expression.

She heard him sigh. "One way or another, this assignment is my retirement. Whether that's from death, or a signed resignation shortly after I return. I will stay long enough to help the three of you, but then I'm out. I've done this long enough. This," he paused, and Clara could only imagine what their facial expressions were, "This," he reiterated, softer, "Doesn't work."

"What if we didn't go back, Nate? What if we took this as an opportunity to leave? Suicide mission, right? Let's go somewhere else. Calyndor maybe? Or even the Isle Kingdom. Somewhere, this must work."

"Reese," he said her name with a groan, "The location isn't the only problem. We don't work."

"You haven't even given us a shot!"

"There's not an us."

Reese didn't respond, and Clara quickly left the doorway so neither of them would catch her. She locked herself in the bathroom, washing her face and changing for the night. She let herself take a warm shower, hoping it would give Reese time to compose herself before she came out.

When she opened the bathroom door, steam wafted out with her. Reese sat on the bed, her legs crossed, with a huge smile on her face. She practically bounced as Clara stepped into the room. Clara continued drying her hair with a towel as she asked, "What are you so happy about?" She kept her tone clear of any judgment.

"I kissed Nate."

"You WHAT?" Clara couldn't help the volume of her voice as she dropped her towel and turned to fully face her friend.

Reese smiled proudly, "Well, he gave me an explanation for why it wouldn't work between us."

Yes, I heard that. Clara thought, but since she couldn't say that, she just nodded. "And that led to a kiss?"

"Well, I didn't have a rebuttal for his reasoning, so I just kissed him. Annnd even better, he kissed me back!"

"Wow, Reese, wow."

"I know, right?? I'm so happy."

"That was fast," Clara exhaled. Her head felt like it was spinning. What was it about this bookstore that led people to interesting relationship choices?

"You're happy for me though, right?"

"Yeah, Reese. Nate seems like an amazing guy. I think he'll do right by you. I really hope it works for you." She smiled, although she could feel how tight it was.

Reese accepted her words and took her stuff into the bathroom. Clara closed her eyes tightly once Reese was out of sight and reminded herself to breathe in and breathe out. In a way, it felt like history was repeating itself. The Raven and the Viper. Destined to be entangled, destined to destroy one another. The Viper would always destroy the Raven.

Clara reminded herself that Reese wasn't like her. Reese had goodness; she didn't. But she couldn't help the feeling that she had no idea what Reese was capable of. The last couple of years, Clara thought Reese had never killed anyone. She was convinced of it, actually. But Reese had. She had killed many people. And for what? Command's orders. She'd killed other operatives. Other Vipers.

Clara inhaled deeply and released it, shaking off the fear. This would be fine.

20 CARRION

It was finally time to present to the king. Raze had been more than a little moody the day before. He snapped at Carrion for every detail that wasn't perfect and worked him even harder than he had until this point. Considering how hard Carrion was pushing himself in training every day, that said a lot.

Carrion rose early and immediately made his way to the training room. Raze was already there, pacing the floor. "A suit was delivered for you this morning." He pointed at the clothing hanging from one of the punching bags.

It was black stretchy material with red stitching. "I suggest you put it on, not just stare at it!" Raze shouted when Carrion hadn't made a move to wear it yet.

"Yes, sir," Carrion called back, removing his clothes quickly. The suit fit perfectly. It was tight over his muscles, but stretched in a way that made it feel intentional. He went through his stretches and warm-up. Raze had taught him it was the start of every good session, and noted how the fabric felt over his body. He didn't feel too hot or too cold, and he wondered if the material had something to do with that.

"The king will be here at 1100. My job here is done." Raze nodded at him, leaving before Carrion had a chance to respond. He was supposed to present to the king on his own?

All of this week, he had assumed Raze would be involved, or at least be introducing him. He stared at the door for a couple of moments, wondering if this was Raze's way of punishing him for some unspoken altercation. But Raze didn't come back. He had no idea what the king expected.

His thoughts raced as he wondered how this presentation would go. King Herring had seemed quite fond of him when he'd awoken from surgery, so he really didn't feel too nervous about his wrath. No, he wasn't scared of making the king angry. He was scared of disappointing him. He wanted the king to be impressed by his performance and feel proud of how hard he had worked. He wanted King Herring to recognize that Carrion valued his orders and would commit himself in every way possible.

With that in mind, Carrion continued to rehearse his drills, keeping one eye on the clock. At 1055, he put his weapon away and stood at attention. The door opened exactly five minutes later, and two guards stepped into the room. They held the door open for King Herring, who followed them in. Two more guards filed in behind him, carrying a chair.

"Carrion, I hope your training with Raze has been more successful than his other," the king's face curled in disgust. "Exploits." *I thought he was the king's personal trainer?*

"Your Majesty," Carrion bowed low, remembering the rules of respect Raze had taught him.

"Stand, son. I'm here to see the progress you've made. We did a lot to keep you alive," King Herring turned to sit in the chair his guards had brought in. Carrion heard him mutter, "Even if some have questioned that choice." The king laid his arms across the armrests, the picture of elegant royalty. Carrion straightened even further.

"Where would you like me to begin, Your Majesty?"

The king waved at him in annoyance, "Raze was supposed to run you through this. Don't tell me he's left you entirely unprepared! That fool!"

"Apologies, Your Majesty," Carrion bowed again, "I was under the impression you may have a specific request. Raze did give me a routine to run through. I will begin there." *Fuck you, Raze. Leaving me here with absolutely no practical training.* Carrion thought, well aware he had just lied to the king. Raze may have taught him well, but he did not give him anything to run through for the king.

He started with the daggers, throwing five perfectly into the bullseye of a target at 100 yards. The king nodded, but gave no other indication of approval. Carrion picked up a sword with the intention of running through the motions of swordsmanship that Raze had so carefully drilled him on.

"Son, don't tell me Raze wasted your time with a weapon so outside the scope of our use! Put that away and demonstrate your gun skills."

Carrion kept his face straight as he did what the king commanded. *So, I was right.* He kept the smirk off his face, not surprised that he understood the king's expectations better than Raze did. Raze didn't seem to have the experience needed for the position he had been placed in.

Carrion picked up the loaded gun and fired the entirety of the mag. Every bullet hit the center of the target. "Now that's a skill we can use." The king stated proudly.

Carrion bowed, replacing the weapon on the table. He then went through the fighting stances Raze had taught him, including flips and evasion tactics. The king finally applauded. "Tell me, son, how confident are you in your abilities to defend yourself?"

Carrion stood straight, hands clasped behind his back. "Extremely confident, Your Majesty. I have pushed myself to the limits in every category Raze suggested, and then some. I have no doubt I can defend myself physically in any situation."

Carrion felt uneasy at the glint in the king's eyes as he replied, "That is a lot of confidence, son." They both stared at each other, and Carrion didn't flinch under the king's assessment, waiting for him to verbalize what he observed. "Guards," the king stated, without taking his eyes off Carrion, "No guns. Take him out."

All four guards stepped forward. They wore no masks, making their faces and necks the obvious target. Their hands were also bare. Their arms, chest, and legs were covered in armor. The armor split at the joints, so those were possible spots as well. No one walked with a limp, and they did a good job of hiding anything they favored.

Carrion backed up quickly, not taking his eyes off the approaching guards. He rammed into the table and grabbed what was left of his knives from the top. "Oh, pretty boy wants the knives?" The first guard sneered. He pulled out a sword, and Carrion's eyes widened.

He took his eyes off the guard just long enough to glance at the king. The king watched, looking almost bored, "Oh, did I forget to mention all of my guards are trained in swordsmanship for the purpose of resolving internal conflict?"

Thank you, Raze. Carrion jumped high over the sword as the guard swung at his waist, landing to the left of the blow. He flicked his wrist and landed the dagger just above the man's collar in his throat. Blood dribbled, then spewed as the guard pulled the dagger out. Shock was apparent in his eyes as he stared at the dagger.

One down, three to go. The other three were smarter, circling him away from his ability to pull more weapons. He flicked the second dagger, and the guard on his right batted it from the air with his sword, the resounding clang ringing through the training room. Carrion sprinted backwards, jumping into the boxing ring. The height gave him the high ground, though all three still approached at the same time.

"Marcus, circle to the back, Derek, take the left side. I'll approach from this corner." One guard stated, and the other two rushed to do his bidding.

The guard who gave the orders walked slowly to the edge of the mat; the other two behind him already had hands on the ropes, ready to jump him the second they got in. Carrion's eyes scanned the room in a second. There, behind the guard giving orders, his sword on the wall. All he had to do was take this one guard. He threw a dagger at his face. The guard dodged it, but didn't dodge Carrion jumping out of the boxing ring and landing a blow to his face. Carrion slipped behind him as the guard grasped his bloody nose and brought the dagger across his throat. The guard fell to his knees when he stepped away, and he sprinted to his sword, knowing the other two would be on him in a heartbeat. He dropped the daggers in the process, but pulled the sword down in time to parry a hit from the guard named Marcus.

Marcus took a wide stance, nostrils flaring as he glanced at his fallen commander and back to Carrion. "You're going down."

Carrion just smiled. With a twist of his wrist, he brought the sword hard against Marcus's, then slid the blade down. He hit the hilt of Marcus's sword with his own, and Marcus cried out as his wrist twisted. Carrion hit it again, and the sword fell from Marcus's hands. Carrion brought the hilt of his sword down on Marcus's head and spun to deflect the blow from Derek. Derek jumped back after the impact and stood with his arms bent in front of him as he and Carrion circled each other.

Carrion grinned, the adrenaline amplifying his mood. He spun his sword in one hand, smiling wider when Derek flinched. He brought the sword down against Derek in a quick succession of moves, not stopping until Derek's sword landed 10 feet away. Derek fell back, pushing himself back with his hands and heels, terror in his eyes.

The king started applauding. "You can leave him, Carrion. Come, stand in front of me."

Carrion gave Derek one more once over, then left him to stand before the king. "Derek, take your weapon and get cleaned up. I expect you to report for your next shift as usual, and mention nothing of this training exercise."

"Yes, My Lord," Derek answered. Carrion didn't miss the shaking in his voice.

He stood before the king proudly. He wondered if he should be angry at the setup, at this additional test. But he didn't feel angry. He felt fulfilled. He felt like the king was allowing him to prove himself, and he could only be grateful.

"That was a brilliant execution of your skills, Carrion." The king nodded at him, pride shining in his eyes. Carrion did his best to bite back the smile he felt pulling at his lips. "Tell me, how do you feel?"

"Your Majesty?" Carrion questioned. *How do I feel about what? Physically, how do I feel? Amazing.*

"Do you regret killing one of my soldiers?"

Carrion felt a sharp pain across his chest, but when he brought it to the forefront of his mind, it wasn't regret for the kill. It was fear that he had disappointed the king by killing the guards. He chose his next words carefully, "My only goal is to serve you, Your Majesty. I do not regret the blood I have spilled in my attempt to prove myself useful."

The king leaned against his backrest, and Carrion's heart raced. Would he be enough? Would the king approve of his attempt, or was this the end? "You did very well, son. You didn't question what needed to be done. Raze may be worthless, but he has found a new purpose in your training. You did well today, Carrion. Are you ready to be my soldier?"

Pride swelled in his chest. "Yes, Your Majesty."

21 CLARA

"Of course, you can't agree on which path to take. That's because you're both so, so wrong." Marsh interjected.

Nate and Clara had been outlining plans on the map for the last hour. Reese hung by the table, but she didn't try to offer suggestions. She just gave encouraging smiles and the occasional kind comment to both of them.

Nate looked at Marsh wearily, "What is the right path, then, Marsh? And you better not be interrupting just to interrupt."

"I'm honestly offended you think so little of me." She responded. She pushed her way between Clara and Nate, and Clara threw her hands up in frustration before taking the seat next to Reese.

"It's not a bad idea for you to have a break," Reese whispered. "Want a cup of coffee?" Before Clara had a chance to respond, Reese was already standing. She poured the cup and handed it to Clara.

Clara smiled, "Thank you, Reese."

Marsh outlined a path between the two that Nate and Clara had been arguing over. "How do you suggest we go that way? There's a massive building there. We can't just go through the building."

"You can if you know the owner. It's a warehouse. We can go through it. I know the owner."

Nate took a step back from the table. "And you only now thought you should mention this?"

Marsh shrugged one shoulder delicately, "It was fun watching you and Clara debate, and I wanted to make sure that my idea would line up with your plans. I observed that it will work, and now I am sharing it."

Nate huffed, but didn't answer. Reese hid a smile behind her hand, glancing between Marsh and Nate. Clara rolled her eyes at the whole exchange. "We're a team, Marsh." Nate finally answered. "You should have shared the idea when you first had it instead of watching us chase our tails for the last hour."

Marsh didn't back down. "As I said, I shared it once I believed it to be relevant. I'm sorry I didn't have the idea within your perfect time frame."

Clara glared at Marsh, but was trying desperately not to get involved. She would, however, enjoy seeing Nate take a piece out of her. To her dismay, he chose a route with more maturity. "I'm going for a walk. Any other ideas you have for our entrance into the labs, please share with Clara."

"Ooo, can I go with you?" Reese bounced up quickly, "It's stuffy in here. Fresh air sounds absolutely wonderful."

"Yeah, I'm sure that's it." Clara teased.

Nate looked at the ceiling, "Yes, you can come. Clara, Marsh, keep deliberating over the map."

Once the door closed behind them, Marsh groaned and sat in the seat to Clara's right, pulling the map in front of them. "So because he's sweet on her, she gets to go with him on a walk, and we are stuck here staring at the same map."

"We are also far more equipped to make decisions regarding said map." Clara reminded her. She traced her finger over the building that Marsh said they should cut through. "I think this would work," she muttered, drawing her finger from the building to the lab entrance.

"Wow, you're actually willing to agree with me on something."

Clara sat back in her chair to look at Marsh, "I don't hate you. I also don't think you're stupid, or incompetent, or anything else you seem to think I believe about you." Marsh was stunned into silence, so Clara took the opportunity to add, "I do think you're a bitch, but that's not an unredeemable quality."

"Pot, meet kettle," Marsh said with a laugh. "I guess we're both bitches."

Clara laughed with her, "We are operatives. Our lives revolve around these…assignments. Maybe being a bitch just comes with the job."

"Maybe." They settled into a silence before Marsh said, "I don't hate you either."

"No? You could've fooled me."

"You are…a lot. And Carver," Marsh inhaled and slowly exhaled, her eyes scanning the ceiling. "Carver was unlike anyone I had met here. I didn't know what to expect when they sent two operatives, but I didn't expect a couple. That isn't done. And the way you treated him frustrated me." Clara felt annoyance rise in her, but she pushed it down as Marsh continued. "But I treated you worse than you treated him. I should have recognized that you had a past and were figuring things out. It wasn't my place to say the things I said to you."

Clara nodded, unable to come up with words that represented the weight of the moment. Who would have thought she and Marsh would ever become amicable?

"My friend who owns this building," Marsh pointed at the building, "He'll be there tomorrow. It would be a good time for us to scope the area and talk to him for a bit. He should let us go straight through."

"What kind of friend is he? Won't he question all of us showing up with you? We aren't exactly a subtle group."

"He's the kind of friend who won't ask questions. I don't question him and his business pursuits, and he doesn't question me and mine."

"That's a nice friend to have."

"If we walk through tomorrow, it'll give Nate a chance to learn more about Noxvalis. He needs a better understanding of how to get around here if he's going to lead this mission. The alleys and city are nothing like the open roads in Quorath."

Clara chuckled, "That's for sure. And the bars here are so loud."

Marsh went silent, and Clara realized her mistake. She took a deep breath, "I did love him, you know. I don't know if that changes anything for you, but I loved him. And I hate myself for where we ended up. I know it's on me, and nothing I can do will change that."

Marsh nodded, "I know. And I don't blame you anymore. I'm choosing to let go of that. You're here, and we need to survive this. So that's enough for me."

The door crashed open, and Reese bounded in, immediately pouring herself a cup of coffee.

"Well, since you both are still at the table, I'm going to guess you found some common ground and figured out a path for us," Nate said.

Reese sat in the seat next to Clara, her energy palpable. Clara gently took the coffee cup away from her, "I'm not sure you need this."

Reese groaned, pretending to pout, but didn't try to take it back. "Butttt it's my happy juice?"

Clara shook her head as she sipped the coffee.

"We did," Marsh answered Nate's question. "Today will be dedicated to planning and rest, and tomorrow we will begin exploring and laying the groundwork for our lab break. My friend who owns the building should be there tomorrow. We'll go there first, and once you see everything, you'll be able to plot out a workable plan."

Nate leaned back against the counter, arms crossed over his chest. "I like it." He said slowly, "And the two of you have decided to work together going forward now?"

Marsh and Clara looked at each other before both looking back at Nate, "We will survive this assignment." Clara said, "We can hate each other again after we survive."

Marsh laughed, "We didn't sound that aggressive when we decided to get along."

Nate joined them at the table. "It looks like we may actually become a team. Marsh, do you need to let your contact know we're coming tomorrow?"

She shook her head. "We'll be fine to just show up."

He leaned back in his seat, pushing his hands against the table. "Is there anything we should know about this contact?"

"That's relevant to the assignment? No," she dodged the question.

Nate narrowed his eyes, and Marsh fully exhaled before continuing. "He's in love with me. Has been for at least the last year."

"Oooo," Reese teased.

Marsh glared, "It's not like that. I went on a handful of dates. He was so, so boring. It was never going to work."

"Will your previous attachment cause any interference in our assignment?"

Marsh lifted her head, tilting her chin down firmly. "It will not. He will be thrilled to see me, and I will handle conversations with him while you cut through and survey the surrounding areas."

"Remind me again why we can't use the alleys on either side?" Reese looked at Marsh sympathetically.

"One isn't a true alley, and is blocked by the buildings. The other ends in a stone wall. Certain businesses on this side of town, especially those with…shadier pursuits, don't like having open alleyways. It provides too much ease for thieves and vagabonds."

"Or people like us," Reese filled in the blank.

"Or people like us," Marsh confirmed.

Nate nodded his agreement before changing the subject. "Marsh, I'm sure you know a few spots where we can pick up food for dinner."

"Of course."

He stood, brushing his hands on his pants. "I would like to get a bit more acquainted with the town through someone who knows the area well. Escort me around, and we'll pick up food?" It could have been a demand, but he asked instead.

"No problem." Marsh stood with him. "Reese, are you allergic to anything?"

"Food related? No. People related? Sure. Some people make my skin crawl."

Marsh rubbed her forehead before following Nate out the door.

Clara crossed her arms on the table and rested her forehead on them. Planning with Marsh was not for the weak-minded. Reese gently stroked her back, continuing to stare at the door where Marsh and Nate had left.

"You don't think she likes him, do you?" Reese broke the silence.

"Does it matter? We've figured out the next step of the assignment. That's what we should focus on."

"You're telling me that, stuck on an assignment with Carver, you solely focused on the assignment? That's not what you told me, so I think you should have a little more compassion for me here."

Clara lifted her head, and Reese dropped her hand, picking at her fingers. Clara met her friend's gaze. "I'm sorry. I'm not being very kind." She breathed in, exhaling heavily. "If I had focused solely on the assignment, I wouldn't have made the mistakes I did last time." She held up a hand quickly correcting, "Not that I think you're prone to making similar mistakes. Just that, this time I'm way more committed to the assignment, and I forget not everyone else views it that way." Reese's eyes widened, and Clara covered her face with her hands, groaning, "That's not what I meant either! It's okay, you have feelings! I don't think he likes her! I'm sorry I shot myself in the foot so many times in this conversation!"

Reese started giggling. "It's okay. I knew what you meant."

Clara leaned back against the table, "Ugh, I'm just so tired. We spent all morning and all afternoon debating over that stupid map, and now my brain doesn't want to form helpful sentences."

"You're doing great. Nate clearly respects you, and you patched things up with Marsh. I certainly didn't see that one coming."

"Yeah," Clara admitted, "Neither did I."

"So we'll get through this."

"For the record," Clara added, "I do think Nate likes you. What happened on your walk?"

Reese pulled her feet into her chair, wrapping her arms around her knees. "He told me we could discuss the status of our relationship when we return from this assignment. But until then, his job is to keep us alive. He can't afford to be distracted, or favor one of us over the others."

Clara grimaced. "Ouch. You taking it okay?"

"I mean, I bounce back, but it definitely sucked to hear. Like, I know I haven't known him for that long. And maybe it is just a fearful infatuation. You know? Like we're going to die, so of course I found a hot man to attach myself to because it makes the dying thing more romantic." Reese finally took a breath, and Clara nodded along to her words carefully. "I don't think it's that, though. I mean, he has soooo many good qualities. The way he leads us? Hell, even the way he rejected me to prioritize the team. That shows responsibility, and that shit is hot."

Clara laughed, and Reese deflated a bit, looking smaller in her chair. "He's the kind of guy I would want to be with in a perfect world. But I know I'm not the kind of girl he's looking for."

22 CARRION

It was his first day as a personal guard to the king. He knew he wouldn't be stationed there forever, but the king felt it was important that Carrion receive a first-hand view of court proceedings and learn his role.

He stood at attention diagonally behind the king's throne on the left side. His posture was impeccable, his breathing almost unnoticeable.

The king had given him more than the bodysuit. While he had never thought armor was something he would desire, the king's scientists had created an impenetrable, flexible armor. Though they did say he would be the first to test it. The armor had molded to his body over the body suit, and it continued to take the shape of whatever position he was in.

He held his posture with pride. After all, he was the king's guard now. He hadn't given much thought to what he had survived. He had asked the king once more, but the king continued to be vague. The king would only tell him it was a miracle he survived and to continue forward. Since then, he decided that not remembering was a blessing. He was honored to serve the king, and whatever came before was irrelevant.

The first person came with a request for the king. Carrion scanned the man carefully, noting any place weapons could be hiding. The man's back was hunched, his skin dark and wrinkled from the amount of sun exposure. His hands were held in front of him, clutched together and constantly shifting.

Carrion immediately categorized him as a non-threat. Too nervous, and no place for weaponry. The man presented his request to the king, and though Carrion listened, he didn't retain anything that didn't interest him.

Person after person filed in to seek an audience with the king. All morning, Carrion stood there. He never flinched. He never changed position. He just watched and waited. At noon, the doors were closed to the public.

The king motioned Carrion forward, "What did you think, son? Speak truthfully, now."

"I think you spend a lot of time having to listen to people who can barely string together the correct words to form their request." Carrion blurted.

The king looked shocked, and Carrion almost added an apology, but the king started laughing. "Carrion, you are right. But know, the mark of a good ruler is listening to their people. Once every two weeks, I let people, preselected by my court officials, in to speak with me. It keeps the kingdom at peace.

Everyone wants to feel like they are in control. Everyone wants to feel like they have power. Very few people have any true form of power. The trick to keeping your power is making those who are powerless think they have power. That is all this is."

Carrion nodded, mentally filing away every word the king spoke. These words were worth something. These words he wanted to retain.

"What do you think about your position here in the court?"

Carrion kept his face blank, "As always, my only desire is to serve you, Your Majesty. Put me wherever you feel best."

"I admire your loyalty. Though I asked for an honest opinion. What do you think about your position here in the court?"

As though triggered by the king's request for honesty, Carrion answered, "I think it is a waste of my skill, Your Majesty. Your people are pre-vetted, and you are surrounded by guards on every side. My presence will not change your safety." The king didn't interrupt, so Carrion continued, "I believe I would be much more useful outside of the castle. I can assess threats faster than any other soldier." Carrion didn't know what he was requesting exactly. But he knew he needed a little more action.

He wouldn't survive stuck in a courtroom waiting for something to go wrong.

"I will grant your request." The king replied slowly, "I, too, believe you can be far more useful outside of my courtroom. But," the king slowed over the word, looking Carrion up and down. "Your surgeries were so recent, I will not send you out on your own. You completed my tests with flying colors, but still, I cannot afford to lose you." The king went silent, and Carrion felt sure his request would be denied before he continued with, "You must have a partner. Alius!" The king shouted.

A man with a neatly trimmed beard and short black hair approached. He dropped to one knee, "You called, My King?" Carrion noted immediately that the man's armor was far more similar to his than to any of the other guards. He narrowed his eyes in suspicion. Who was this man the king trusted more? Alius didn't raise his gaze from the floor until the king spoke again.

"Alius, you may stand. I have a new assignment for you." Alius's gaze finally met Carrion's, and the two men nodded at each other. The king motioned to Carrion, "This is my newest," he paused as if deliberating what word he would use, "Soldier. He has requested to be put in an area with more action. Your new assignment is to teach him about Noxvalis and how our soldiers maintain order here." Carrion didn't understand why the king would hesitate over calling him a soldier. He filed the pause away with the rest of his thoughts from today, determined to unpack it all later.

Alius nodded. "Carrion," the king addressed him, and Carrion's heart pounded, "You are dismissed for lunch. Alius will find you after lunch, and you will begin your work together."

Carrion nodded to Alius and bowed to the king as he said, "Yes, Your Majesty." He walked back through the courtroom, pausing at the exit door once he was out of sight.

The king's voice was soft, but Carrion could still pick out his words. "You are familiar with the work of my scientists."

"Of course, Your Majesty," Alius responded, and Carrion rolled his eyes. He was supposed to be working closely with the king. Why would the king remove him from this discussion?

"Carrion completed the operations eight days ago." Alius didn't respond, but the king added, "Shocking, right? He is our most successful yet, and the product of the only vial they left." The words spun across Carrion's mind, but he couldn't grasp them enough to make sense of them. "I want to know what his limits are, and if his loyalties are true. Your job is to ascertain this."

"Yes, Your Majesty," Alius responded.

Carrion carefully turned the door handle and slipped out. He walked towards the guards' dining hall, his steps fast. What did the king mean by "he is our most successful yet?" and "the product of the only vial they left?" Carrion took a tray of food and sat as far from the other guards as he could.

He ate his food without noting any of the characteristics as he tried to put the pieces together. He could feel it in his gut; something wasn't right. What had happened before his accident? His head started pounding as he tried to remember. He closed his eyes tightly, begging his mind to remember the before. Blue eyes? Dark hair? Grasping, grasping.

Then it was gone, and he was left with a splitting headache. He groaned inwardly, steadying himself with deep breathing. After a few seconds, the intensity passed, as did whatever he had been thinking about. When he opened his eyes, he couldn't remember what thought had triggered the headache. He shrugged it off. He had what he wanted.

Alius met him in the dining room shortly after he finished his food. "I will escort you into the town and teach you our ways. Guards live by a specific code, and if you are going to be one of us, you need to learn this code."

Carrion followed Alius through the halls and outside. He couldn't help feeling like a trained animal. He nodded and followed wherever he was told, learning the behavior required for his survival. Beyond that, he didn't know what his goals were or where he was headed. So he kept following, but he kept his eyes open. He was prepared for things to go south. *The product of the only vial…*the words surfaced in his mind, unbidden, but he stayed focused on Alius.

23 CLARA

Marsh had them rise early, and Clara was only halfway through her cup of coffee before it was time to leave. She chugged the last half, coughing as it hit the back of her throat. Nate stared at her, "I'm pretty sure there were better choices to be made there."

Clara shrugged, taking a sip of water to soothe her throat. "Time to go, right?"

He shook his head. Reese stepped into the room, filling up a water bottle. She kept her back turned towards Nate, but Clara didn't miss the way Nate's eyes tracked her. Men were such idiots. Whether he wanted to have a bias or not, his eyes didn't watch Marsh or Clara the way they followed Reese.

Marsh tightened her ponytail, "So, ladies," she grinned as she glanced at Nate, "I'll distract Jacob while you take the opportunity to go through the building and see where we need to end up. We need a solid plan by the end of the day. I'll make sure Jacob is okay with us using his building as an entry point once we have our plan."

They all nodded. "Clara, I want you to walk all the way to the labs and scope out the guards and entrance. You'll have to move quickly to be back in time to not cause suspicion with Jacob." Nate instructed. Clara agreed. "Reese, you'll scope out the alleys behind and ensure there won't be any surprises the next time we're there. We need to know all entry and exit points. I'll scope Jacob's building, and as much of the surroundings as possible in the time we're there."

Marsh shifted from foot to foot as Nate turned to her, "How much time can you buy us?"

Marsh inhaled deeply, "At least 20 minutes if I play my cards right." Clara heard the strain in her voice and didn't particularly want to know what this portion of the assignment was costing Marsh.

"That's plenty." Nate either ignored her discomfort or didn't notice it. "Team, we'll have 20 minutes. Clara, that means you're going to have to move fast to get there, survey, and get back in time."

"Understood."

"Anyone have any questions?" Nate took his time looking at each of them. Reese shifted next to Clara, but didn't say anything. "Excellent."

Marsh twirled the edge of her ponytail, her eyes glued to the map on the table. Reese took a step towards her, murmuring, "Are you okay with this?"

"Hmm?" Marsh looked up quickly, her eyes wide. "Okay with what?"

"With distracting Jacob. It seems like you may have a bit more of a history than you wish to share with us."

Marsh quickly dropped the concern in her features. "Oh, I'm totally fine. Jacob and I are still friends. It won't be a problem at all."

Clara wondered if Reese could hear the false tone in Marsh's voice, or if it mattered. They had to fulfill this assignment, and to do that, they had to get into the building. Marsh had to play her part. She was the only one who could.

Her heart sped up as they left the Midnight Quill behind. She counted her breaths and tried to rein in her emotions. She was being silly. This was just an assignment, like all the others. Not like all the others. Close enough?

She breathed deeply, noting the elaborate buildings she was enamored with the first time they were here.

When Nate came to walk beside her, her breath caught. She

turned, expecting Carver, but the hair was too dark, the body too big. Her heart sank in disappointment, even as she tried to contain it. Nate watched her wordlessly. She refocused straight ahead. She could do this. For Carver's sake.

"Are you sure you're prepared to be back in the field?" Nate's voice was low, quiet enough that Marsh and Reese, leading the way, wouldn't hear him.

Anger simmered beneath Clara's skin at his implication, but when she exhaled, she could recognize the concern and truth in his words. "I'm not sure of anything yet, Nate. I don't think I'm a liability, and staying behind isn't going to help anything."

Nate didn't respond. Clara's brain kept spinning over words as if she needed to find further justification. "I want to redeem myself. I want to do better. I'm trying."

"I know." Nate's response was simple, and did nothing to quell the anxiety rising within Clara. *I know? What do you know? You have no idea what it feels like to be back in this city. You have no idea what it felt like to leave him behind.*

She clenched her fists hard, leaving crescents in her palms but not breaking skin. She didn't think there was anything she could say to change Nate's mind, so she didn't try. She let the silence weigh over them, hoping things would be different this time. This time, she could do what she signed up for.

They stepped out of the main city street and onto a side street. Within a few hundred feet, the sound of people gave way to the sound of heavy machinery. Smoke drifted in the air, casting a pall over the day even as the sun tried to break through. Reese coughed, but Marsh looked just as comfortable here as she had in the main part of the city.

The industrial sector was about as Clara had expected. The buildings rose around them, the streets becoming more and more narrow as they walked deeper. It was a massive cage, with entry and exit points that hid in plain sight. She inhaled, careful not to choke on the smoke. Her skin crawled, but she kept her hands at her sides, refusing to itch her arms. She would focus on the assignment ahead.

A door slammed as they walked by, and a lanky figure stepped out.

He blew his cigar smoke as he watched them with dead eyes. Marsh kept walking, ignoring him entirely. Clara couldn't help but wonder what kind of existence that would be.

Marsh paused in front of the doorway, her eyes briefly closing as she exhaled before stepping through. They followed. Clara blinked slowly as her eyes adjusted to the darkness.

Electric lights flickered, buzzing throughout the cluttered space. Broken crates lined the right side of the room, and a pile of fabric lay forgotten on the left. The air was dry and musty, like this section of the building had been unused for quite some time. There was no machinery, nothing to make it look like this room was useful.

"This room wasn't exactly part of the operation." Marsh mumbled, "He used it to store…things he wished to forget about. I kinda told a guard, and the room's been empty ever since." She muttered the last part, but Clara caught it.

Marsh nodded towards the door at the end of the room, opposite the one they came through. "That door leads to the main building." Reese stepped forward and squeezed Marsh's shoulder, and Clara rolled her eyes. This was the easy part of the assignment, and whatever history Marsh had with Jacob couldn't be worse than the history Clara had with Carver. Marsh betrayed Jacob? Well, he was alive and free, so that was quite the improvement to Clara's situation.

They walked forward, steps silent. At the doorway, Clara felt the energy from the other side. She heard voices and movement, and the clang of metal as it was moved. "What exactly does Jacob do?" Clara asked as Marsh's hand clasped the doorknob.

Marsh swallowed, "Best not to ask too many questions." She opened the door. They stepped into a well-lit room. These lights didn't flicker. The space was full and meticulously organized.

"Marsh!" Clara turned towards the man as he barrelled towards Marsh with his arms outstretched. He wrapped her in a hug, lifting her off her feet. His cheeks were rosy from exertion, and he towered over Marsh, both in height and form. His voice was jovial, his smile wide and genuine as he held Marsh. Clara shifted her weight to her other foot, shooting a glance at Nate.

Nate took one step forward, and Marsh grunted as Jacob set her down. Jacob's gaze sharpened, and though his smile didn't falter, his jovial air did, "And you've brought friends."

"Jacob, this is Nate, Clara, and Reese. They've been visiting me."

Jacob tilted his head respectfully, "A pleasure to make your acquaintance."

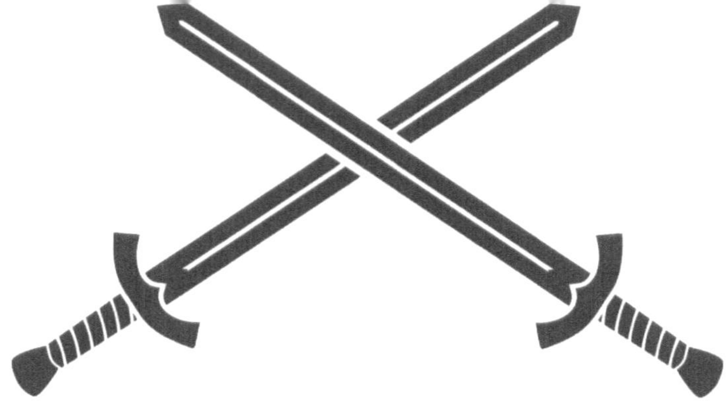

24 CARRION

The fresh air made him feel more alive. He breathed in deeply, his sense of smell categorizing each scent that wafted through the air. There was so much more to observe out here, away from the king's stifling palace.

Carrion didn't miss the edge Alius walked on around him. Even though they weren't around people yet, Alius stood braced as though waiting for a fight. Carrion could only assume he was the fight Alius was waiting for. Why? He wasn't sure. The king's commentary rang in his head, refusing to leave, no matter how much he tried to focus. Something wasn't right.

He kept pace with Alius, keeping his commentary to himself. Alius was much taller than he looked in the throne room, at least a head taller than him. His shoulders were broad, making Carrion feel like he needed to puff himself up a little bit so he didn't shrink beside him.

"We're going to spend today getting you used to the city. Noxvalis is a hub of stores, people, and deals. Anything someone wants to purchase can be purchased in Noxvalis. Because of that, we maintain a steady stream of traders from neighboring kingdoms, though our primary is Calyndor."

Carrion blinked hard, shutting his eyes tightly as a flash of pain shot through his brain. Brown hair, blue eyes, and that skirt…he tried to hold on to the image, but it disappeared, taking his pain with it.

Alius didn't slow his pace, but he did give Carrion an assessing look. "Because of the steady stream of traders and the exports we provide, our security must be top-notch. Plenty of fights have broken out in the streets, and there's always someone more willing to steal than to pay for their goods. Additionally, Noxvalis offers exports of a more…sensitive nature. We've had at least one hostile agent infiltrate previously. The king is determined that it not happen again." Alius went silent after this proclamation, continuing to assess Carrion's response.

Carrion simply nodded. "People always want to get their hands on the next big thing." He looked around as they walked, noting the intricacies of the buildings. It was beautiful. The craftsmanship was beyond anything he had ever seen, though he could admit he didn't remember what he had seen.

"For today, we are going to be stationed at the corner of the market. We won't be the primary response. I want you to have the opportunity to observe Noxvalians, traders, and the overall attitude of the market."

"Yes, sir," Carrion responded without a hint of disrespect. He was, of course, at the king's disposal, which currently meant he was at Alius's disposal.

Alius slowed his pace as they approached the market. Though Carrion would have assumed their armor to be a deterrent towards people, the people in the market didn't seem to notice or care. They continued to weave around them as if they were any other citizen or trader.

Carrion stepped carefully through the people, trying to follow the path Alius wove. It took a few minutes for them to make it out of the center of the market and to the corner Alius had mentioned.

The rooftop on the neighboring shops extended to shade the corner. As much as Carrion was enjoying the sun on his arms, he knew in a couple of hours he would be grateful for the rooftop extending over them.

Alius stepped into the shade, his posture perfect, his face impassive as he began to watch the marketplace. Carrion stood next to him, shoulders back, trying to keep his face as straight as Alius's. The various scents registered in his brain again now that he was paying attention. Fried foods, sweat, odors, some type of chemical? The last one gave him pause, but when he started to look more intently, Alius glared.

"The job here, Carrion, is to blend in until we need to stand out. No need to scare the shoppers. We need to maintain our reputation of being a *welcoming* kingdom. Where do you think our wealth comes from?"

Carrion didn't answer, assuming the question to be rhetorical until Alius doubled down, "Well, Carrion?"

Quickly knocking the surprise from his face, Carrion answered, "Exports, like you said. I assume we import many of the products we use, and the processes here make them worth more than when they came in. We're the industry, yes?" The use of 'we' felt strange on his tongue, but he didn't let that show. He was a Noxvalian, was he not?

Alius nodded, his lips tightening into what could almost be called a smile, but even that felt forced. Carrion didn't think he was the type to smile much, or at all. He couldn't blame him. Smiling didn't come naturally to him either. "Good. I'm glad you've been listening. Now, we stand here and wait."

Carrion kept the same perfect posture Alius held. The sun shone brightly onto the market, and people rushed around, squinting and sweating as the day continued to warm. As Alius said, no one seemed concerned by their presence. The occasional person, a trader usually, saw them and either nodded or made sure to walk a few feet further away from them. Carrion didn't mind the space. He observed each person who walked by, waiting for an infraction that would allow him to participate.

25 CLARA

Within two minutes, Jacob lost interest in their party, aside from Marsh. He turned away from them, effectively dismissing them. Reese hesitated a moment, looking at Marsh with her eyebrows drawn in. Nate stepped into her field of vision, shaking his head at her.

She followed him wordlessly.

The room they were in took up most of the building. Machines stood against all of the walls, ringing with their efforts. Clara tried to catch a glimpse of what the machines were actually producing, but she didn't get much of a look before Nate gave her the same withering look.

"I'm coming, I'm coming," she muttered at him as she followed Nate and Reese out the door. The whole building felt like a series of parallel doors. One more door, and they were in the alley behind the building, just like they were supposed to be.

"Alright, team, be fast, be safe." Nate clapped his hands together like it was some kind of mantra. Clara resisted rolling her eyes. Reese stared at him, fully engrossed, before they all parted ways.

As Clara left them behind, she quickened her pace. Sprinting would be too obvious if someone stepped out of one of the other buildings, but she wouldn't make good enough time if she walked. She kept her head low, deciding the cover was more important than observing each building. Marsh seemed to have a pretty good idea of what was on this street anyway. But the deeper into the alleys she walked, the less noise she heard.

Supposedly, this lab was at the end of one of the alleys. She visualized the path Marsh had drawn for her, turning down the streets where she had been instructed. Several of the alleys ended abruptly, and she had to backtrack to remember the correct turn. She stopped. If Marsh was correct, the lab should be down the alley to her right.

She looked at the buildings bordering the alley. One would be far too short, but the other was made of brick and had jutting window ledges. Bingo. She rolled her shoulders a couple of times, taking the opportunity to look around. No one was in sight, and these buildings were soundless.

She walked to the alley that was parallel to the one she needed to see. She'd climb the building on this side, then crawl across the rooftop to get a vantage point. She didn't have long, though. With another breath in and out, she started climbing.

She paused at the first windowsill, stretching her hands. She hadn't been as consistent with her pull-ups in the weeks following her first trip to Noxvalis. But she could do this. With her resolve intact, she continued scaling the wall. Her heart pounded, but she reminded herself she was doing this for her redemption. She would make Carver's death worth something.

Her hands stung as she pulled herself over the top, but she barely noticed. Her focus stayed trained on making it across the roof soundlessly so she could assess the lab. The rooftop was surrounded by a stone barrier, the inside meant for people to be one. A mini garden was even set up in the corner with a few chairs. The plants had long since died, and the chairs were rusted, but at some point, the effort was there. She walked quickly. When she was a few feet from the other side, she crouched before reaching the rooftop wall. Slowly, she peered over.

She had expected to see four guards standing outside, the same as the other lab. But instead, there were only two, all at perfect attention even though the alley was silent. Had the king not fortified this lab? Did it remain untouched despite her previous venture?

That being said, she did note the impressive physique of the guards. Each of them would make Nate look small. She noted the keypad, similar to the one she dealt with at the other lab. Something about it was different, but she couldn't quite pinpoint what.

A door slammed a few alleys over, and if possible, the guards were even more at attention.

She walked down the inside of the rooftop wall, careful to keep herself from visibility. Once at the corner facing the main alley, she peered back so she could see under the cover of the lab roof. A pin pad was there, but there was an additional measure of security she didn't quite recognize.

She watched for as long as she felt she could, but nothing changed. No one approached; there were no new noises. The whole area remained incredibly untouched by change. The guard's posture didn't break, the doors didn't open, nothing happened.

She chewed on her bottom lip. It didn't feel like enough to report. But she was past the halfway mark on the amount of time she had to spend here already. So what could she do?

Nate's face came to mind, and the punishment she would face if she were late. He needed to be able to trust her. She squeezed her nails into her palms. He needed to trust her more than he needed whatever information she could garner (or most likely wouldn't garner) by being late.

She turned away from the wall, listening intently for anything different as she trekked back to her starting place. She was hoping something would happen so she could turn back and prove herself valuable, but nothing did.

She reminded herself that this was just a surveillance mission. She knew how to find the lab now and had a few ideas for access points that she mentally stored.

She climbed to the ledge, carefully dropping her legs over the side as she hung from her hands. Her feet found purchase on a brick a few feet above the highest window ledge. She put her weight on it and began to climb down in a similar pattern to how she climbed up.

Her heart raced in frustration. She was hoping this would be far more successful.

Her feet hit the ground with a thud, and she brushed her knees off as she turned back to Jacob's warehouse. "Hey!" A male voice shouted at her.

She glanced at him. He stood there carrying a few boxes out of a neighboring building. "Are you lost?" He asked.

"I think I took a wrong turn." She answered, trying to look innocent enough. Panic flared in her chest, but she didn't let it show in her face.

He nodded. "What building are you looking for?"

"Uh," her mind stuttered. She tried to recall the buildings Marsh had pointed out on the map. "Weston's?"

The boy tilted his head at her, but only responded, "It's back that way." He nodded the way she needed to return, and she was beyond relieved.

"Thank you. I better hurry. They're expecting me." She tried to smile in thanks, but it felt forced on her lips. Instead, she gave him a brief wave before turning on her heels to walk back towards Jacob's.

The boy didn't follow her, and as soon as she turned around an alley, she sprinted the remaining alleys to Jacob's. She reached the back door and almost ran into a waiting Nate, "You're late." He said, checking his watch.

She took a couple of deep breaths before responding. "I ran into someone on my way back. Had to be careful." It was the only explanation she provided him.

"Find out anything?" He stepped aside so she could enter. The room was empty aside from him and Reese.

"It's somehow less secure than the previous lab. Two guards. The buildings on either side are no longer operable. They utilize the same keypad security the other lab did, but there's a secondary measure I didn't get a chance to examine. No one came by. After I was back on the ground, a kid came out from one of the buildings across the alley. He was the only activity there the whole time."

Nate crossed his arms over his chest. "Well, this should be interesting."

Clara nodded. "Did you find anything?"

"Not particularly. All of these buildings shut down by sundown, so if we're planning a break-in, night is going to be our best friend. We'll see if Marsh got anything from Jacob."

Clara looked at Reese, but Reese just shrugged instead of jumping into the conversation.

Nate led the way back through the doorways until they reached Marsh. Clara had planned to try to examine Jacob's machinery a little closer, but she didn't get a chance. When they stepped into the room, Jacob quickly took a step back from Marsh.

Her face was flushed, and anger was written across her posture. Jacob glanced nervously between her and them. Marsh's hands were at her side, but Clara didn't miss the clenched fists. She grit her teeth. Marsh seemed okay, though, so there was that at least. Nate strode across the room quickly, Reese and Clara on his heels.

"Everything okay?" He asked.

"Obviously," Jacob answered immediately.

Nate didn't even spare him a look. "I was asking Marsh."

Marsh's shoulders began to relax. "Everything is fine."

"See, I told you!" Jacob chimed in. Clara wanted to punch him. But she didn't think that would assist with their assignment, so she resisted.

"Now," Marsh concluded her sentence.

26 CARRION

The day threatened to be consumed by monotony. He scanned every person that passed, every person he could see in the marketplace, even. He observed every building, filtering through and categorizing every piece of information he could find.

He didn't know how guards did this all day. This was the action? All of his training for this?

The previous days had blended into a single stream of consciousness until the fight with the guards. That was the first moment he truly felt alive. He could feel the adrenaline pulsing through his veins, his heart pumping. He had never felt as fulfilled as he had in that moment. Everything before that moment had faded into a wash of gray, and everything else was dissolving into the same color.

Alius didn't speak, so Carrion kept his thoughts to himself. His mind raced. He could admit this was more interesting than his day spent with the king, but it seemed patience was not one of his strengths. However, he was determined to prove himself, so he would do whatever it took. Apparently, this is what it took.

The sun began to fade behind the taller buildings, and still nothing happened.

Carrion scanned his eyes over the crowd of people, tilting his head at the one abnormality. A young woman, not older than him, stood still in the sea of people. People wove around her, and a dark-skinned woman with braids was pulling at her arm, but she wouldn't budge. The woman's lips parted, mouthing a single word. He narrowed his eyes on her lips, but he didn't make out the word in time.

The woman's hair was braided over her shoulder, her blue eyes catching on his. A jolt spread through him, and he took a single step forward. A large crowd passed in front of them, obscuring his vision of the woman. When his line of sight cleared, she was gone.

Alius looked at his foot, now out of alignment, and then his eyes made it to Carrion's face. "Carrion?" He questioned gruffly. "What is it?"

Carrion shook his head, stepping back into position. "I thought I saw something concerning."

Alius placed his hand on the hilt of his sword. "What did you think you saw?"

Carrion knew how dumb it would sound if he professed a young woman to be dangerous just because he caught her staring at him. Though his gut clenched, and his heart hadn't slowed down, he answered, "I'm certain it was nothing to be concerned about. I watched the situation until it was over. Nothing we need to involve ourselves in."

Alius grunted. "Don't leave the position unless we're getting involved. That's the rule."

Carrion rolled his eyes internally, but didn't dare let that show on his face. A brief drunken sprawl broke out as the moon waned across the sky, but all the moments in between were awash in gray. Though Carrion would have loved to be involved in settling the dispute, one look from Alius and he maintained his position. He watched as two other guards stepped into place.

Finally, Alius said, "It's time to return."

They walked in silence back to the barracks. Once they reached the door, Carrion hesitated. "The king has decided you should continue bunking alone." His jaw flexed, "Against my recommendation. You will be returning to your previous room." His room was small, next to the training room.

"I'm not bunking with the other soldiers?" Carrion asked, hoping he didn't sound impertinent. Alius noted his hesitation, and Carrion was surprised he didn't roll his eyes with the attitude he had when he said, "Over time, you will be fully integrated as a soldier. For now, you will be my shadow. Breakfast is at 0600, and I will be there to pick you up at 0630, so eat quickly."

Carrion nodded. Alius led him back through the castle to his small room. "One more thing, Carrion." Alius stepped into Carrion's space, his voice low and harsh. "You aren't special. So drop whatever you think you have that's better. You're a soldier. You follow orders. Don't forget it."

"Understood," Carrion responded, keeping his shoulders back.

Alius gave him one more once over before finally exiting, and once he was out of sight, Carrion released a long exhale, grateful to be without his supervisor. He wasn't tired enough to call it a night, but what were the other options? His room held only the small bed pushed against the wall and an old dresser with the few items of clothing he had been given.

He sat on the edge of his bed as he thought back through his day. The king's words and the girl's face kept coming to mind. What was he a product of? A vial? Was he an experiment? He pushed the thought away. Surely not. The king seemed to value him too much.

He grabbed a clean pair of shorts from the dresser and headed into the training room. He ran through a few rotations with his sword, enjoying the pull on his muscles. Once he was sweating, he reset the training room and walked to the far end and through the door for the showers.

There were ten showers lined up. In his time this past week, he hadn't encountered anyone else in the training room or the showers. It was starting to feel like the space was his.

He pulled a shower curtain back, stepping inside. The water sputtered when he turned the handle, but eventually the stream solidified. He couldn't consider it to be a warm shower, but it felt nice over his sore muscles from the prior days of training. He rolled his shoulders as the water ran down them. His mind felt empty for once. No thoughts, no wondering.

He stepped in front of a mirror to run his hands through his hair so it would dry properly. The skin on his shoulder was pink, pulling tight when he leaned forward. The pull wasn't painful, but he could see it stretching taut in the mirror. He turned to examine it better, noting a red line parallel to his spine under his shoulder blades on both sides. How had he not noticed it before? He guessed he was too exhausted from Raze's training to pay attention.

He reached his hands back trying to feel the wound, but either he couldn't reach it, or there wasn't anything to feel. He rolled his shoulders a few more times, but he still didn't feel anything unusual.

He recalled the king's words. He had been in an accident. What kind of accident? What kind of wounds left those marks but healed so quickly? *Our most successful yet…product…vial.* He heard the words over and over in his head, but still couldn't make sense of them.

Eventually, he shook his head in the mirror, letting the issue drop. Maybe he could ask the king about it at some point in the next few days. If not, maybe Alius would be willing to share information with him.

His footsteps were silent as he padded to his bed, covering himself with only the thin sheet. He closed his eyes and drifted into sleep. The only dream he remembered in the morning was a fragment of a girl with black hair and blue eyes. The girl he knew he had seen.

27 CLARA

"You pulled me away from him! It was him!" Clara sobbed at Nate once they were safely in the bookstore. She didn't know how she had held it together until then, but Reese had held her up with an arm around her waist, and they made it back.

Marsh had taken to chewing on the ends of her hair. Clara could barely focus on Nate as he blurred in her vision. "Stick with the mission, Clara." He grit his teeth, and Clara launched herself at him, her teeth bared.

He grabbed her wrists, pinning them to her sides. She didn't try to break free, just yelled at him. "We came here because of him. How could you leave him? It was our opportunity to save him! He wasn't dead." She broke down sobbing on the last word, falling to her knees.

Reese quickly stepped forward and put her arms around Clara's shoulders, holding her while she cried. "It wasn't him." Nate stepped past them and poured himself a glass of water. "You left him here weeks ago. It may look like him, but it isn't him, Clara. We didn't come here to save Carver. We came here to save our kingdom. A feat you didn't fully succeed in last time. This time needs more success. I need you to pull yourself together and handle this."

A slap resounded through the room. Clara sniffled, her vision clearing enough to see Nate's eyes narrowing on Marsh, and Marsh staring at him in bewilderment. Reese covered her mouth with her hand. "That's not a fair thing for you to say, right now. I get it, you're the oldest, you've seen a lot of shit. But she loved him. You're condemning him to continue living in this hell without even recognizing that saving him is a possibility?"

Nate touched his cheek where Marsh left a handprint, flexing his jaw. Her face was bright red, matching the handprint on his. His nostrils flared as he breathed. Clara attempted to pull herself together as Reese tightened her arms around her shoulders.

"I trained him for the last three years." Nate made eye contact with each of them, staring at Clara as he continued, "Don't you think I would do everything in my power to save him if I thought it was possible?" Tears streamed down Clara's cheeks as she nodded. "I will not condemn more of you to die trying to save someone that's already gone. Do I make myself clear?"

He looked around the room again, and everyone nodded their agreement. "I will reiterate my earlier sentiment. We are a TEAM. I understand the wrench this has thrown in that trust, but believe me, we cannot save Carver. Trying to will only destroy us, too. I need you to trust me on this point."

Clara's voice wavered as she said, "What could they have done to permanently change him in a month?"

Nate shook his head. "Consider him dead. The alternatives are not things you want to imagine."

Tears filled her eyes again, and she blinked quickly. "There's nothing we can do to save him." It could've been a question, but they both knew it wasn't.

"I'm sorry, Clara. It is the reality of Noxvalis. There is nothing we can do."

Clara inhaled deeply, sitting up on her own and pushing out from under Reese's arm. "Then," she took another breath. "We have to complete our assignment." She locked eyes with Nate, feeling herself break inside as she said, "We make his death count for something."

"We will." He finished his water as his eyes scanned over the room. Reese and Clara didn't move from the floor, though Clara continued to support herself. Marsh had taken to leaning against a wall, her ankles and arms crossed in front of her. "Do we need to take a break before we dissect today's excursion?" The words came out tightly, but Clara knew he was offering them for her. She was grateful, but she was stronger than that.

She pushed herself off the floor and poured a glass of water. She took a seat at the table as she answered, "I'm ready if you are." The other three took the remaining seats, each with their own drink.

A knock sounded on the door, and they all tensed. Clara glanced at Marsh, "Are we expecting company?"

She shook her head no. Whoever it was knocked again. "It's your house, Marsh. You're the least suspicious to answer it," Clara shrugged. Marsh rolled her eyes as she stood.

She glanced at them, "I suggest keeping your faces turned away from the door in case there is trouble. We don't need more people to recognize you."

They all turned inward, ensuring their faces wouldn't be seen from the door. Clara listened for the conversation, only catching small bits and pieces. The man's voice sounded familiar, but she couldn't quite pinpoint it. She glanced at Reese and Nate, but both of them were focused on listening as well.

"Is it better to trash or burn books?" Clara heard a muffled male voice say.

"Neither, information should be preserved." Marsh responded slowly.

"Yes, but some information is too dangerous for that."

How does someone else know that code? Clara remembered when she spoke those same phrases to Marsh.

She heard Marsh close the door, and they all immediately turned. She had brought the man inside. Clara jumped to her feet, knocking her chair back in the process. "What is he doing here? Why did you let him in?"

"He knew the code?" Marsh's eyes darted between the two of

them. "Why do you look like you recognize him?" She shot back at Clara.

Clara took a step forward before stopping. The man shifted his weight, his hands clasped behind his back. "I saw her in the alley earlier. I've been waiting for you. Command told me you were coming and you would need my help."

Clara's eyes found Nate's. He shrugged almost imperceptibly. This was news for their whole team. "Explain." He deadpanned.

The man's eyes widened as they all stared at him, and Clara could practically feel the fear radiating off of him. Interesting. "I confirmed the lab report for Command. They, um, they asked me to work near the labs, so I've been an errand boy," he paused here to roll his eyes skyward, "for a large company in a building off of those alleys. Command got a message back to me saying to expect a team, and described you, Clara."

Clara, Marsh, Reese, and Nate all glanced around at each other. What were they supposed to do with this? No one seemed inclined to respond, so finally Clara answered, "How do we know you're telling the truth?"

He slipped his hand into his pocket, they all braced, and Clara and Reese had weapons in their hands almost instantly. He held his hands up, paper in one as he shied back. "Please don't, I was only going to show you the missive they sent me." He continued to hold himself back while reaching his hand forward with the paper. Clara recognized it from all the missives she'd received from Command.

She stepped forward and took it in her left hand, continuing to hold her dagger in her right hand. She opened it, holding it far enough in front of her that the others could read it. "He's right," she was the first to admit. "Command told him we were coming and to join us when we got here. His name is Ryker Ericson." She inhaled, holding her breath.

Reese muttered, "But why didn't they tell us?"

Marsh shook her head, "I still don't trust it. Anyone could fabricate a Command edict, right?" She looked around the room for agreement.

Ryker sighed, "I'm telling you the truth."

Marsh jabbed him in the shoulder with her finger, "We didn't give you permission to speak. The adults are talking."

Ryker's jaw dropped before he swallowed hard and answered, "I can help. That's all I want. I want to help."

Nate stepped forward, putting himself in the middle. "Well, team? What do we think?"

Clara looked around him to Ryker as she crossed her arms, flipping her dagger in her hand so it still pointed in Ryker's direction. "What do you bring to the team? Why are you so convinced we need you?"

He shrugged, shifting his weight to his right foot. His eyes darted to Marsh first, "She's a Raven," then to Reese, "Viper," then to Nate, "Raven," then finally landed back on Clara, "And you're a Viper. The Eclipse. A pleasure to make your acquaintance. You know what you don't have? A Spider. This lab is highly technologically advanced. You can't just blow shit up and assume you'll have any measure of success."

Reese nodded her head, "I mean, he has a point. We are missing a Spider."

"One vote from Reese," Nate said, turning to Marsh.

Marsh shrugged, "We just figured out our team dynamic, I can't say I'm thrilled to change it. But…"

Nate looked to Clara next. "I'll admit, a Spider's help would be useful. I don't trust them, though. Spiders are crafty bitches. He could just as easily kill us as help us." Clara exhaled heavily, "At this point, our options are to trust him or to kill him. I highly doubt Marsh wants blood on her carpet."

"Yeah, I'd really like to keep it the blue color it is." Marsh replied, "But I have a tarp in the back if that's the direction we decide to go. I'm really here for whatever."

Ryker's throat bobbed. "Guys–"

Nate stepped in front of him, and Ryker silenced instantly. He cowered back from Nate, as Nate towered over him. Nate stood there assessing him for longer than felt necessary. The girls exchanged glances, and Clara rolled her eyes when she mouthed, "boys," at Reese. Reese hid a smile behind her hand.

"He lives." Nate finally declared. "But you're on a very short leash, buddy. One wrong move," he drew his finger across his throat. "Clara enjoys it."

Ryker looked from Nate to Clara, and Clara flipped her dagger, catching it with two fingers by the tip as it flipped. "I promise," he swallowed, "The dagger will not be necessary for anything. I am here to help. That's all I'm here for."

Clara smiled, "I believe you. For now."

28 CLARA

It took a few minutes before everyone was settled enough to continue their conversation. Marsh dragged in an extra folding chair, giving Ryker a seat that was lower than everyone else's at the table.

"May I have a glass of water too, please?" Ryker looked up at Marsh.

She huffed, but grabbed another cup and poured him a glass. She wasn't gentle about it, and it splashed over the edge, leaving a spot on his pants. He didn't comment, just shifted in his chair as she put the pitcher back.

"Marsh, what happened with Jacob?" Nate's first question was something Clara hoped Marsh was prepared for. She took a sip of her water as Marsh sat back down.

"We had a brief...misunderstanding." Her words were soft.

"Explain." Nate didn't give her any room to back out of the questioning.

Marsh rolled her neck, "I called off our friendship primarily because he was too...interested in me. He made, let's just say, unwelcome advances? More than once. It wasn't a fun time. He assumed that my resumed acquaintance with him meant I was desirous of those...advances."

Clara looked around the table, noting how sympathetically Reese looked at Marsh. Marsh continued, "When it became obvious to him that I was not interested in his advances, he became angry. You walked in after a few minutes of that."

"Ah. Does this mean we need a new plan for accessing the labs?"

Marsh started tugging on the ends of her hair again. Reese chimed in, "Nate, give her a moment. Don't be so assignment-focused!"

Clara interjected, "No, he's right. We all need to be assignment-focused. Including me. If we can't use Jacob's building to get access to the back alley, we could scale one of the neighboring buildings and cross via rooftop. The one I climbed wasn't difficult, and the roof was flat, which made for easy access."

"We can use Jacob's. He agreed to let us come back, once, provided I let him take me to dinner." Marsh answered.

Reese crinkled her nose, "Gross."

Marsh shrugged, "I agreed primarily because the next time we're there will be for retrieval and exit. Nothing else. By the time he comes to collect his dinner, we'll be long gone."

Nate shifted, "Solid plan, provided we can accomplish our assignment in one pass. Clara, please bring Marsh up to speed."

Clara cleared her throat. "The lab seems to be lower security than the previous one. Two guards, a key pad, and one additional measure of security I didn't get to see in use. I wouldn't be surprised if it were biometric, though. The buildings on either side of the alley leading to the lab are empty. We can easily cut through those or scale and drop from the roof. However, any noise or interruption will be easily caught. There is absolutely no traffic. I saw one person on my trip, and he's now at this table."

Nate nodded as Marsh processed the information. Reese chimed in, "The buildings behind Jacob's are quite busy. They close after dark, though. Regardless, quite a few have low security measures. We could use them to hide or store things as a last resort."

"Ryker, do you have suggestions for how to get past a biometric scanner?" Marsh asked.

"Of course," he agreed easily. "Shouldn't be a problem."

"Clara, Reese, how efficient are you? How quickly can you dispatch the guards?"

Clara looked at Reese, who shrugged. "Sixty seconds," Clara decided. "That's the time it will take to land in the alley and dispatch them."

They sat in silence, processing their options.

Ryker shifted, pushing his glasses back up his nose. "The main square of Noxvalis has paved roads, but the alleys remain dirt." He tilted his head back and forth, "How common are strong winds in Noxvalis? Uh, dust storms? Maybe even the little dust devil tornadoes? I haven't explored the alleys enough to know."

Marsh scratched her nail across the table top, "Pretty common. The winds can start up between buildings, affect one alley and not the other. It isn't abnormal at all."

"Then it would work," he murmured, mostly to himself.

Clara sat forward, "What would work, Ryker?"

He finally looked up and met her gaze, "I've created dust bombs before. It wouldn't be hard to reproduce them here. I need a few basic supplies, but I'll be able to get those or tell you where to steal them from. If we threw a dust bomb in the alley, it would mimic the dust storms that are normal for Noxvalis anyway. We could use the dust as a cover for you and Reese to dispatch the guards without giving them time to alert anyone."

"Brilliant, Ryk," Nate smiled. "That just might work."

Ryker cocked his head at Nate, "It *will* work. Provided Clara and Reese can dispatch the guards as quickly as she claims."

Clara rolled her eyes, "Consider it done."

"Won't be a problem," Reese added with substantially less sass than Clara in her tone.

"Excellent," Nate answered. "We can't have anything go wrong here."

This time. Nothing can go wrong this time, Clara thought. But she only nodded. They went through the plan again and again until it was late in the evening.

29 CARRION

Carrion woke up early enough to stretch and prepare for the day before heading to breakfast at 0600. Though Carrion had stood all of the previous day and laid awake for hours that night, he didn't feel tired. In fact, he felt absolutely wired.

He could feel the buzz beneath his skin, desperate for him to do something. Anything. He needed to feel alive again. The fight with the guards that spurred him down this path made him long for that feeling again, though he wasn't quite ready to cross Alius to get it. He'd remain the obedient soldier. For now.

It had occurred to him in his midnight thoughts that if he could take out four guards, he could certainly handle Alius if the need ever arose.

He walked through the food line and tried to smile at some of the guards near him. He approached a table with an empty spot, but the guards quickly moved into it, preventing him from sitting with them. He passed them quickly, but found most tables acted the same. He walked to the furthest table in the room and sat alone.

He scarfed down a full plate of food, surprised by how hungry he was. Then he cleared his dishes and tray, and waited at the door for

Alius. Alius arrived promptly at 0630. "Are you prepared for today, Carrion?"

"Yes, sir," Carrion answered.

"Excellent. I need to know you can do your job without distraction. As guards, we must be focused at all times. Yesterday's step was out of line; don't let it happen again."

Yesterday, the day he saw the girl with black hair and blue eyes. The day something other than adrenaline felt real. But it wasn't. "Yes, sir," he responded again.

Alius eyed him with disregard, but finally nodded. "We're stationed at the same spot for the rest of the week. Though yesterday was busy, prepare yourself because the next two days are historically even busier."

"Are we going to step in if there's a disruption this time?" Carrion couldn't help the bounce in his step as he followed Alius out the door.

Alius didn't turn to look at him as he responded, "We are going to observe. You are not yet equipped to deal with the general populace."

Carrion felt his excitement deflate, but he tried to mask it as his energy still bubbled beneath his skin. "But Raze–"

Alius cut him off, "Raze trained you for one specific purpose. To pass the king's test. You succeeded. Congratulations. Don't continue questioning me, soldier, unless you would like to be placed somewhere even more mundane."

Carrion shut his lips with a snap. He knew he was valuable to the king. The king had saved his life. The king had, according to himself, brought Carrion back from the dead. The king had given him the training to survive and a position within his palace. Why, now, was he subject to taking orders from Alius? He didn't like it. But Carrion still wanted to serve the king. So since the king had ordered him here, he would do everything in his power to make the most of it.

They made it back to their spot from the day before. Carrion kept his posture straight, his eyes observant. He recalled the instructions Alius had given him and resolved to be the perfect soldier Alius wanted.

He watched each person and sorted through each of the smells, but none stood out to him. His eyes tracked each girl with dark hair, but none of them was the girl from the day before. The girl he'd caught glimpses of in the few pieces of his dreams he could remember.

If Alius noticed his intent, he didn't comment. But still, Carrion was relieved when they headed back for the night. "The king told me he wants you to be proficient in every area of surveillance. Tomorrow we will begin our lab rotation." Alius said, his words tight and careful.

Carrion glanced at him from the corner of his eye. "You disagree with him?"

Alius gritted his teeth. Carrion could feel the restraint in his choice not to respond. Finally, he answered, "Don't take this the wrong way, Carrion, but this is a strange choice. You aren't someone who's grown up here. You've been trained into a weapon, and now you're being given access to all of this?" Alius shook his head. "Forget I said anything. I'll be back at 0630 tomorrow."

"I wasn't born here?" Carrion stopped walking forward.

Alius's eyes narrowed. "A slip of phrase." His words were more careful, "You didn't grow up in the guard training as all of us did. Hence, you weren't born here."

The comment pierced Carrion more than he thought it should, and he couldn't help but wonder what other truths were beneath Alius's statements. "Is that why the other guards won't talk to me?" He regretted the question as soon as he asked it. He could feel the insecurities hovering over his body, and once he asked the question, it felt like he had claimed them as his own. That wasn't his intent. He swallowed hard, but he couldn't pull the words back into himself.

"I don't concern myself with the other guards." They had reached the training room, and Alius was turning to leave. As he stepped away, he met Carrion's eyes, "And you shouldn't either."

Carrion closed himself in his room, waiting until he was sure Alius was far gone. He had memorized the routes they had taken and was convinced he could slip into the square without being caught.

His steps were silent as he walked through the hallways, and the one time he heard steps, he pressed his back into the wall and held his breath until they faded. He reached the exterior doors with a sigh of relief. The night was anything but quiet as he walked. The further he walked from the palace, the louder everything grew. He passed several bars on the way and considered going in, but it didn't feel right. He was looking for something, even if he couldn't articulate what.

The streets were full of drunken revelers. No one noticed one more person among them. He paused in front of one bar. It was loud, people were drifting in and out, and the girls on the corner attempted to charm every man who came near.

He wasn't impressed, but something about it felt familiar. He knew this bar. Something had happened in this bar. He stepped to go inside, trying to remember why he'd been here.

Sharp pain shot through his head. He doubled over in pain, grasping the sides of his skull. He breathed deeply, trying to find some relief.

One of the girls put a hand on his shoulder, "Sir, are you okay?"

He could hear the concern in her voice as he straightened. He blinked the pain away as she came into view. Her silver tassels revealed more than they covered, and he swallowed hard. "I'm fine," he told her, shaking her hand off.

He walked away quickly, heading back to the palace. Why had he ever left in the first place? He couldn't remember anymore.

30 CLARA

By evening the next day, Clara didn't think she had it in her to rehearse the plan one more time. When they broke for dinner, she slipped out. She didn't have a plan in mind...yet. She just needed to get away, even if it was just a walk.

She wandered through the streets, blending in with the other people out at night.

The girls still stood on the corner with their frills and beads. Clara gave them a large berth as she passed them, blending into the shadows near the building walls.

Her mind spun over the events of the past 36 hours. Yesterday morning, she learned Carver was alive. But not truly alive. His body was there, yes, but she had never seen his eyes darken the way they did. He was broader, his muscle mass somehow extremely increased. She could tell there were other alterations done to him, but she couldn't quite pinpoint what. More than anything, she had wanted to run across the street and touch him. Confirm that it was truly him when she stood in front of him with his body beneath her fingers. But her team had pulled her back.

She understood why. It was the right call. She had promised this assignment wouldn't be destroyed by her recklessness, and she needed to hold to that.

Eventually, she stood in front of the bar where she had seen Carver kiss Marsh in. How was that only weeks ago? It felt like a lifetime now. She inhaled deeply, trying to stay in the present and not step back into that moment.

She put one foot in front of the other as she walked in, but she didn't even feel like the same girl anymore. If she walked in and saw him with another girl this time, she would only be grateful he was truly alive.

The bar was close to packed when she walked in, but she found a corner stool and ordered a drink. She knew from her last experience she wouldn't enjoy it, so she wasn't quite sure what brought her in this time. She sipped it carefully, cautious not to choke on the taste. She looked around the room, relaxing into the chaos. Here, she was just another face in the crowd, not someone with responsibility.

The bar doors flew open, and a large group of men walked in. They were laughing and shouting, pushing each other around. She didn't miss the bartender's subtle shake of his head as they approached the counter.

Clara's heart rate skyrocketed, even though she wasn't quite sure why. She resisted the urge to shrink further into the wall as the raucous party took up at least half of the counter space. They didn't seem to have much regard for the people already sitting there, instead prioritizing their own needs and space.

Their voices boomed in the bar, and though the bartender looked annoyed, he didn't dare comment on it. Guards. *These are guards.* The pieces finally clicked into place. She would have realized sooner if she hadn't been so caught up thinking about Carver and the last time they were here. The way the bartender looked at them, but didn't say anything. How people moved around them to give them their own space. The callous disregard the guards held for everyone else in here.

She took another sip of her drink, knowing it wouldn't calm her racing heart. She kept her eyes glued to the counter, aware of how close they were in her peripheral vision. *If I leave without finishing my drink, it will look suspicious.* Clara reminded herself that the guards had no idea who she was and no reason to suspect her of anything. She settled into her chair; she hadn't done anything wrong.

If I'm stuck here, I may as well eavesdrop. She tuned into their conversation, which mostly revolved around work and women. Very typical of men. "Carrion, you're the new guy." One man shouted, "I think you need to find a woman in here to hit on!" The other men jeered and called their appreciation. "What about the girl at the end of the counter?"

She almost choked on her drink. She did not want one of the guards to hit on her. She didn't know how far they would try to go, and she couldn't afford to blow her cover. She finished her drink and stood up, but a guard stepped into her path.

His dark eyes met hers, *Carver. CARVER?* His eyes were even darker than they had been, the pupils practically fading into the irises. His jaw was wider, his face filled out. The dark circles were practically non-existent. He was clean-shaven, and his hair was exactly the same. He was still him...but he wasn't. She could feel it in the way he looked at her. He didn't know her anymore.

She swallowed hard, now desperate to leave. She would destroy everything if she stayed. "I'm sorry, I have to go." She tried to push past him, but he caught her wrist, holding her there gently but firmly.

"Please, stay." His voice was deeper than she remembered, a rasp on the end of his words. "Let me buy you another drink."

She shook her head, her hair momentarily obscuring her vision. He pushed a strand back from her eyes when she looked back up at him, and a shiver ran down her spine. *I'm going to throw up.* "I'm so sorry," she repeated, "I really have to go."

She pulled her wrist from his, and his grip tightened for a moment. Her eyes widened, terrified he was going to keep her here. Maybe, if she were honest, she was excited that she was forced to stay. Because in front of her stood the man she loved. In front of her was the opportunity to ruin everything and destroy Quorath. What a price. He let her go. She stepped past him, calmly walking to the exit.

She heard the men laughing at him for letting her go. They taunted him, but he took it good-naturedly. It took everything in her not to look back as she walked through the exit. She kept her head forward and her shoulders straight, even as her heart begged her to turn. But her heart was a foolish creature, driven to emotion best left untouched. She ignored it.

She resisted every feeling until she made it to the alleyway and turned the corner so she was out of sight. Then she sprinted back to the bookstore.

In the bookstore alley, she leaned her back against the cold concrete wall, resting her hands on her knees. She breathed deeply, her heart racing so fast she could barely get enough oxygen. The tears came hard and fast, and she let them fall. It was all she could do to alleviate the pain in her heart.

Nate was right, that wasn't Carver.

31 CARRION

At breakfast the next day, Carrion heard a group of guards talking about going out drinking that night. He still hadn't made any progress befriending anyone and was determined to prove he was a guard just as much as they were.

That night, he slipped out of the palace again. This time, he followed the group of guards that had already left. He stayed a distance behind them until the square came into view, then he caught up. "Hey guys!" He said when he approached, and the group fell silent, stopping in their tracks.

The guards exchanged glances before one spoke up, "What do you want?"

Carrion shrugged, "To join the group and get a drink?"

The man who spoke was at least a head taller than Carrion, his shoulders wide as he crossed his arms over his chest. "How do we know you aren't here to report us for dereliction of duty?" A few of the other guards nodded.

"Why would I report you for dereliction of duty? You aren't on duty, therefore you can't be derelict?"

"You could still be a spy. We all know you're Alius's pet."

Carrion swallowed, "I follow the orders he gives. Doesn't mean I like him, or that I'll keep to those orders when he's not in sight." He knew the words were dangerous, but he didn't have a lot of options.

The massive man thought it over before saying, "Alright, you can join us. But we're keeping our eyes on you, Carrion."

Carrion nodded, about to ask for the man's name, but the group turned and continued, this time with him beside them. The man on his right, a smaller-statured guard with blond hair, smiled and said, "I'm Jasper," as he held out his hand.

Carrion shook Jasper's hand, "I'm Carrion."

"Oh, we know." Jasper laughed. "Everyone knows. It isn't often they let soldiers like you join us in the dining hall. You're something of a rumor."

"Soldiers like me?"

Jasper shook his head, "I'm glad you joined us tonight!"

Carrion just smiled back, a little tired of receiving the same response every time. Why was it so strange that he was a soldier? *The red lines on my back?* He flexed his back almost involuntarily at the thought. He wasn't the same as everyone else. That much was becoming apparent. He couldn't help but catalogue every detail of everyone in the group.

He matched their pace, smiling and laughing along when the moment called for it. They let him join in their revelry, and he played the perfect part. It could be said he fit in, except he recognized the role he was playing. Just like he did with Alius. He played the role expected of him. What did that say about him? Who was he really?

They reached the same bar he had paused in front of last night, the doors open wide. The corners were strewn with girls in beads and lace, and his face flushed as he drew his eyes back to the group. The girls noticed their large party of men and tried to draw their attention, and though a couple of the men hollered at them, the party as a whole made it inside.

When he walked in, the scents filled his awareness, and the lights almost overwhelmed him. He was right last night. He had been here before; he just couldn't remember when. Why had he been here?

He cocked his head, trying to take it all in, but the group was moving on without him. Jasper grabbed his arm, pulling him back into the throe. Carrion plastered his smile back on.

He took a deep breath, trying to calm his mind. He didn't need to process all of this input, even as every detail filtered through his mind. The music was loud, and the song felt like something he had known before. He hummed along as they walked. Every table was full, and their group displaced people on their way to the bar. People seemed more than happy to move out of their way. *I guess citizens prefer to keep their distance,* he thought.

He hadn't fully calmed himself before another guy said to him, "Carrion, you're the new guy." He nodded at the obvious as the man slapped him on the shoulder, "I think you need to find a woman in here to hit on!" The other men jeered and called their appreciation, with Jasper agreeing the loudest.

"What about the girl at the end of the counter?" Jasper suggested.

He turned, and *not a chance. It's her.* He knew her. He still couldn't remember how he knew her, but he *knew* her. The girl with dark hair and blue eyes. Today, her hair floated around her shoulders instead of being braided back. She didn't meet his eyes until he stepped in front of her.

He forgot the group of guys encouraging him when she looked up, and he was right. Her blue eyes pierced him to the core, and something twisted in his gut. "I'm sorry, I have to go." He could hear the hesitancy in her voice, the nervous tick of her jaw as she tried to look confident. She tried to push past him, but he caught her wrist, holding her there firmly. He needed to know who this girl was. It could be the key to unlocking his past. And something, something inside him wanted her to stay here with him.

"Please, stay." He knew he sounded pathetic, but attempted confidence, "Let me buy you another drink."

She shook her head, her gorgeous hair falling over her face. He couldn't help himself; he reached out and pushed a strand back. She looked up at him, fully catching his attention with those blue eyes. Her lips parted. He definitely knew her.

"I'm so sorry," she said again, "I really have to go."

She tugged at her wrist, and his grip tightened on instinct. He could keep her here. But he wouldn't. He let her go, and she left without looking back. But Carrion, on the other hand, stared at her retreating form until she was long gone.

"Dang, man, harsh rejection!" Jasper grasped his shoulder with all the fervor of a man several drinks in. "Don't take it personally, though, man!"

Carrion shook Jasper's hand off, trying to shake his disappointment off along with it. He turned back into the group, smiling along with them, though he'd never felt this miserable. He turned her features over in his head, again and again, but he couldn't make sense of them beyond knowing he had dreamed about her.

But people don't dream about faces they've never seen before. He had seen her. At some point. *Before.* And then he was back there. To the before. What happened before his accident? Before his surgery?

He spun every piece of information he had around in his head. *Alius's distaste. 'It isn't often we get a guard like you.'* **Like you.** *Red lines on my back. Her. Red lines. Vials. Product. Experiment. Raven?* His head started spinning, bringing a gut-wrenching pain with it. He grimaced, his knees buckling at the sharp pain as he put a hand to his head.

He squeezed his eyes together, trying to push past the pain to put the pieces together, but then they were gone. He couldn't remember what he was trying to figure out. "Man, you good? You haven't drank near enough for that!" Jasper laughed at him with another aggressive pat on Carrion's shoulder.

Carrion straightened, dropping his hands from his head. The pain receded as he focused on Jasper, "Damn right," Carrion grunted. "I have to get back." He turned without another word and walked back to the palace. He couldn't stand the thought of the king discovering he was gone. He had to be the perfect soldier. As he focused on his job, every memory of *her* sank back into the dreamworld–where it belonged.

Clara only pretended to sleep that night. Lying awake in the room she shared with Reese, letting Reese's breathing lull her into something some people may have considered rest. Her body was still, but her mind was racing a hundred miles an hour. Her heart had never felt this tight, and she didn't know how to change it.

How could she let go of him when he wasn't dead?

A plan began to form, the tendrils of thought just out of reach. She could, but she couldn't. She could try to save Carver, but she couldn't damn her team or her kingdom. She could try to let him go, but she couldn't actually forget him. She could; she almost sat up in bed at this thought; she could complete the assignment, but not return with her team. She could stay here. She could try to save Carver.

Nate would never let her, but she had to try. He couldn't keep her from staying once the assignment was over, and Carver was worth whatever price she had to pay. With that decision, her mind settled enough that she managed to fall asleep, at least for a short amount of time. It wasn't long before Reese threw the blinds open, announcing, "Rise and shine, let's murder this bitch!"

Clara sat up and couldn't help but laugh. "Is this your motto?"

Reese shrugged, "It works when we have a lot to do. Might as well bring some joy into the trials."

Clara smiled ruefully as Reese locked herself in the bathroom. *Am I still capable of happiness?* She wasn't sure anymore. To be entirely honest, she hadn't been sure in a while. She was focused. She was driven. She was a perfectionist and the antagonist in her own story, but happy?

She wanted to say that happiness was for people who didn't know any better, but as she started stretching, she could hear Reese humming in the bathroom. It felt like a prick in her heart. She had chalked Reese's happiness up to a lack of assignments; it's easier to be happy without blood on your hands. Now she knew it wasn't the case. Reese had been through hell, yet somehow she was still…happy?

Clara stretched her shoulders out, but the tension there didn't abate. She knew it wouldn't. Even when she chose not to act on her emotions, they affected her. It was something she couldn't pretend against anymore.

When Reese finished, Clara readied herself quickly, avoiding the mirror. She knew the circles under her eyes would be darker. She didn't want to remind herself of the night before. Instead, she focused on her breathing and fixed her gaze on the shower tiles as she braided her hair tightly. She rolled her shoulders a couple more times, straightening her spine as she walked out.

She was a feared assassin. She could handle whatever was thrown her way. *This is going to break me.* She wouldn't break. She would keep her head up and finish her assignment.

The five of them gathered in the kitchen for coffee and the pastries Ryker had brought. It was very smart of him. He seemed to be winning points with Marsh because of the food. Clara was only slightly surprised that it was that easy.

Nate and Ryker talked through the details of his design. "It will take me a day or two to acquire the materials I need to make the dust bombs and break the security." Ryker motioned to the pages in front of him. He'd brought his journal today, along with all the additional pages of notes that were now taking up half of the table.

Clara didn't realize she had zoned out, thinking about her plan to rescue Carver, until Reese nudged her, "Clara?"

Clara sat up straighter, "Sorry. Didn't sleep. What?"

Marsh rolled her eyes, but there was sympathy there. Nate gritted his teeth but answered, "Are you still prepared to dispatch every guard in our way?"

She tilted her head, almost offended at the question. "I'm an assassin, Nate. Of course."

Nate didn't back down, "You're a loose cannon. You'll have to forgive me if I need additional confirmation."

Clara bit down on her lip as anger flared in her chest. *I can't get kicked off this assignment.* She breathed in deeply before plastering the fake smile—the one Carver taught her–on her face and responded, "Confirmation, given."

"Scary," Ryker muttered under his breath as he shuffled through a few more pages he pulled out of his bag.

Clara kept the smile pasted, but glared at him until he met her eyes. He quickly looked back at his pages, his face flaring red. Clara dropped the fake smile, landing on a real smirk.

Nate didn't comment until the exchange was over. "Marsh, do you know where to go once we're in the labs?"

"I've been asking around, subtly, of course. I think I've got a good grasp on it."

"Thinking you have a good grasp on it isn't enough. We have one shot at this. One shot. That's it. We can't blow it."

"I know where we need to go." All eyes snapped to Ryker, who shied away under the attention.

Nate's eyes narrowed on him, "Oh?"

Ryker shrugged. "I got bored one day and wanted to see if I could get into the lab."

"What?" Reese's jaw dropped. "You're still alive, so that's a good sign."

"Elaborate, Ryker. I don't have the patience for this. Cards on the table. Now." Nate's voice was harsher than Clara had ever heard it.

"I dressed as a scientist. They're all nervous people anyway–scientists that is. I walked right past the guards and scanned in with the system I made. It didn't flag the system, and just like that, I was in. I didn't stay long, though." He coughed, "Was concerned they would ask for an ID."

"You built a system to break into the labs but didn't manufacture your own ID?" Marsh asked incredulously.

"The IDs they use are chipped with a material I couldn't get my hands on!" Ryker defended, "They don't look at the IDs, they scan them."

"Ryker," Nate picked up a page between his thumb and pointer finger, looking from the page to Ryker. "You showed up here a couple of days ago." Ryker nodded, "Don't you think this information might have been relevant yesterday?" Nate didn't raise his voice, but Clara could feel the anger radiating from his words. She was relieved. She didn't trust Ryker at all and was a little concerned about how quickly they had included him in their plans. She was glad Nate was pushing back. She had decided long before this she didn't trust Spiders. So far, Ryker had only emphasized her belief.

"The information isn't any less relevant today." Ryker sat back in his chair. He wasn't confident, but he was certainly trying to fake it. Clara could see it in how carefully he kept his posture, but his breaths were still too fast for it to be real confidence.

Nate flexed his jaw, and Ryker flinched almost imperceptibly. Clara would have missed it if she hadn't been staring at him.

"It's not a good idea to test me."

"I'm not testing you. You're ascertaining my loyalty; I'm ascertaining yours." Ryker responded, his voice soft.

"There's four of us and one of you; it doesn't seem like testing us would be in your best interest."

"Not the way I see it."

Reese shot Clara a look, and Clara shrugged. She was content to let the men hash it out. Her loyalty, ultimately, was to herself and Carver. If Ryker had what they needed to get in, she was willing to use him, but she wouldn't trust him beyond his own interests.

"How do you see it?" Nate practically grit the words out, and Clara was impressed by how restrained his volume was.

"I can walk away right now. I built a life for myself here, and it isn't a bad one." A lie, Clara didn't miss the hesitation in his words. The first sentence was true, but the second one wasn't. "If I decide you aren't trustworthy, I don't lose anything. From my understanding," Ryker paused here, nervously looking around the table. "Command doesn't want you back. They're happy to have you die here or there. You're hoping to change that by fulfilling this assignment. Therefore, you need me, far more than I need you."

Nate smiled, and somehow that was more chilling than his glare. "I think you missed my point. You're not just among Ravens. Two of the best Vipers are here as well."

Clara watched as Ryker paled. She tossed a dagger in the air and caught it by its tip. Ryker flinched again. When she didn't say anything, he relaxed into his chair, leaning back with all the confidence he didn't have. Reese didn't pick up a weapon, just shrugged with her arms crossed over her chest.

"Threatening me isn't the way to earn my trust." Ryker protested.

"We just established that you're the one who needs to earn our trust," Marsh answered. "Stop withholding information. If our plan goes sideways, you're right there with us. I may not be an assassin, but if you're the reason we fail, I'll make sure you die with us. Is that enough incentive?"

Ryker looked around the room, his eyes wider than when he first met them. "Excellent." Nate said, "I'm so glad you've decided to join us and be fully forthcoming moving forward."

"As if I was given a choice," Ryker mumbled under his breath.

Clara circled the conversation back around, "You can get through the locks without a key card. We won't have IDs, but once we're in, do you know exactly where they would keep the radioactive material?"

Ryker thought for a moment, his eyes looking up to the ceiling. "Yes. I think I do. All of their weapons material was down the right hallway. It's just a matter of finding which room it's stored in and moving it."

"With three of us inside, we should be able to search quickly. Without a trigger, the material should be stable enough to move." Nate pondered his statement before turning to Ryker, "But in case there are any issues, can you build a case for us to use in transporting the material without harming ourselves?"

Ryker nodded immediately. "That's easy."

Nate turned to Marsh, "We move on this in three days." He looked around the table. "Can everyone be prepared by then?"

Everyone nodded, and Clara's excitement grew. Three days of preparation, and then she would be able to make a plan to save Carver.

33   CARRION

"You wanted to see me, my king?" Carrion knelt to one knee and bowed low. The king had summoned him, and Alius had escorted him to a small room to the side of the courtroom.

"Alius says your performance and loyalty remained unmatched."

Carrion remained on his knee, though a smile played across his lips with the praise, "My only desire is to serve you, my king." The king stood before him, with a table to the right. The table was unset, though a towel covered something on it.

"I know. You may stand now."

Carrion stood, facing the king. He had never been directly in front of the king while they were both standing. The king was a formidable figure. His shoulders were as broad as Carrion's, but he was at least a couple of inches taller. His sheet of gray hair added an edge to his entire persona.

"I summoned you because my team has finally ascertained that your effects do not present any danger."

Carrion shook his head in confusion, "Your Majesty?"

The king sighed, clasping his hands behind his back. "When you were found, you had several items on your person. I had my team analyze the items. Now, I am returning them to you."

Carrion couldn't remember any items he would have had, and he didn't really know what the king was talking about, but he nodded regardless.

The king motioned to the table to the side of them. The king removed the towel, revealing a few coins and…and a gold necklace with a red jewel. *I know that necklace.* The king watched him, and Carrion felt his skin crawl. This was a performance, wasn't it? He didn't know what the king expected, but clearly, he was watching for something. Carrion scrubbed all emotion from his face.

"Thank you, my king." He picked up the coins and slipped them into his pocket. As much as he wanted to examine the necklace, he resisted the urge. He picked it up and slipped it into the pocket with all of the coins.

The king watched his every motion, but didn't comment until Carrion was fully facing him again. "You stand to become one of my best soldiers."

"High praise, Your Majesty. I can only hope to serve you well."

"You do. You've come a long way from the almost dead young man I found all those weeks ago." The king's eyes remained fixed on him.

"May I ask," Carrion paused, trying to find the right words. "What happened to me that I ended up in the care of your staff?" He was careful not to elaborate beyond that.

"You had a bad accident. We don't know beyond that. They found you almost dead. They weren't even sure if they could save you." Carrion's heart tugged at the sympathy he saw shining from the king's eyes. *I can trust him.*

"It's just," Carrion hesitated.

"Speak, boy. I have other matters to attend to."

"Of course, my king." *This can wait until another time.* Carrion bowed low again, "I only wanted to thank you for saving my life, and for keeping my items safe for me."

"You're dismissed," the king said with a wave, "Alius will continue to keep me informed of your progress."

Alius nodded, bowing to the king as they left. Once they were walking down the hallway, he said, "You're not going to find anything out about your past by asking questions. Best to let it stay in the past."

Carrion scoffed, "You're telling me that if you woke up from an accident with no memory of your past, you wouldn't try to figure out what happened?"

"Sometimes your brain knows best. Maybe it's protecting you. If I were you, I would let it go."

"Why are you giving me advice on this? You seemed annoyed by having to train me."

"You're not all bad."

Carrion chuckled, "From your reports to the king, it sounds like you might even think I'm good."

"Don't push it, or your next report will be a lot more honest."

Carrion just shook his head, unconcerned. "Where are we headed today?"

"We're doing a rotation at the biochemistry lab today." Alius's pace stayed fast, but Carrion easily kept up with him.

"Biochemistry lab?"

"It's where all of our bio weapons are designed." Alius sighed, "How was that not obvious?"

"I think there are quite a few basic things I've forgotten along with my history." Carrion played the card for sympathy, but Alius didn't bite.

"Your lack of memory around your past shouldn't affect your understanding of words. Pay more attention, and you'll do better."

Carrion followed Alius out of the palace and through the forest. "The lab is on the other side of the forest? Are you sure you aren't just taking me out here to kill me?"

"Can we go back to the first day when you were scared of me and didn't talk at all?" Alius huffed.

"I was never scared of you. I was just trying to figure out what was going on."

"Uh huh. And yes, I am sure that the lab I've patrolled countless times is this way."

The guards in front of the lab didn't abdicate their posts until Alius and Carrion were standing before them to take their places. They exchanged nods, then the guards trekked away. "It's a new rule," Alius explained as they took their positions. "We had a break-in. Since then, guards aren't allowed to leave their posts until the replacements arrive."

"That feels like common sense. Why was it not always a rule?" Carrion asked.

"When a kingdom is as strong as Noxvalis, there is the temptation to become complacent. It creeps in slowly, but before anyone has time to catalogue it fully, everything is done in that spirit. No one had dared attempt an invasion on Noxvalis in at least three decades. Our king has known war, obviously, but never has anything shown up at his door, until now."

Carrion nodded, adding the information to his mental file about Noxvalis. The more he learned, the better he could serve. This was what he reminded himself whenever the information felt less than useful.

Alius became his usual stoic self, and Carrion followed suit, although he allowed his eyes to take in everything around him. His breath caught, but he quickly returned to neutral before Alius had a chance to comment. But this…this lab. It felt familiar. Another place he was certain he'd been to before. The hill coming out from the trees.

He'd been there before. A flash of pain hit in his head, and he breathed in carefully, trying to appease it. If Alius noticed, he didn't comment.

Carrion straightened. He was here for one purpose, and one purpose only. He was a soldier.

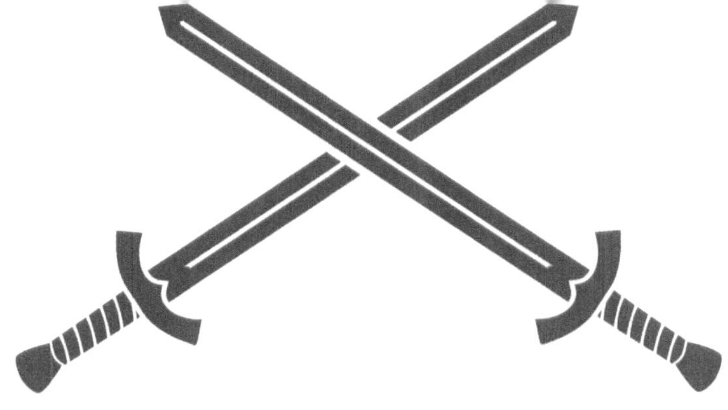

34 CARRION

Night couldn't come quickly enough for him. They'd been standing for hours when Carrion was convinced he'd been here before. But again, he couldn't recall anything else. He pushed the thoughts aside. It wasn't worth causing a scene. Once he was back in his room, he lay down on his mattress, his eyes closed tightly as he pictured all that had surrounded them at the lab.

A bang rang through his head, and he tried to grasp the sound. Before...before that sound had surrounded him. He tried to put himself back in that moment, wondering if perhaps he could trick his brain into remembering. Along with the bang, the smell of smoke assaulted his senses, and he was convinced the two coincided, but he couldn't put the pieces together.

He stood up, about to change, when the coins clanked in his pocket. He took them out, his fingers pausing on the necklace. He put the coins with the rest of the stuff, but left the necklace in his hands. Another piece from his past. Something else he recognized but couldn't grasp. He shifted the chain through his fingers, back and forth, stroking his finger over the ruby.

What was he looking for that he didn't already have?

Her.

35 CLARA

The day had finally come. Today, they were breaking into the lab.

As Clara stretched, she practically bounced on her toes in elation. Carver had been such a weight on her shoulders the past few weeks, she'd forgotten that she was still alive. But today, with an assignment at the tips of her fingers and a plan in place, she felt alive.

It wasn't easy to move on without Carver. Even this assignment felt like she would be better partnered with him—she'd obviously do it differently this time. Yet for the first time since she left him, she had hope that she could save him. She could fix everything she had ruined. She had cost him so much, and now she had an opportunity to change it.

Reese stepped out of the bathroom, squeezing her hair out with a towel. She chewed on her lip before finally asking, "Do you think we actually survive this? Like, is there any hope for Nate and me? Or are we doomed just because we're soldiers?"

"I think all soldiers are damned, Reese." Clara grimaced inwardly at her honesty when Reese's face fell. "That being said, there's still hope. We have a solid plan and an even better team. I do think we can survive this, and when we survive this, I think there's a really good chance you and Nate will work out." Reese looked appeased, and even

Clara was impressed by how well she BSed. She did believe they would survive, but she also believed that all soldiers were damned. The best she was hoping for was saving Carver from Noxvalis. She wasn't hoping for a happy ending. Happy endings didn't exist for assassins. She literally killed people.

A smile played against Reese's mouth, and Clara was relieved to see her friend happy again. She deserved that. "You're right. I think we can do this." Reese breathed in deeply as she hung her towel up in the bathroom. "We got this. It's just an assignment."

"It's just an assignment." Clara reiterated. She locked herself in the bathroom, once again avoiding the mirror. She took the time to braid her hair tightly against her scalp, ensuring it wouldn't come loose to wreak havoc before she left.

The bedroom was empty when Clara stepped out. Reese had already headed downstairs. Clara knew she should follow, but she couldn't help but pause and survey the room. Tears filled her eyes when she thought about the pallet Carver had made on the floor and her belligerence in every interaction with him.

She inhaled sharply, forcing herself back into the present moment, and left the room. Today was not the day to reminisce. Nate and Reese were in the kitchen already, talking in hushed tones. Clara stepped back to avoid interrupting them, but the floorboard creaked, and Nate caught her eye. "Clara, how are you feeling about today?" His tone was harsh, and Reese's smile was gone.

Having been spotted, Clara gave up trying to give them their moment and poured herself a cup of coffee. "We have a really good shot at success. Far more than a 'suicide squad' should have." She smiled, trying to interject some levity.

Nate's eyes narrowed, and Clara almost choked on her coffee. "We have a solid plan and a great team." She looked between Reese and Nate. *What is going on with them?* "Why? How do you feel about today?"

"I think if we all survive, it will be a miracle."

"Damn, Nate," Marsh huffed as she walked into the kitchen. "That's the team spirit our team leader has? No wonder we failed."

Reese's face cracked into a brief smile until her eyes looked up to

Nate again. Clara could hardly stand the oppressive feeling in the kitchen. "Is there something that has changed the potential outcome?"

"We have reason to believe that going forward, labs will be monitored by…creatures. At the very least, a creature." Nate stretched his neck.

"And that changes something for us? Creatures die just like men do." Clara leaned against the counter, wrapping both hands around her coffee cup. She looked at Reese for support, and Reese shrugged.

"We have no way to prepare for what kind of creature could be there. You know better than I do the types of monstrosities Noxvalis has created. If we end up face to face with one of those, I don't like our odds." Nate answered, his jaw flexing.

"I've seen those 'monstrosities'," Clara rolled her eyes as she said the word, "They are creations. They were once people. They're broken. Believe me, it won't be any harder to dispatch a creature than to dispatch a well-trained guard. Everyone has a spot to hit, and blades will work on anything with flesh. And personally, I think people are far more threatening."

Nate looked around the room. Unprompted, Marsh chimed in, "I agree with Clara. We've come too far to give up here. Like she said, the creatures will die by blade just like guards would."

Nate's eyes landed on Reese, and even across the room, Clara could see the question in his eyes. "I'm not going back. We came here for this assignment; let's finish it."

"Ryker," Nate said, his voice filled with such authority, Ryker visibly flinched.

Why does Command trust him this much if he's this easily shaken? Clara couldn't help but wonder.

"Uh, my opinion," Ryker started.

Nate cut him off immediately, running his hand down his face as he stared at him, "Wasn't asking your opinion. Show us what you brought for the mission."

"Oh, right." Ryker set his bag on the table and began pulling things out.

Clara's eyes widened. She crossed her arms over her chest, waiting for the explanations.

"These four are the dust bombs. We should only need one, maybe two, but I made extras just in case." Nate picked one up, and Ryker immediately tried to take it from him, then dropped his hands. "Please, please be careful. The release mechanism doesn't take much. I don't think Marsh wants that going off in her kitchen."

"I absolutely do not." Marsh stepped forward and took the bomb from Nate's hands, setting it gently on the table.

The next thing Ryker pulled out was a small metal square. It had a few wires and odd ends sticking out of it. "This is the tool that will give us entry to the lab. I just have to plug these into the keypads, and it will disable the passcode so we can get in. I also took the liberty of creating these." He pulled out two batons, handing one to Clara and Reese.

Clara flipped it in her hand, weighing the balance. "This is way less effective than a blade," Reese said.

"Agreed. Why would I ever choose this?" Clara added.

Ryker held his hand out, asking for it back. "Because, if you push this invisible button on the side here," he slipped his finger over the button, and the tip of the baton lit up with electricity. "You can stun someone. Less bloodshed, less evidence."

Reese looked at Clara, shrugging her approval. Clara merely grunted. "It's an option," she said.

Ryker smiled like she had given him the greatest form of praise he could hope for and handed the baton back to Reese. Clara made a mental list of the rest of the items Ryker brought, including the lab coats he had snagged. Most of the tech would require Ryker to operate, so she stopped trying to remember how it all worked. It worked, and that was enough for her.

"Alright, team," Nate said once Ryker put his tools back in his bag. "How are we feeling?"

They all looked around the room at each other before each shrugged. Ever the optimist, Reese chimed in, "It will be a breeze."

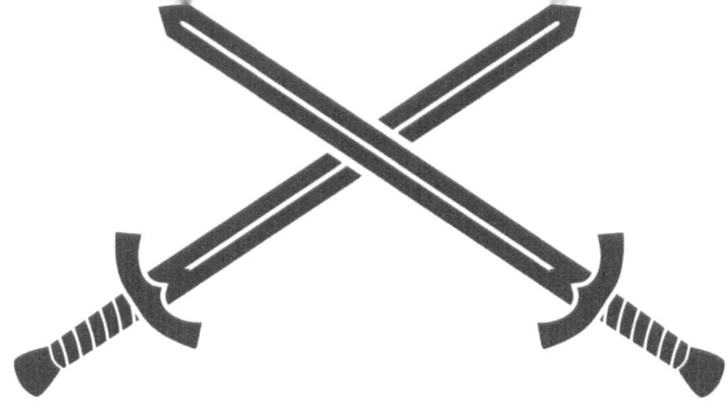

36 CARRION

Carrion woke up the next morning feeling energized. He dressed quickly and put the necklace in his pocket. Although it wasn't heavy enough to provide a weight against his leg, he felt its constant presence all the same. He could even feel the bounce in his step as he walked to the dining hall. If one small piece of his past could bring this much hope and this much desire to keep moving, what would happen when he discovered all of his past? The thought brought a warm sense of comfort into his chest, but with no new pieces of information, he didn't try to remember anything else.

As much as he wanted to follow Alius's words and let go of the past he couldn't remember, it also felt like an anchor to the life he had now. He had a past. He had something he had gone through to make it here. He wasn't just floating aimlessly, another face among the guards.

After he filled his tray, Jasper waved him over to his table with a few other guards. Carrion slid in across from him, nodding to the guards he recognized and the ones he didn't, which was most of them. "Dude, did Micah tell you about the girl he went home with at the bar?"

Carrion shook his head as he took a bite of his food. "He thinks he may have actually found 'the one'." Jasper laughed heartily. "It's a fling, but it's funny to hear him talk about her. He thinks when we go out again this weekend it'll be a huge romantic evening for them."

Carrion kept eating. *What do I even say to that?* "You alright man?" Jasper finally took a bite of his own food, watching Carrion down his.

"Yeah. Just have to eat quickly, or I'll miss my post."

"Ah, yeah. Alius is such a prick. Sucks you got stuck with him."

"He's really not that bad," Carrion felt the impulse to defend Alius. He may not have liked Alius, but he was dedicated to the king. "He's a very thorough trainer. Definitely making me a better soldier."

"Yeah, well, he's the one guard that all the new recruits hate. He's strict as hell. Did you know that one time he caught one of his trainees sneaking out so he threw him in the dungeon?? For a week?? Like that's some crazy shit."

Carrion chuckled, "I'm not worried."

Jasper looked mildly impressed, "I want to believe you, but man, you just sound naive."

Carrion scarfed down the rest of his food. "Haven't had any issues so far. But I gotta go." He grabbed his tray off the table, tossing the trash and adding the tray to the pile of other dirty trays. He walked quickly to the entrance, briefly wondering if he should be afraid of Alius. He did sneak out. Did Alius know?

He beat Alius to their meeting point, but only by 60 seconds. "What are you waiting for? Let's go." Alius demanded as soon as he saw Carrion was already there.

Carrion straightened from where he was leaning on the wall, quickly walking after Alius. Their hike today was much further. They walked for over an hour before they reached their destination. Alius filled him in as they walked. "Today, we are stationed at the weapons lab. Usually, the lab entrance has four guards. Today it will only be us. The king wants to make sure you feel confident at every post, even if it was only you."

"Why would it ever only be me? Isn't that how mistakes are made?" *Probably shouldn't have asked that.* But the words were out, and there wasn't anything he could do about it.

Alius's hand tightened over the hilt of his sword. "You are one of the few soldiers gifted enough that the king would consider giving you your own post."

Since Carrion hadn't learned his lesson about asking questions, he responded, "Did you just call me gifted?"

"Don't make me regret it." Alius gritted out.

Carrion followed Alius through alleyways and backroads, and he took note of each turn they took, forming the mental map in his mind. The air smelled of smoke, and it only thickened as they drew closer to the lab. He started taking shallower breaths so he wouldn't choke on the smoke. Alius didn't seem bothered by it.

When they reached the lab, Alius nodded to the guards, and Carrion copied his motions. The guards bowed slightly and relinquished their post. Carrion and Alius took up their spots, posture perfect.

The buildings were so tall next to them that the sun didn't quite reach his face. The shade felt nice after the warmth from the previous few days. A gentle breeze flowed in and out of the alleys, but other than that, they were surrounded by silence, and Carrion was finding he didn't do well with silence.

Even the forest post had more noise. There were squirrels, birds, the caterpillar he watched climb all the way up the tree in his boredom. But here? There was nothing. The most excitement so far was the gentle dust cloud the wind stirred up. Even that was quickly thrown down.

After a few hours, Alius broke the silence. "This will be your first 24-hour post."

"24-hour post?" Carrion questioned.

Alius's mouth straightened into a perfect line. "It is exactly what it sounds like. Please, use your brain today. Don't make this 24 hours longer than it has to be."

Carrion faced forward again. 24 hours in this alley would be a long time. His brain spun and spun, until finally it landed on a topic of interest. The necklace. Her.

He must have known her previously. That was the only explanation. And the necklace? He wouldn't have bought that necklace for himself. Even the possibility was ludicrous. But for her? Surely he would have bought the necklace for someone like her.

Then he was thinking about her. He was thinking about her dark hair and blue eyes. He was thinking about how small her wrist had felt in his grasp and the way his heart had raced when he recognized her. He was thinking about how, though he never remembered his dreams, he knew she was in most of them.

These thoughts helped the time keep passing. The daylight eventually faded. Each of them took a few moments to relieve themselves; the other standing guard in the meantime.

Nighttime brought a chill in the air that Carrion hadn't prepared for, but still enjoyed. The night was oppressively silent. The buildings that had pumped smoke all day had turned in for the evening, and there was nothing. Carrion squinted at the sky, hoping to make out a few stars. Though the moon's light was bright enough to filter through the smoke, the stars did not have that same ability.

Eventually, his thoughts circled back to where they always seemed to go. Back to her. He heard a scritch in the dirt and leaned forward to see where it came from.

Then the alley filled with dust.

37 CLARA

They left the bookstore shortly after nightfall. They kept their pace casual, walking in groups of two, with Ryker awkwardly walking in front. Clara was paired with Marsh. At first, she was annoyed by it, but once they started walking, she realized she didn't hate Marsh as much as she used to.

"Are you going to be okay with Jacob tonight?" The plan still hinged on Marsh's relationship with Jacob.

"He told me where his spare key was and that we could use his building one night. He didn't ask for more information; I didn't volunteer." Marsh sighed deeply, "I can only hope he isn't pulling a late night tonight."

"He didn't seem like the best…friend the last time we were there."

Marsh chuckled dryly. "That man never wanted to be my friend. He wanted to shag me. That's all he really cared about. And I thought about it, a time or two. Especially that summer he got really weight-conscious and was actually a normal size. I thought, maybe it wouldn't be so bad. I almost did it too. That's why he was so angry with me. He felt very led on, and that I owe sex to him now."

"Very male of him," Clara rolled her eyes as she stepped over a branch in the path.

"I understood where he was coming from. I mean, I guess I led him on? It just didn't feel that intense." Marsh shrugged. "Living here for the past few years wasn't easy. I think people crave community, and it shuts a part of us down when we don't have it. This time with our little group, even if it is a suicide squad, has been nicer than I expected it to be. I wasn't sure what to expect."

"Neither was I. I'm glad we came to a truce."

In front of them, Ryker stumbled before regaining his footing, and Marsh and Clara laughed softly. "You never knew he was here in Noxvalis?"

Marsh laughed again, "Never. Though even if I had, I probably wouldn't have spent time with him unless forced."

"You seem to get along with him well enough now," Clara lifted a shoulder.

"Well, the last couple of days forced me to spend time with him. He's more enjoyable the more time spent."

They passed through the square silently, weaving between the groups of people still out on the town and the stumbling drunks. Clara lost sight of Ryker in the blur, but when they reached the next alley, she saw him at the very end of it. Relief filled her chest. As wary as she was of Spiders, she preferred it when he remained in her sights.

She looked over her shoulder, but Reese and Nate hadn't reached the end of the square. "They're fine," Marsh whispered as they continued. The smell of smoke was lighter at night. Or maybe Clara was more prepared for it. She had no way of knowing for sure.

"I think it's so funny we landed on the name suicide squad." Marsh broke the silence again a few moments later. They weren't far from Jacob's building anymore.

"It's pretty accurate. It's a fool's errand. Either we survive, or we don't."

"This was a punishment for more than the missing vial, wasn't it?" Marsh voiced the question Clara had pondered.

Clara glanced around, but no one else appeared in the dark alley. "My assignment last time wasn't to steal the vials."

"Oh?" The shock was loud and clear in Marsh's voice. "Command seemed pretty focused on the biological weapon."

"They wanted me to execute the king," Clara said it as bluntly as she could.

"No, they didn't." Marsh's voice softened.

Clara shrugged, "It was the orders I was given. The vials were a pretty excuse for the trip, and if we returned with them, it wouldn't be a loss."

"The only loss would be…" Marsh's voice trailed off.

Clara could say what she wouldn't. "The fact that Carver and I were still alive." She shook her head, "I was specifically instructed to leave him to his own devices once we broke into the lab. I was supposed to head directly towards the palace through the underground tunnels in that lab. He was supposed to die retrieving the vials; I was supposed to die executing the king."

"Just to play devil's advocate, do you think there's any way they thought you would succeed? You are a pretty fierce assassin."

Clara pierced her with a glare, and Marsh's eyes widened, "Be honest with yourself, Marsh. We're all liabilities."

Marsh nodded. "We're the only ones who have been in Noxvalis. We're the only ones who know the truth about the creatures they're creating."

"Yup. Command hides the truth because people would panic if they knew."

"We can't go back, can we?" Marsh voiced what no one in their group had.

Clara shrugged. "They wouldn't want us back. Our best bet is to take the materials to Calyndor and hope they will give us entrance."

Marsh sighed, "What kind of life would that be? A life without war?"

"Not worth considering until we finish this. I may not be willing to return to Quorath, but I'm not willing to damn the civilians there either."

The door to Jacob's building was cracked open, the key already removed. Ryker should be inside. They were silent as they reached the doorway. Clara crossed the threshold first, her hands over the easiest daggers for her to slip out. The room was quiet, and when Marsh followed her in, Ryker stepped out of the shadows.

"Somehow, you were further behind me than I thought."

"Now we wait for Reese and Nate." Clara rolled her shoulders, stretching as they waited. Her nerves hummed with excitement. But this time, a new emotion rolled through her stomach as well. She'd never feared for her life before, and until Carver, never had a partner to fear for either. Nausea churned in her stomach.

She bounced on her toes, trying to push away the anxiety. She could feel it crawl up from her stomach, wrap around her chest, and slowly make its way to control her throat. She started counting her breaths. She was fine, this would be fine. She played through their plan until the anxiety settled enough she knew it wouldn't control her.

Nate stepped through the doorway, Reese following behind him. "Alright, team. You know the plan." Everyone nodded.

They wove their way through the alleys until they reached the street leading into the lab.

Ryker nodded at Clara and Reese, and they nodded back. Clara began counting down in her head. She and Reese pulled the fabric bandanas over their mouths and noses.

Ryker threw the dust bomb. *Three. Two. One.* The guards started coughing, and Reese and Clara jumped in. She took the one furthest from their side. It was the first detail she noticed. There were only two guards instead of four.

She held a knife to her guard's throat as his eyes widened. *Shit. Carver.* The knife slipped from her fingers, and he threw her off his back, still coughing up dust. She landed hard, stirring up more dust. Her mask slipped in the tussle, and she coughed, trying to clear the dust from her throat. The guard Reese had attacked lay slumped on the ground, the blood soaking into the ground. Reese turned, her eyes meeting Clara's before she stepped up to Carver.

"Reese, don't!" Clara called. She pulled the baton from the holster on her thigh, pressing the button Ryker had shown her as she jumped to her feet. She pressed the electricity into Carver's neck. His eyes rolled back, and his knees gave out.

"What the hell was that, Clara?" Reese turned on her.

Clara rolled Carver's body over, so his face was visible. "It's Carver."

Nate stepped into the alley, shaking his head at her. "That's not the mission, Clara." His eyes softened as he reached Carver's body, but he only shook his head again. "Ryker, you're up."

Ryker stepped up to the lock and began inserting his wires. A soft whirring sound filled the alley. Clara stayed perched over Carver, terrified that if she moved, someone would kill him. "We can take him with us," Clara said.

Nate pinched the bridge of his nose. "Clara, it's not him. Look at his body. If they've done this much to his physical body, imagine how much more they've done to his mind."

"We can take him with us." Clara forced the words out again.

"We have no way to contain him. He'd slaughter us as soon as he wakes up."

Clara couldn't force the words into her head. This man was Carver. The man she loved. Nate looked between them, "Clara, you and Marsh stick to the plan. Keep guard out here. Say goodbye to Carver. We can't take him. Reese, lead the way inside. Ryker, lead us to the radioactive material."

The door chimed softly as it opened, and Nate, Reese, and Ryker disappeared behind it.

38 CARRION

She's in this dream again. Somehow, I know it is a dream. I know because she's walking towards me with a smile. She wouldn't smile at me.

Her hair is down and flowing around her shoulders, and she wears a colorful skirt with a tight tank top. She is beautiful. I have the necklace in my hand again. The gold feels cool between my fingers. Am I sure this is a dream?

I hold it out to her, but she's gone. Once again, I am left with the memory of those blue eyes and dark hair. Her.

39 CLARA

Clara held her hand against Carver's cheek. His face was smooth, his jaw wider than before. They had changed him. This wasn't enough. She couldn't say goodbye. A single tear fell.

"I want to take him too," Marsh admitted. "I don't know how we can. Nate is right. How do we get him out of the city?"

"Maybe he will remember me?" Clara's voice cracked as the tears came with more vigor. "Maybe he will want to come with us?"

"He didn't remember you in the square the other day." Clara's heart fell with Marsh's honesty.

"I've seen him since then," Clara whispered the admission. "In a bar. A group of guards dared him to hit on me."

Marsh exhaled forcefully. "That wasn't part of the plan, Clara. You could have endangered us all."

"I didn't mean to. I meant to get a drink. But then," Clara brushed Carver's hair off his forehead gently. "He was there. It was him. But it wasn't. I know that."

Tears filled her eyes. "Clara…" Marsh started.

"What if we took his armor off and took him with us? We could get him back to the bookstore, couldn't we?"

"Right, cuz carrying a limp grown ass man wouldn't raise any suspicion."

"Okay, I'm not looking for negativity. You want to save him, too. Help me think this through."

Marsh started pacing through the alleyway. "I don't know, Clara."

Clara ran her fingers through Carver's hair again, her stomach twisting into knots. He was here. So close, yet so far. When he woke up, he'd be gone.

He stirred beneath her fingers, and before she had a chance to react, he grabbed her wrist. "You're not a dream." He said gruffly, coughing and clearing his throat of dust.

Clara left her wrist in his grip but quickly grabbed the baton in her other hand, readying it just out of his field of vision as she leaned over him.

"No, I'm not a dream." She swallowed hard. "Do you know who I am?"

He pushed himself up onto his forearm, bringing his face to eye level with hers. His lips twitched as his eyes scanned hers. She didn't back off. *This is a bad idea.* She pushed the thought away. This was Carver. He wouldn't hurt her.

He slowly shook his head. "But," he licked his lips, "I think I did."

She nodded. "You did."

"So you know me?" His eyes narrowed.

"I do." Her voice caught on the last word, and she ducked her head. "I did." She wasn't sure why she corrected herself, but she didn't know this version of him, and she couldn't claim to.

He pushed himself back from her, taking in the full view of the alley. "Alius," he exhaled, anger crossing his face when he saw the body behind Clara. Clara held out her empty hand.

"It was self-defense."

Carver's eyes darkened, "You killed my commander. Why?" He blinked hard.

This was her chance. Could she convince him to join them? Could she jog his memory?

"Carver," she started softly.

His eyes met hers, confusion clouding them. "My name isn't Carver."

Clara ducked back like she'd been hit and stood to her feet. Carver continued, "My name is Carrion. I am a royal soldier for His Majesty King Herring."

Carver didn't move to stand, and Clara didn't bring her weapon to the front. Not yet. They continued to assess each other. Clara wanted to believe he wasn't a threat to her. Marsh remained silent behind her. "You were my partner." Her voice was soft, but still it filled the emptiness of the alleyway.

Carver shook his head. "I'm a Noxvalian soldier. I never would have had," his eyes flicked harshly between her and Alius's body, "An assassin as a partner."

The bitterness in his tone pierced Clara's heart, but she held her ground. "You were a Raven. I am a Viper. We were paired together. But before that..." her voice grew even softer. She shouldn't voice it. She still didn't know how she was supposed to feel. But if saying the truth could help him remember, she had to try. "You were mine. We were in love."

"Were." He whispered the word. He reached into his pocket, and Clara brought the baton forward, holding her position.

He smirked at her, "I'm not a threat to you. Yet. If I were, you'd be dead already."

Clara's eyes widened, and she heard Marsh gasp behind her.

He pushed his hand deeper into his pocket. "In fact, the only reason you aren't dead yet is because I'm curious. You see, I bought this for someone. I don't know who. I can't remember. I was in an accident, and the before is blurry. Tell me," he pulled his hand out and let a necklace dangle from his fingers. "Do you recognize this?"

The delicate gold chain hung from his fingers, the ruby pendant hanging towards the dirt. Her mouth opened as she struggled to find the right response. It was the necklace she saw the first day they wandered through the festival. It was the necklace she wanted. How did he know?

She closed her mouth, swallowed. Opened her mouth, but still couldn't find the words to say. She closed her mouth again. All the while, he lay casually on the ground, propped up only by his forearm. His eyes continued to scan her, his lips tightening when he saw the baton in her hand, but he didn't comment on it.

"Yes," she got out. "When we came here for our assignment, I noticed it at one of the stands. I thought it was beautiful. I had no idea you bought it for me."

His eyes widened, and for a moment, Clara thought she glimpsed the innocent boy she used to know. Then his eyes hardened. "You're lying." He spat out.

Reality came crashing in. She couldn't fail this assignment. She couldn't let her friends be hurt. She didn't know him anymore. He slipped the necklace into his pocket as she stepped forward. She pushed the baton on, quickly stepping to him, but he grabbed the end of the baton, careful to keep his hand far enough back that the electricity wouldn't touch him.

"I thought you might threaten me." He stared her down, not budging as she shoved the baton towards him. It didn't move at all. "If you threaten me, you are certainly a threat to the crown. I handle threats to the crown."

He yanked the baton towards himself, pulling her on top of him. The air rushed from her lungs as she made impact, but she quickly recovered, squirming away from him while keeping a hold on the baton. He let her go, and she moved back from him.

She jumped to her feet, but he was faster and was already in front of her. "I suggest you drop your weapons and turn yourself in."

He leaned over her, and she took a step back. Her heart racing, "Carver," she whispered, searching his eyes for any recognition. "It's me, Clara."

He grimaced, but he kept stepping into her space. He grabbed her wrists, twisting them behind her back as he forced her against his chest. She couldn't see his face anymore and looked around desperately for Marsh.

Clara was close enough to the building wall on the other side that an idea finally hit her. She threw her legs up, and as soon as her feet hit the building wall, she kicked as hard as she could, throwing herself against Carver. He stumbled back, but quickly regained purchase, holding her wrists even tighter.

Electricity crackled, and Carver's grip loosened as he fell to the ground.

Clara fell forward, landing on a knee. She knew it would be bruised later, but for now, the adrenaline was too high for her to feel anything. She quickly stood and spun to face Carver. Marsh stood over him with the baton.

"This clearly isn't effective enough for him, but we can keep him knocked out until we're ready to go."

Clara didn't have any words left. As the adrenaline faded, her wrists began to ache, and her knee voiced its disapproval of her landing. She simply nodded at Marsh.

40 CLARA

Marsh had to electrocute Carver two more times before Reese, Nate, and Ryker made it back. The door closed behind them, and they exchanged glances. "Are we good?"

Nate nodded, and Reese cracked a smile. "We have everything."

Nate examined the alley, noting Marsh standing over Carver.

"Take his armor off." He nodded to them, holding a set of cuffs up. "Marsh, do you think we can make it across the square and to the bookstore without anyone noticing he's cuffed?"

Clara immediately started taking Carver's armor off, struggling briefly with the weight of it. Once she unclasped it all, she was able to slip it off his body. Marsh gave her space, weighing the options in her head. "I don't know," she said honestly. "But I don't want to leave him either."

Nate nodded. "I thought that would be the consensus. We are going to cuff him, and try to hide his hands under my jacket. It should fit on him and let us hide his hands. It's a huge risk."

Clara examined the cuffs before slipping them on Carver's wrists and clasping them. They were black, a bright color running across each side. "What are these?" She asked as she took Nate's jacket. Marsh came to Carver's other side, and together they pulled him to his feet. Clara threw the jacket over Carver, pulling it down around him while Marsh supported his weight.

The sleeves hung limp, but the jacket primarily secured his hands cuffed behind his back. With Marsh and Clara on each side, they could hopefully pass him off as drunk. "It's an unbreakable alloy they created. When fused into the metal of the cuffs, it makes them entirely unbreakable. The only way to open them is with the key Nate has." Ryker answered her question. "Reese actually found them in a room next to the radioactive material. She thought they might come in handy, and I recognized the design from some paperwork I've seen."

"Time to go, team," Nate commanded. Ryker and Nate took the lead, with Clara and Marsh following with Carver, and Reese bringing up the tail.

The walk to Jacob's building was silent. No one stepped out of the buildings, no lights turned on. It was just them. Clara's body tensed when the wind whistled between the alleys, but she quickly calmed herself.

They made it to the backdoor of Jacob's building before Carver woke up enough to be a problem. He threw his head back wildly, causing Marsh and Clara to lose their grip on him. He landed in the dirt, his hands still bound behind his back. He was on his feet in an instant, seething at them.

His arms flexed as he pulled at the restraints, but they held firm. Clara didn't wait for someone else to step in this time. As long as they were in the alley, they were vulnerable. And he had seen all of their faces now. He would either come with them, or they would have to kill him.

She stunned him.

As she and Marsh hauled him inside to Jacob's, she turned to Ryker. "How many times can we shock him with this before it becomes an actual problem for his brain?"

Ryker shrugged. "I'm guessing we're going to find out."

He narrowed in her field of vision. "Why don't you take a guess."

"With the amount of electricity and the frequency you are applying it," Ryker looked at the ceiling, his eyes moving back and forth as he thought it out. "I think you should be good for five more times before it becomes a problem."

"And then?"

"Hasn't been tested. This is a much higher voltage than a normal taser. I didn't design it to be gentle or safe. It's designed to be a weapon."

"You couldn't have told me that earlier?"

Ryker threw up his hands. "What do you mean, told you that earlier?? How was I supposed to know we would be kidnapping a soldier?"

"We didn't kidnap him," Clara groaned, letting Carver's weight slip toward the ground.

"Yes, because he so obviously wants to be here," Ryker muttered, scuffing his toe against the ground.

"Quiet!" Nate snapped and the room fell silent. "You're acting like this assignment is over! We still have to make it out of Noxvalis!"

Marsh and Clara rearranged Carver's weight and followed Nate as he walked through the building. *He's right. Damn, when did I become such a bad operative?*

41 CLARA

They made it back to the Midnight Quill several hours later. Carver kept waking up, and they kept having to silence him. Nate suggested gagging him, but that was quickly vetoed. They had to duck into random alleys a few times to avoid the occasional guard patrolling the streets.

Nate put a kitchen table chair in the middle of the room and tied Carver to it as he started to wake up again. "I don't have a good feeling about this." He muttered.

Clara took his place in front of Carver when Nate stood, but quickly took a step back when Carver growled at her.

Marsh looked on from where she leaned against the counter. "If he was a little shaggier, I'd say we could pass him off as an aggressive puppy."

Clara couldn't find it in herself to smile. "Carver, you have to remember us."

"I don't." He spat the words, and she grimaced, taking another step back. "I already told you I don't know you. I have a job to do. And you're all," his eyes scanned the room, and Clara could've sworn he didn't miss a single detail. "Criminals! You don't deserve mercy from the king. I should kill you all."

"We may have to rethink our strategy of taking him with us." Clara could hear how reluctant Marsh's words were.

Nate just shook his head. "We can't afford to wait this out here. We have to get out."

Clara glanced around frantically. She was so close to saving him. She couldn't leave him. "I'm staying."

"What do you mean *you're staying*?" Nate walked towards her.

Clara didn't back down. "The assignment is over. Take Reese, Marsh, and Ryker, and get the hell out. I'm staying."

"Clara, he's past saving."

"I don't believe that. If I believed he was past saving, I would have left him in the alley."

"I can't leave you behind, Clara. You know that."

Clara chuckled bitterly, "You're willing to drag me, but you won't drag him?"

Nate ran his fingers through his hair, huffing out a breath. "Ten minutes."

"What?" Clara answered.

"You have ten minutes to convince him to come with us. If he doesn't agree to come with us willingly in ten minutes, we leave him. As for you? I'm your commander here, and you will obey. Otherwise, we'll stun you and take you with us, allowing you to endanger your friends here more. Is that what you want?"

Clara was shocked by the fervor in his voice and the way everyone crowded around him. He had their support. She believed every word he said. She believed he would drag her out. She believed that he would endanger the rest of their team if she chose to disobey.

She lifted her chin. "Fine. Ten minutes. Not a second less." She nodded, their agreement done.

Nate addressed the team, "Alright, everybody. Ten minutes. In ten minutes, you better have your asses packed and be ready for a long night of walking. We have to get far enough from Noxvalis that their scopes can't see us. Everybody out!"

The room cleared, and only Reese paused to give Clara a soft smile. "You've got this," she mouthed.

I have to be able to do this. How could she convince him to come with them in ten minutes?

42 CARRION

Carrion's brain felt like it had split. Genuinely had split. Like, there were two entirely separate people on either side shouting that their side was the most correct. One side reminded him, endlessly, of his reverence to the king. Over and over, the king's accolades played through his head. He respected the king. He honored the king. He *owed* the king. It was only because of the king that he was even alive. He owed the king his loyalty, and he didn't leave debts.

The other side of his brain wasn't shouting, as much as it itched. It was the smallest itch that slowly festered in your unconscious until the feeling became conscious and could almost be called pain. Now, here, before her, the feeling was pain.

He looked at her, and he *knew* her. But he didn't. He couldn't. He was loyal to the king, and she was...very much not. So he couldn't have known her. He never would have betrayed his country like that. But her. She was in his dreams. He had a necklace that may have been for her. How would he ever know?

He couldn't remember his past, that was true. That gave her that much more credibility, but still, it was hard to believe he knew her and didn't remember her. Was he her partner before? What she said to him rang through his head, drowning out the shouts from the other side.

Violent pain erupted behind his eye, and he blinked to try to refocus his vision.

When his vision returned, she was in front of him. She had pulled up a chair and was now at eye level. The rest of the room had cleared. *When did that happen?*

"Carver?" He met her gaze, almost as an instinct.

"That's not my name."

"Carver," she said, softer this time. "I need you to remember me."

He forced himself to keep his eyes on hers. She was the threat in this room.

"Carver, I need you to remember me so you can come with us. So you can come home."

He wasn't confused anymore. His home was here. He served the king. These criminals wouldn't let him go unless he played along. Once they set him free, he could kill them all. They stole something from his king, and he would get it back. He had to play the role she expected. If she wanted him to be Carver, he could be Carver.

He shut his eyes as if thinking. *I can pull this off.* When he looked back into her eyes, he could see the plea there. He replayed their earlier conversation in his head again, "Clara?" He murmured, barely letting the word out.

She dropped out of the chair to her knees, cupping his face with her hands.

"Carver? Carver?"

He tilted his head from side to side as if shaking loose a memory. "Clara?" He said again, more confidently now that he knew she believed him. "Where, where am I?"

She let out a sob, and it took everything inside him not to turn away in disgust. She didn't let go of his face. This woman, who had stolen from his king, and she wouldn't let go of his face. He continued to play along.

She finally got control of herself and answered him, "We're at Marsh's bookstore. Command sent us. We're here to get a weapon.

But we're leaving now," she finally took a breath, "And we saved you, so you can come with us!"

He smiled at her, trying desperately to keep his true emotions hidden. Saved him? They didn't save him. They kidnapped him!

"I've been waiting for you, Clara."

"I've missed you so much, Carver. I'm so sorry. I can't even imagine what you've been through. And I'm so sorry for how I handled it last time. I'm so sorry." Her voice broke again as a fresh wave of tears surfaced.

He inhaled deeply, like he was coming back to himself. "I'm sorry, Clara, but I..." he paused for dramatic effect as if searching for the right word, "I don't remember much." He squeezed his eyes tightly, faking the pain. "It might, it might take a while for it all to come back to me."

Clara sat back on her heels, and he immediately registered the look of disappointment that crossed her face before she caught herself.

Disgusting. But he could do his job. How proud would the king be if he infiltrated their enemy's ranks and returned with their heads on pikes? How proud would he be if Carrion not only returned with what was stolen but took back from them as well?

So he forced a sympathetic look, "I remember enough," he couldn't force himself to tears, but he got as close as he could. "I want to go home." His voice was soft, barely a rasp as it left his mouth.

She fell for it, and inwardly he smiled. "Of course, Carver. I'm just so relieved we found you. I have to go pack my things, and then we'll head back."

"I can't wait." He forced the enthusiasm into his tone. She stood and kissed his forehead before she walked away. "Hey! Wait! I need you to unlock my cuffs."

She looked over her shoulder at him, "I'll be back."

43 CLARA

She didn't leave to pack her stuff. She left to find Nate. Because he was right. Whoever that person was, it wasn't Carver anymore. Carrion had stripped away the man she loved. But if Nate agreed to take him with them, maybe she could figure out how to get Carver back.

She found Nate in a heated discussion with Reese, but they silenced as soon as she walked in. Reese kept glancing her way, and she could feel the tension between them. She still hadn't fully learned how to be the friend Reese needed. She gave Reese a tentative smile before turning to Nate.

"He's agreed to come with us."

"Because that's exactly what we need on this assignment. A psychopath who's waiting for an opportunity to murder us." Nate didn't mince words, and Reese grimaced.

Clara just brushed it off. Nate wasn't wrong, and she didn't feel the need to fight with him on it. "We keep him in cuffs. He'll come with us willingly. This gives us the opportunity to restore him over time. He's seen our faces. We can't leave him here, at least not alive. I'm not willing to kill him." She pierced Nate with a look, "And I don't think you're willing to kill him either."

"I would." Reese's voice was soft, and Clara couldn't help the look of betrayal she gave her when she turned. "He's a danger to us. I'm not letting him destroy you again."

"We're not killing him." Nate's voice was gruff and final.

"If we take him with us and we can't bring him back to himself," Clara took a deep breath to prepare herself for the words she knew she needed to say next, "We can give him to the Spiders. They can ascertain what Noxvalis did to him, and maybe, maybe, use that information to better prepare us for this war."

Nate didn't respond for a while, and Clara felt convinced she had lost him. Her heart felt like she was running a marathon; her breaths were coming in shorter and shorter gasps of air.

"Fine. If you can convince him to willingly come with us while wearing the cuffs, we can take him."

Clara smiled, relief flooding through her system. It felt even better than the adrenaline she usually relied on. She had a chance.

She walked back to Carver, her entire body feeling lighter. He looked at her desperately, but she knew how careful she had to be. She had to let him think she believed him. She had to convince him this wasn't her decision. "I'm so excited to take you home." She believed these words as she said them, even more when he looked up at her. He looked like Carver at that moment.

Then he blinked, and she could see him slip into his act of Carver. "Oh, thank God. Please, please, take these godforsaken things off of my wrist."

She chewed on her lower lip, "Our assignment leader is pretty strict on the integrity of our assignment. He's the only one who can remove them," true since Nate had the key, "But once we're further down the road, I'm sure he'll undo them."

Clara didn't react to the anger that crossed his face. When he settled on despair, her heart cracked, but she stayed firm. This wasn't Carver. "It's literally rubbing my wrists raw. Please, Clara, I want to come with you. I can't make it out of Noxvalis with my hands tied behind my back."

"It's out of my control, Carver," she begged him to understand. As much as she was acting to prove she believed him, she was begging him to come with them. He had to agree so she had the chance to save him. If he didn't come with her now, he'd be lost to her forever.

He looked at her with the most despair she'd seen from him, and even though she knew it was an act for him, her heart broke. "I'm so sorry," she reiterated. "But I don't have a choice."

He nodded. His voice was gruff when he answered, "I don't understand. But I'm not staying here. I want to go home."

44 CLARA

It was still the middle of the night when they slipped into the shadows between the alleys. For Clara, it felt like hours had passed. There were no guards, signals, or signs that their assignment had been discovered. Aside from one of the guards being Carver, it all felt too easy. *It's a trap,* she couldn't help but think. She was fairly certain she had brought the trap with them. Though finding Carver while completing the assignment felt like a wink of fate more than a warning sign. She ignored every feeling that it was anything else.

Carver stayed silent as they led him through the alleys they traversed to get here in the first place. His posture curved forward from his hands cuffed behind his back, but he didn't present further commentary as they walked.

Marsh took the lead, with Nate at her heels. Ryker followed them, and Reese took up the rear. Clara's responsibility had become Carver. She knew Nate still felt it was a bad idea. He had mentored Carver for years, and she believed he cared about Carver as much as she did. But Nate's job wasn't to take care of Carver. His job was to lead their assignment and protect them.

They reached the wall less than an hour later. Ryker was careful with their cargo. He carried it in the satchel he had built purely for this. It was padded and protected to keep the radioactive isotope from moving and causing a reaction. Although Ryker claimed it wasn't dangerous without a trigger, Clara wasn't quite sure what counted as a trigger, and she was still concerned that too much movement was all the trigger needed.

They reached the doorway, and Marsh slipped through first. Nate followed. Ryker leaned through on his stomach, passing his bag to someone at the bottom before climbing back to standing, and dropping through feet first. Clara heard him grunt as he landed.

"So this was how you got in," Carver muttered.

Clara glanced at him, wondering if it was a slip for him. "Easier than faking a marriage, for sure." She quipped.

His face twitched. She couldn't tell why. Did referencing their last assignment bring any memories to the surface for him? Were his memories just buried, or were they actually erased? Since she couldn't know for sure, she would keep commenting to try to jog something.

"Remember? You threatened to kiss me because the PDA might make the guards uncomfortable enough they wouldn't even check our papers."

His blank stare pierced through her. He ignored her comment. "How am I supposed to get down there with my hands tied behind my back?"

"Slide through on your stomach, we'll make sure you don't break anything," Nate told him from the bottom.

Ryker had steadied himself, and the satchel returned to his shoulder. "Now, Carver. We don't have time to waste." Nate repeated.

Carver clenched and unclenched his jaw, but did as was instructed.

"You're up next, Clara."

Clara slid through the opening, holding on to the bottom of the doorway before she dropped to the ground, landing on her feet. Adrenaline rushed from the brief fall, and as Reese came through the doorway, pulling it closed behind her, she smiled. They did it.

45 CARRION

Alius's comments were all starting to make sense now. His hesitancy to trust Carrion, and the training he made sure Carrion was well-versed in. The guards' standoffishness also made sense. He wasn't a Noxvalian. He wanted to be. This was his opportunity. Once he returned with their stolen goods and their lives, the king would finally accept him. He could do it.

So he allowed them to keep his hands bound behind his back. This was the rhetoric he told himself. The truth was, he was confused why he couldn't break through the restraints. He had tried to when Clara stepped out of the kitchen, but they wouldn't budge. He didn't know what was different about his cuffs, but he could feel when he pulled at his wrists that he couldn't do anything about the binding. He was actually stuck. He settled the panic in his mind by reminding himself they were at far more risk than he was.

Clearly, he had known this girl, Clara, previously. She was the "girl of his dreams". Quite literally it seemed. Regardless of what she said, their past hadn't been enough for her to save him. He didn't need saving anymore. She still loved him. He could tell. He would weaponize that love to succeed and make the king proud.

They trekked through the forest, and she kept one hand lightly grasping his forearm. He wasn't sure if it was for her own comfort or if it was to keep him from running. They walked until the walls of Noxvalis were no longer visible, and the sun was rising on the horizon. The world was cast in pinks and oranges, and as he stared at the sunset, he could feel a memory start to surface. A rooftop. The color orange. A girl laughing. Clara laughing.

The memory brought a feeling of stress up in his chest. Something wasn't right. He tried to grasp the memory threads as they passed through his mind. The second he started to pull on the memory and remember, shooting pain erupted in his head. *They don't want me to remember,* he thought, but when the pain faded, so did the thought.

He was here to kill them. Nothing else mattered.

"You okay?" She asked him softly.

He growled, "I'm your prisoner. Of course, I'm not okay."

"Alright, team, let's break here. Relieve yourself, drink some water, eat some jerky, and then we keep moving. I know you're tired, but we have to get out of the range of the guards."

Everyone nodded.

Nate approached them, "I'll take Carver off your hands for this."

Clara hesitated, shifting her weight. She didn't release Carrion's arm. Nate continued to look at her, and finally she stepped away from him, "Okay." She turned and walked into the forest. She was no longer visible to Carrion.

Nate stepped fully into his face. "I'm assuming you would also like to relieve yourself."

Carrion turned enough to show his restraints, "Hard to do so when I'm bound."

"I'll help you, but I'm not unlocking those."

Nate grabbed Carrion's arm, and instead of the gentle touch from Clara, practically dragged him into the forest. "You don't remember me, do you?"

Carrion wracked his brain. Clara had told him his name was Nate, but no other information came to the surface. "Nate."

Nate nodded. "You've heard everyone say my name. Good job keeping up."

Carrion grimaced inwardly. He needed to turn this around. "I told Clara, I don't remember much. It's all slowly coming back."

Nate pushed him against a tree. The bark dug into Carrion's fists as he clenched them. Nate placed his forearm against Carrion's throat, pushing just enough for Carrion to know he was serious. "I know you're not Carver."

"I am. I was tortured. I was changed. But I'm still Carver." It was the closest to honest he could be. He wasn't Carver. He was here on assignment, same as then. The loyalties had shifted, but regardless, he remained a soldier.

Nate shook his head. "No, you're not. I heard you introduce your-self as Carrion. Whatever that bastard Herring did to you, you're not the same person I knew, and you're certainly not the same person Clara knew. I'll admit, you're doing a fucking good job of convincing the team you are Carver. I don't believe you. I won't believe you. I'm delivering you to Command so you can live out your life in a cell. I am the only one on this team who can release you. And I won't. I suggest you give up whatever plot you hatched before joining us and accept your fate."

Carrion just shrugged, the tree continuing to dig into him as he did so. "I don't believe in fate. I thought I would never escape Noxvalis. And yes, I didn't remember anything at first. But it's coming back." It wasn't. If anything, he remembered less than he did before. But Clara seemed to be convinced, and he couldn't afford for Nate to ruin that.

Nate dropped his forearm, but he didn't drop his posture. "You can spew whatever bullshit you think will help your case, as long as you accept those restraints aren't coming off. You were like me, Carver–Carrion. A Raven. Ravens don't kill. They don't murder. They collect information. I have all the information on you. I've never killed anyone, but if you dare hurt any member of my team, I will personally watch you bleed out."

Carrion swallowed hard, knowing that Nate meant every word he said. "I promise, Nate, even though I don't remember much, I will do what's right. For you, and for Clara."

46 CLARA

Clara ended up appreciating the moments alone. She walked deeper into the forest, marking her surroundings with a couple of broken branches so she could make it back. Once she was out of eyeshot, she fell to her knees, letting the damp underbrush take her weight. Tears filled her eyes, but she breathed in and out deeply, refusing to let them fall.

She couldn't walk back to Carver, to Carrion, to whatever the hell that creature was, with a puffy face and swollen eyes. No, she needed to be stronger than ever before. She needed to be the Clara he would remember. Strong, level-headed, a little crazy, aggressive, brutal. Her. The woman she was the last time she saw him.

Somehow, it was harder to be strong now that he was her enemy than it was when he was trying to protect her. It was easy to write off his attempts and protection and convince herself she needed to push him away. She had pushed him away. Quite effectively, it seemed.

She took a few minutes to compose herself, relieve herself, and stretch before she walked back. Carver stood a few paces away from Nate. Nate had his back against a tree, his arms crossed over his chest. Marsh had returned, but Reese wasn't back yet.

"As soon as Reese is back, we need to keep moving."

Clara nodded. "How far do we want to get today?"

Nate shrugged. "Ideally, we walk until we can't keep moving for today."

Reese yawned as she joined them in the clearing. "Sounds fun," her voice was devoid of her usual enthusiasm, but they were all tired.

Ryker walked up front with Marsh this time, with Reese and Nate trailing behind Clara and Carver.

Clara wasn't sure what to do with the man beside her. Now that they were further from Noxvalis, she didn't try to keep hold of his arm; instead walking beside him with her hands pressed to her sides. For the first hour, he didn't try to make conversation with her either.

Clara focused on the sounds of nature around her, forcing herself to focus on any noises that stood out. If they hadn't been caught by now, they probably wouldn't be, but they couldn't be too careful.

Eventually, Carver broke the silence. "How…long?"

Clara glanced at him in surprise. She hadn't expected him to speak up. "How long, what?"

His face contorted momentarily as if trying to grasp the right words. If she could have helped him, she would have. "How long have I been in Noxvalis? You said I was captured, right? How long?"

She nodded slowly. "It's been a few weeks." This wasn't something she wanted to talk about. Those weeks were miserable for her, and she didn't want to know how much worse they were for him.

He absorbed the information without further comment. Then, a few minutes later, he asked, "Were we in Noxvalis together?"

"Yes."

"How did you escape?"

She felt the question like a dagger in her heart. "You saved me."

Again, the silence fell between them. Again, Carver broke it. "Why would I save you?" The question wasn't harsh or mean. But the directness of it caused Clara to flinch.

"Only you would know the answer to that." She dodged the question. *Because you loved me,* were the words running through her head, but she wouldn't admit that. She didn't know for sure that he had saved her because he loved her.

"Oh. I mean, I can think of a few reasons I would save you." Clara stumbled at the flirty tone in his voice, and he chuckled.

"I'd reach out to catch you, but I can't."

She shook her head, "Thanks for the offer."

47 CARRION

This was supposed to be easy. He was supposed to convince her that he remembered, and she needed to free him. That shouldn't have been a hard task. But he couldn't remember, and she seemed to grasp that at least a little. He needed to figure out how to actually win her trust.

She stopped holding on to his arm. Thank God. Though some secret part of him missed the connection. As he stepped over branches and the leaves crunched beneath his feet, his mind felt scrambled.

In part, he felt like when he first woke up in that room with the white coats buzzing around him. Before the king walked in and gave him a purpose. He woke up, and he didn't remember anything. He didn't know what he was supposed to be doing or who he was supposed to be.

He felt that same kind of confusion again. On the one hand, he knew he would make the right choice and kill them all. On the other hand, she was something he hadn't fully prepared for.

As they approached a tall tree that had fallen across the path, she grabbed his arm to steady him as they walked over. Her fingers lingered a few moments too long, and when she let go, he could still feel where her fingers had been. This was insane. He was going insane. Why else would she be affecting him like this?

"How long have we known each other?" He asked her. Maybe her stories would jog enough of his memory.

"You and your mom moved into the house on the back of our property when we were teenagers." Clara's voice was tired, so he kept pushing.

"And we were friends?"

She shrugged, refusing to look at him. So more than that, then. They were definitely more than that. She picked a leaf out of her hair as they kept walking. "I think you almost proposed to me once. But yeah, we were friends."

His feet stumbled, but he managed to catch himself before he landed face-first in the forest floor. He had loved her. What did that feel like? What did love feel like? Did he still love anyone? He thought of his interactions with King Herring and the loss of Alius. No, he didn't love anyone. Everyone served a purpose, as he would serve his. Emotions were not a necessary piece of it.

He ignored his own ramblings about feelings when he realized he could use this. She clearly still had feelings for him. He could exploit those. Flirting seemed to be the right route.

She had moved towards him when he stumbled, but once he caught himself, she stepped to the side again. "Until our assignment here, we hadn't seen each other in three years."

His mind spun across this fact. If she was telling the truth and he had loved her, why would he have allowed three years to pass without seeing her? A memory flashed across his mind. *"You're weak."* His words echoing in the room when they left his mouth. Her tears. His cold shoulder.

This was the first memory he could feel in his body. He could feel his heart break for her, and the stab of guilt that he was the one who made her cry. Pain shot through his head and then shuddered through his body. But this time, it didn't take the memory with it.

His vision was blurry, so he stopped walking. "Carver?" Her voice felt far away. Finally, he brought himself back to the present moment.

"I broke up with you. Didn't I?"

Her eyes widened in shock, her mouth opening into a perfect "o." She nodded.

"I called you weak. And you cried. Then I left."

Again, she nodded. "Yes."

Nate caught up with them in the time it took him to recover. "Clara, why don't you walk with Reese for a bit? I'll take care of Carver."

Clara exchanged a glance with Nate before nodding and setting off to close the distance between them and Reese. "Are you actually remembering things?" Nate's voice was low but adamant once the girls were out of earshot.

"Yes," Carrion admitted honestly. He didn't know why the memories were returning now or how to keep them.

"Hmm," Nate answered. "Regardless, I can't let you out of your restraints until Command does a full evaluation on you. And, if you are Carver, you wouldn't want to be free if there was even a chance you could hurt Clara."

"I'm not asking you to free me," Carrion would take the opposite approach. Nate was suspicious because of how quickly he had asked to be set free. He could remedy that.

"Have you had any memories of me come back?"

Carrion shook his head no. If he had known this man in his past life, he didn't know him well enough to bring the memories into this life. "I remember her, Clara. Why would I remember you?"

"I'm the reason you're still alive, boy." Nate's voice was cautious, careful.

"How so?" Carrion challenged him.

Nate didn't deign to look at him. "Maybe one day you'll remember. For now, your only job is to keep up. I suggest you walk faster."

48 CLARA

"Are you okay?" The concern was evident in Reese's eyes.

Clara yawned, the tiredness hitting her in a way the adrenaline didn't allow for when she was walking with Carver. "I don't know. Is that a question I need the answer to right now?"

"Nope. If you don't know, we'll leave it at that."

"Are you okay?" Clara returned the question.

Reese lifted one shoulder. "We're alive, right?"

"Yeah."

"What happens when we go back? We all knew this was a suicide assignment. I think going back is the wrong call."

"What's our other option?" Clara asked, yawning again. She wasn't processing the information as quickly as Reese was talking, but she was trying to keep up.

"We talked about this in Noxvalis, remember? We go to Calyndor. Ask the queen for refuge. Offer our services." Reese said decisively.

Clara slowed her pace, "Have you talked to Nate about this? I know we talked about it, but I kind of thought we were kidding. What about our parents?"

Reese chewed on her bottom lip. "I've thought about that. But they're safest if Quorath assumes we're dead. Be honest, do you actually think that Quorath would never use them against us? We know too much. It's just a matter of time."

Clara let the information settle in her mind. Slowly, she answered, "I think," she paused, "I think you're right. They would use our parents against us. I haven't even seen my mom since 2nd year. It was strongly encouraged that we break all contact."

"I remember," Reese's voice was soft.

"What did Nate say? I assume you talked to him already?"

"Nate thinks anything except going back to Quorath is too much of a risk. Especially now that our party includes Carver."

Clara shook her head, feeling her braid bounce across her shoulders. She yawned through the words, "I disagree, and I'll tell him so."

"He's in charge, does it matter what we think?"

"Let's pause and find out."

They stood still, watching as Nate and Carver walked towards them. "Why are we stopping?" Nate's tone held all the suspicion Clara was hoping to avoid.

"Reese is right." Clara didn't wait to jump into the conversation.

"You've recently become notorious for doing things your own way. Of course, you think Reese is right." Nate responded.

"That's not what this is!" Clara took a deep breath as soon as she heard the defensiveness in her tone. "What do you think happens to the team that returns from a suicide mission? Be honest, Nate. You know Command better than any of us. Is this really how you want to go out?"

"Clara, now is not the time to talk about this."

"Nate," Clara's voice was just as firm, "Now is the only time to talk about this."

"I'm your assignment leader. The decision is made. We're going back."

"I think we should vote. The assignment is over. We got what we came for. We don't need you to remain our leader."

Nate gritted his teeth as he flexed his jaw. Clara glanced at Carver, but he didn't seem overly engaged in the conversation. He looked up at her, and her heart lurched. She quickly fixed her gaze back on Nate.

"Are you sure you're doing this for the right reasons?" Nate looked pointedly at Carver. Clara didn't look at Carver again, keeping her eyes on Nate.

"Nate, I'm telling you, we can't go back. You know it too."

"We'll take a vote."

They kept walking, catching up to Marsh and Ryker.

"Do we feel like he," Reese nodded her head towards Carver, "Should be privy to this conversation?"

Clara shrugged, "He's coming with us either way. It's not like he'll be unaware of what decision we make."

"Wait, what are we talking about?" Marsh's voice was flat, exhaustion clear in every word.

"I don't think we should go back to Quorath. We should seek refuge in Calyndor. They can keep the radioactive materials safe, and we can disappear." Reese spoke up.

Ryker scratched the inside of his wrist as Marsh said, "Why?"

"We called this a suicide assignment. It wasn't an accident." Clara answered.

Marsh shrugged. "There's nothing for me in Quorath. Why not?"

Ryker shifted his weight back and forth. "We aren't going back?"

"We're taking a vote," Nate replied. "Clara made the fair point that we're out of Noxvalis. We're all adults. We've all taken multiple assignments. It's only fair that everyone has a say in where we go from here. So, what do you think?"

"Calyndor." Reese immediately responded.

"Agreed," Clara said.

"If they're going, I'm with them," Marsh answered with a yawn.

"Ryker?" Nate questioned.

Everyone looked at him, and he stared at the ground, still scratching at his wrist. "I don't know. Don't ask me."

"You're far too opinionated not to have an opinion on this," Clara stated. "And Nate, we already have the majority. Time to admit it."

Ryker finally looked up, tears in his eyes. "I left Quorath when I was so young. I have no idea if my parents are alive or not. I wanted to see them again. But it's not a guarantee. I understand your desire not to go back. I won't be the one to stand in the way of that."

"Ryker," Reese said carefully, "You could be a danger to your parents if we go back. Quorath could use them against you."

"I know that," he paused, thinking it through. Finally, he exhaled, "We should go to Calyndor. I won't endanger my family."

No one spoke for a few minutes. Nate broke the silence, "It's not my first choice, but we'll go to Calyndor."

49 CARRION

After they decided where they were heading, Carrion was still stuck with Nate. Nate really didn't seem to like him. A decent amount of Carrion's plan involved being able to charm his way out of the cuffs. From the beginning, Clara was his best shot at that. Nate didn't seem willing to give him any grace at all. If Nate had his way, Carrion was pretty sure he'd be dead.

"How did I know you?" Carrion asked, breaking the silence. Nate's jaw flexed. If Carrion had to win Nate over, well, he'd win him over. Nate didn't answer him. *Well, this is going great.*

They kept walking. Carrion rolled his shoulders. They were starting to ache from how tightly his arms were pulled behind his back. He thought he should be as tired as everyone else, but so far, he felt okay aside from his shackles.

The sun was bright overhead, and his throat was beginning to ache from the lack of water. Time to try a new approach. "I know you want me dead, but I'd really prefer a bullet to dehydration."

Nate looked at him sharply. Carrion continued, "I haven't had water since we started this trek, and it is not a cool day."

"I'm not letting you die of dehydration. Just making sure you keep up a good attitude for the walk." Nate grunted, but he came to a stop and screwed the top off his water bottle.

Carrion wouldn't have put it past Nate to make it difficult or spill the water on him, but Nate held the bottle carefully while Carrion drank. "Thank you," Carrion said once he was finished.

Nate grunted again and resumed walking.

Carrion quickened his pace to keep up. "Did you know Clara before the assignment?" Carrion felt his heart skip over her name, even as he looked ahead to watch her laugh with Reese. He did know her. It wasn't enough. He wasn't that person anymore. How could he walk the line between convincing them he was Carver and Carrion?

King Herring's face flashed in front of his mind. He steeled his emotions, locking them away again. He would serve his king.

Nate sighed deeply. "You aren't going to let us walk in silence, are you?"

"You could always put me back with Clara," Carrion responded casually.

"Not happening."

"You're protecting her. Why are you protecting her? You knew me, you said you saved my life, but now you're willing to damn me?"

"Carver, Carrion, whatever the hell your name is, I suggest you shut up. You have no idea what you are talking about. I did everything I could to protect you, but there's no coming back from Noxvalis's experiments. You know that as well as I do. It's cruel what you're doing to Clara. You're forcing her to hope that the old you, the Carver we knew, is in there somewhere. He's not."

Carrion didn't respond for a moment, trying to figure out how to twist the conversation around. "I have pieces left."

"It's not enough."

"The more I'm around her, the more the pieces return."

Nate didn't respond, and Carrion took a break from pushing.

50 CLARA

The next morning, Clara told Nate she wanted to be in charge of Carver. "If there's even a chance the real him is still in there, you have to let me try." She pleaded. "All that can happen now is I get hurt. You have the key to his restraints. You're in charge of this. Just let me try."

Nate gritted his teeth. "I think it's a bad idea, Clara."

"Thank you," she answered.

Carver was standing at the edge of where they had made camp. Even with his arms held behind his back, he kept his head high. She expected the circles under his eyes to have darkened, but he still looked the same as when they took him, aside from a couple of scratches courtesy of the trees.

"Thank God," Carver grinned when she approached.

Her foot paused, and she almost twisted her ankle on the next step. "You're happy to see me?" She questioned.

She put both arms through her pack, hiking it higher on her back as she watched him. "Nate isn't a fan of me. And, what man isn't happier to be walking with a pretty girl than another dude?"

She rolled her eyes, but she couldn't hold back her smile. "Oh, I'm a pretty girl now?"

He nodded aggressively. "The more I remember of you, the prettier you become. You were always pretty. From the first day I saw you in the square."

Clara didn't miss how the first time he mentioned seeing her, he was Carrion. It was to be expected, of course. He didn't remember Carver.

They took off a few paces behind Reese and Nate. "You recognized me then." He said softly, "I could tell."

"I recognized you." She confirmed.

"You should have walked over and kissed me. Made me remember you."

She laughed, sharp and rushed. "You think that would have worked? You would have arrested me on the spot."

He looked at her from the corner of his eye. "Why do you assume the worst of me?" He pouted. "I wouldn't have arrested you…at least not until after I kissed you back."

She laughed again, "At least you seem to be in a more agreeable mood today."

He nodded. "I do remember pieces. I want to keep talking to you so I can remember the rest." He paused, thinking. "You told me that once I threatened to kiss you to get past security, right?"

She smiled, reminiscing, but kept her eyes on the ground as she stepped over some thicker brush. "Yeah, you did. And I threatened you right back."

"Oh?" He grinned, "What, did you tell me you could show me something else you could do with your tongue?"

Her jaw dropped. "Carver!" She laughed, "Nothing so crass as that. Who do you think I am?"

A smile played across his lips, and she couldn't help but watch. "A feared assassin, I'm sure."

Again, she rolled her eyes. "Indeed." She stepped up onto a tree in their path, easily dropping to the ground on the other side. She turned to Carver, putting her hands on his arms to steady him as he made the same movements over.

She didn't move her hands when he landed in front of her. He didn't pull away. She looked at him fully then. She saw all of the modifications, of course, but staring into his eyes, it was still Carver. If only he could remember.

She dropped her hands before she did something foolish and turned away.

He hurried after her. "I understand why I loved you." *Loved.* Past tense. He shook his head almost immediately, "Sorry, slip of phrase. That wasn't what I meant."

"It's fine," she assured him.

"I just mean, you're amazing. You vouched for me even when I wasn't treating you or anyone else, well. You've stood by me. You're also gorgeous. Any man would be extremely lucky to have you."

Her heart melted a little at that, and she understood what Nate meant when he said this wasn't a good idea. Maybe he was right. She'd let him walk with Carver tomorrow.

51 CLARA

Walking to Calyndor added an extra day to their trek, though it likely thwarted any attempt to find them in time. But finally, they made it. They were all more than exhausted, and Clara's blisters had blisters from the walking. She had finished walking the first full day with Carver and then asked Nate to walk with him for the rest of the journey. Her heart ached, but she recognized it was better for everyone involved. Nate was kind enough not to tell her he was right, and Reese was appreciative of her company.

Clara still wanted to save Carver, but she didn't think a trip where he was cuffed was the right opportunity. Nate wouldn't let him take the bonds off, and Clara couldn't stand seeing the raw lines on his wrist or the blood that had coated his hands. It broke her heart. There had to be a better option, but Nate wouldn't hear of it.

Calyndor was gated similarly to Noxvalis, but the guards stationed weren't checking papers or asking questions. "Great, so we're here." Marsh muttered, "How do we convince them we need to talk to their queen?"

Clara shook her head as she attempted to take in all the details. The guards were finely ornamented. Even in the sun, they wore their full, colorful garb. Their metal helmets were complete with a bright orange plume. If she had been less tired, Clara would have laughed at the absurdity of it.

"Let's keep Carver in the middle so they can't see the restraints. We'll figure out our next steps once we're inside." Nate took the lead, and Reese joined him. Clara and Marsh stood on either side of Carver, and Ryker walked behind him.

The guards didn't flinch as they walked by. Clara was amazed by how little security Calyndor had. They were known as an affluent kingdom, yet their security left much to be desired. She could have slipped in and done anything she wanted with none the wiser.

Nate led them past the gates and towards the buildings. The architecture of Noxvalis was something to behold, but somehow Calyndor was more stunning. The buildings were various colors and made of an array of different materials. Some were stone, some were brick, some were wood. The colors all tied together into a massive kaleidoscope as they walked towards the town square. Before they reached the center, Nate steered them towards two tall buildings on the side and the alley between them.

He kept walking through the shadows until they reached another alley behind the buildings. He turned right. Nate kept turning through alleys until Clara was thoroughly lost. Finally, he stopped.

"Well, we're here. The only contact I have in this city is 100% loyal to Quorath and not worth our time. Does anyone else have other ideas?" Nate sounded beyond exhausted, and Clara felt the same.

"Carver and I met a couple when we were on assignment the first time. Julia and Mark. He worked for the queen." Clara chimed in.

"What if we just walked up to a guard, told them who we were, and asked them for help in seeking an audience?" Marsh asked.

Clara rolled her eyes. No way would that work.

But Nate shrugged, "Worth a try. Stay here, and I'll see what I can do."

"I'm coming with you," Reese stepped up.

Nate looked around the group, "Everyone okay with that? Marsh, Clara, do you both feel comfortable keeping Carver…?" His voice trailed off. Clara could fill in the blanks. They needed to keep Carver contained. They needed to ensure he didn't do anything reckless.

Carver huffed loudly. "We're good," Clara replied calmly.

"Alright."

Nate and Reese left the alley. Ryker and Marsh instantly jumped into a conversation regarding the experiments at Noxvalis. They kept their voices low, and Clara didn't want to try to listen in. She took a few steps away, leaning against the brick building.

Carver followed her, but couldn't lean against the building with his hands bound behind his back. Instead, he stood in front of her. She remembered another similar moment. Him in front of her in an alley in Noxvalis. The moment he had grabbed her wrists and held them against the wall.

Her heart sped up from the memory, and she blinked quickly to push the images away. His lip quirked, "What were you just thinking about?" His voice was soft enough that it wouldn't carry to Marsh and Ryker.

She shook her head, "Nothing I should admit to." She muttered.

He laughed. "That dirty? Wow, Clara, I'm impressed. Especially after you told me your mind didn't go there."

She laughed with him. She loved the sound of his laugh.

She observed him from this angle. While leaning back against the brick, she was almost a head shorter than him. He was so much broader than he was before. The circles under his eyes were entirely gone. His cheeks had filled in quite a bit, but his jawline was still sharp. Again, she noted, his eyes were exactly the same. After studying him, her gaze landed there, and he stared back at her.

His lips parted before he cleared his throat. "Aren't you going to tell me?"

"It was a memory with you," she admitted.

"Oh, now you *must* elaborate." He grinned at her. This was the Carver she remembered. The happy-go-lucky golden retriever. Even the Carver on their assignment wasn't *hers*. He was what Command created. But somehow, somehow, this act, this was the Carver she remembered. Was it possible that it was actually him?

"We were on assignment," she didn't mention Noxvalis. She was careful to avoid anything that could set his progress back, best he only remember the good moments. "And you pulled me into an alley to lecture me."

His smile froze. "I can't imagine me lecturing you."

She laughed, and his smile widened, "Believe me, it happened."

"I believe you," he whispered. "What happened next?"

She adjusted her position against the wall. "I tried to fight you. You grabbed my wrists and held them above my head against the alley wall. And," she paused, the current moment and the past moment blending together. She missed him. She loved him. Even though he was here with her now, he wasn't her Carver. She might never get the chance to tell him how much she loved him.

"And?" He pressed.

She shook her head, trying to push past the moment. She didn't want to admit the truth. But what if the truth helped him remember? She took a deep breath, "Anddd, I kissed you."

She looked up at him, watched as he blinked rapidly while he absorbed the information.

"Not what you expected?" She tried to laugh.

"I don't know what I expected." He sighed, his smile fading entirely. "Clara, I'm so confused."

She stood up straight, stepping towards him and away from the brick wall. "What do you mean, Carver?" Her voice was careful. She was careful. She was walking on a ledge. One misstep, and she'd lose herself forever. She knew that. But this was Carver. She had to try.

"I feel like there are two lives in my head," he admitted. Clara didn't know if he was telling the truth or if he was trying to win her trust. Either way, she would try to help him. She would give him the chance she hadn't given him on their assignment. "You're in one life, but it's almost more of a dream than a life. It's here, and then it's not. I know you, I know in my gut that I know you, right? But I don't know you. I can't remember anything about you." His eyes widened. "Except, green. Green, right? That's your favorite color. Green." He said the final word more confidently.

She nodded, taking another tiny step towards him. The space between them was almost nonexistent, but Clara was far too aware of how close they were to Marsh and Ryker. She wouldn't do anything that would make the team question her ability to handle this situation. With that in mind, she took a big step back, holding her hands behind her back until she pressed against the brick again.

His eyes stayed glued on hers through the movement, and her heart ached. "Yours was orange," she answered.

"A sunset," he murmured.

Then he doubled over in pain.

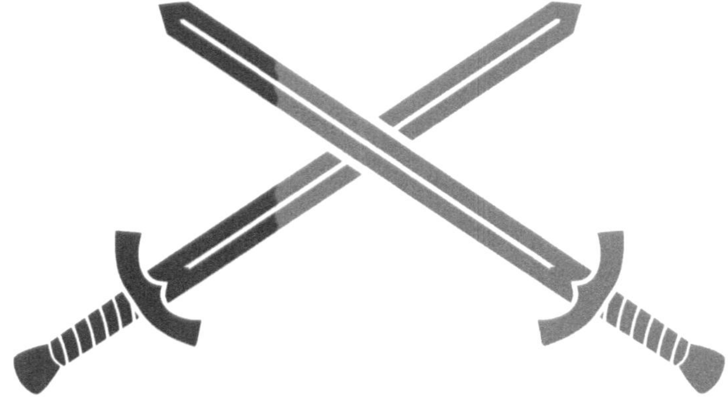

52 CARRION

He was here for an assignment. He was going to return to Noxvalis. To the king. His assignment involved earning their trust. He would do what he had to do. This is what he told himself as he started his conversation with Clara.

He positioned himself in front of her, not quite towering over her, but taking up her field of vision and her attention. He told himself it was for his assignment. But something shifted when she said she was remembering a moment with him.

He saw a flash of that moment. He felt his fear for her in his chest as if he were back in that moment. He remembered what happened next before she said it. For a moment, he convinced himself it was a fantasy. She was attractive. Of course, he wanted to kiss her. Who wouldn't? When she confirmed it, it was as if he felt his gravity shift.

Where previously memories had been threads he couldn't grasp, that memory, the one of him pinning her against the wall and kissing her, became real. It became solid. It was a current memory. With it came the next memory. Green. Again, he thought he made it up.

When she said orange, images of him on a roof with her passed through his mind. But those threads brought the return of that sharp pain through his head.

He doubled over, unable to stand under the severity. She reached out for him, her hands firmly grasping his shoulders as he gasped for air. She knelt before him, her blue eyes wide with worry. He wanted to tell her it was okay. He couldn't get the words out.

He closed his eyes against the pain, trying to breathe through it. When he opened them, he couldn't remember the previous moment or how he ended up right there. He stared at the girl in front of him, trying to figure out how he knew her. Clara. His assignment.

He straightened, trying to pull himself from her grasp. He needed to earn her trust, not her affection. Those aren't the same thing.

"Sorry, I don't know what happened," he said. His voice sounded far away.

She dropped her hands, retreating until she was leaning against the wall once again. It was interesting. He didn't expect her to enjoy being entrapped. From everything he'd gathered, she was a killer. Why would she allow herself to be cornered? She should want the advantage. "Are you okay?"

He licked his lips, trying to fix the dryness of his mouth. "Yeah, I'm fine now. Just a weird moment."

She nodded and paused before responding, "We were talking about sunsets."

"Sunsets?" He questioned.

She tilted her head, "Sunsets." She confirmed.

He could feel it. This was a test. He was failing. He missed something. He tried to grasp at the threads, but they were gone. A memory of him pinning her hands over her head remained, but he couldn't place it in reality. *Is it a memory or a fantasy?* He paused on it for a moment. Pinning her hands over her head would make sense in a fight scenario, which is what he was betting it came from. Did it make sense in any other scenario?

It didn't matter. He only needed her trust enough so he could kill her. He took a deep breath, focusing on the part he needed to play.

"What happened?" Her voice was soft as she scanned his face. She knew something was different. He knew something was different, too, but he didn't have an answer for her.

"Nothing happened." He lied.

Her eyes narrowed. *She knows.* He swallowed. Shrugged. Tried to recall how to behave normally. "My head just started hurting."

"Did it hurt because you started remembering?" She stepped towards him again and reached her hand out as if to cup his face.

This time, he took a step back. Her hand hung in the air between them. She didn't drop it, but she didn't try to touch him again. "I don't know why it happens." He shook his head, "I don't remember why it happens, and I forget it happens quickly after."

"They did this to you." He didn't mistake the fire in her eyes.

"Everything okay over here?" Marsh stepped to them.

He didn't like anyone on the trip. They were all part of the assignment. But Marsh, well, he had a special dislike for her. "Everything's fine," Clara didn't take her eyes off of Carrion. Carrion turned to Marsh and Ryker, forcing Clara to drop her gaze he was starting to squirm beneath.

"Ryker suggested we check in," Marsh said.

Ryker's jaw dropped, but he quickly found words to fill his mouth, "Not true. I just saw Carri-Carv-Carri- ugh, him, double over."

Carrion pierced Ryker with a glare. Pride swelled in his chest as Ryker took a step back. Clara shoved his arm, "Knock it off."

He stopped glaring. "Wow, I'm shocked he listens to you," Marsh said with her arms crossed over her chest. Further proof of why he disliked her. "So well trained," she cooed.

"You knock it off too," this time, he could hear the exhaustion in Clara's voice. She practically sagged against the wall. "We've come a long way, and we may still have more to do. The last thing we need is infighting."

"I mean, I agree," Marsh replied. "Even if it's fun."

"Do you think they're going to be back soon? I don't exactly feel inconspicuous here." Ryker said, rubbing his hands over each other.

"They haven't even been gone for half an hour," Marsh answered. "I don't think we should expect them back for a bit."

"We're in an empty alley," Clara rolled her eyes at Ryker's comment. Carrion couldn't look away from the movement. It felt familiar. Beyond the anger and the determination to fulfill his assignment, he felt something in that motion. "We're about as inconspicuous as it gets. Not like we're going to blend in with other people when we have someone in cuffs."

"You could," Carrion shrugged as innocently as possible, "Let me out of my cuffs."

"Not a chance," Clara said. At the same time, Marsh said, "Absolutely not," and Ryker said, "I don't think I'm comfortable with that."

"You're not comfortable with that? You don't understand how uncomfortable these are," Carrion protested. He wasn't sure his efforts would get him anywhere, but sympathy could go a long way. At least for people capable of sympathy. That wasn't an emotion he'd felt. It was an emotion he primarily saw in Clara's eyes when she looked at him. It was an emotion he could abuse.

"Far more comfortable than a knife in your throat," a deep voice said from the end of the alley. Clara was on her feet away from the wall in an instant, her palms across her daggers on instinct. Carrion watched intently, impressed by her seamless movements.

53 CLARA

"Well?" Clara challenged Nate.

"We were told they don't typically grant audiences with the queen, but if we come with them, they'll present our case to her tomorrow."

"Where does that leave us for tonight?" Marsh asked.

Reese came into view, a guard walking with her. "Everyone," she announced with a smile, "This is Portia. She's a guard here and has volunteered to help us find a place to stay tonight so we can take our information before the queen tomorrow."

No one said anything. Clara caught Nate's eye and raised her shoulders in question when he looked at her. He nodded in response. "Thank you, Portia, for your willingness to help us." Clara finally said.

"The honor is mine. Anything to serve my country." She answered with a smile.

Clara didn't smile back. The gold uniform was accented by spots of bright orange fabric, the same color as the plume. There was a fabric patch over each joint, and stitched across the heart of her armor.

"Do you know Mark and Julia? I don't know their last name. Mark said he worked for the queen."

Portia tilted her head, "I recognize their names. I believe he is on her council. Do you know them?"

Clara nodded, "I met them a few weeks ago. I'd love to see them again. They can also confirm what we're sharing about Noxvalis."

"I'll see if I can get in contact with them," Portia told her.

"Thank you," Clara responded.

"Is everyone ready?" Portia asked with so much enthusiasm that Clara almost pulled a dagger out. She did not have the energy to deal with this.

Portia turned to lead them, Reese directly behind her. Nate pushed Ryker and Marsh to go next, then joined Clara and Carver toward the back. "Everything going well?" He asked her in a low voice; she knew Carver could hear. Nate wasn't even pretending he believed Carver's story.

"Don't act like that," Clara said. It was the politest response she had. "Carver is wonderfully behaved. You have nothing to worry about." She smiled at Carver, but even she didn't believe her own words. *He'd probably kill me if we released him. Maybe I deserve it.*

Nate grunted. "Don't be naive," he muttered. He moved behind her, leaving Carver to follow directly behind Marsh and in front of Clara.

They walked quickly, keeping up with Portia as they wound through all the alleys. It felt like a never-ending maze. Every time Clara thought she was starting to understand the pattern of the buildings or understand the color scheme, another random store popped out.

At the back of one of the alleys, they passed a massive purple building that was covered in blue spots. The sign said, "FUN," and absolutely nothing else. Clara had no desire to explore a building like that, and Portia didn't pause in her quest, so it wasn't an option anyway.

"We're almost there!" Portia's cheerful voice reached all the way to the back of their line.

Clara paused her pace long enough to start walking next to Nate. "How does someone with that disposition become a guard?"

"I don't think that's important right now."

"I don't like the way you talk to Carver," Clara said quietly.

Nate gave her a side eye, and Clara's anger rose. He matched her volume as he responded, "Clara, I don't like that we brought him at all. You know that this was a bad idea. You know it. You keep pretending it's not. You keep pretending he's the man you knew."

"I don't," Clara protested.

Nate held up a hand. He continued in the same whisper tone, "You do. You're hoping if you treat him the same, he'll remember who he was before. You want to flirt and bring him back. It won't work."

He had her there. She was hoping she could make Carver remember and change things. "I've been in this a long time, Clara. I knew someone who was abducted by Noxvalis. I saw him once after, but it wasn't him. My partner had to kill him before he killed us." Clara swallowed hard. Nate continued with more sympathy in his tone, "I know you don't want to think like that. I have to, because I know you won't."

"I've thought about it," Clara admitted. She kept her eyes fixed on Carver's back. She'd asked herself the question multiple times over their trip here. In fact, she kept asking herself that question. She wondered if she could do it. If Carver, Carrion, whatever, endangered Nate or Reese, could she take him out? She still didn't know. She didn't want them hurt, but she wasn't fully convinced she could hurt him.

Nate shook his head. "I'm going to tell the queen what he is. It should be her decision. He's a risk to all of us, and his life isn't a decision I want either of us to have to make."

Clara's eyes caught onto Carver's wrists as he walked ahead of them. They were engulfed in angry red, and the muscles across his shoulders were taut from being held back for so long. She could only imagine how much it pained him. Walking couldn't be easy for him at this point either.

They weren't treating him like someone they were saving. They were treating him like a prisoner. That's what he was now. She couldn't trust him not to hurt her or her friends, so he had to be a prisoner.

"Okay," Clara responded quietly.

"Just like that? Okay? No big fight or argument?" Nate sounded shocked.

"You're right," Clara responded. "We can't save him. He wasn't someone savable. I don't know why he agreed to come with us, but it can't be for a good reason." The flash of him standing in the alleyway came to mind. He was Carver for a minute, but after he doubled over, he was Carrion again. She could see the difference in his eyes. Soft to hard. He knew her, and then he didn't. "I thought he would start to remember more. It's not fair to keep him in cuffs while we hope he remembers more than he did. I mean, what's the other option?"

"I don't know, Clara. That's the problem. We can't exactly blend in here while we have a prisoner."

"At least they can't hurt him anymore." Her words came out so soft she barely even heard them.

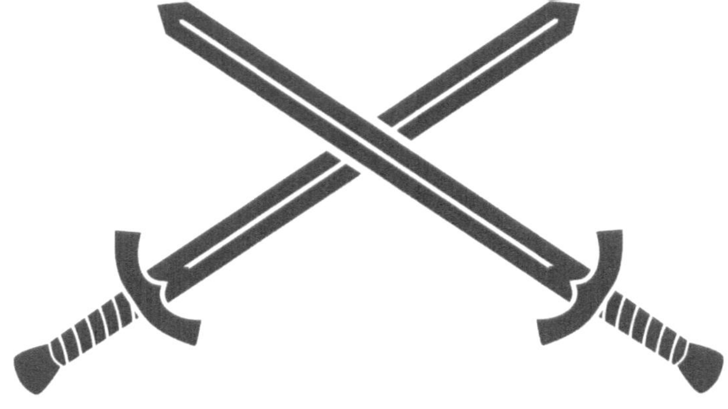

54 CARRION

Carrion listened intently to every word Clara and Nate said. As soon as she had started talking in a hushed tone, he knew it would be relevant to him. They were planning to give him over to the queen. If they did that, he'd never be able to complete his assignment. He had to stay with them. He had to get out tonight. He had to convince her that he was Carver.

I am Carver. He tried to make it stick in his head. What did Carver feel for her? Aggression? Is that why Carver pinned her hands above her head? If Carver was cruel to her, why did she care so much? Why did she look at him with such sympathy?

His mind spun across all of the words until he thought he was going to be sick. He had one shot. Tonight. The sun started setting in the distance as they walked towards their destination. The orange and pink rays peeked over the city walls, the one time they were visible, and then it was gone, and they were left walking the alleys in the dusk. Orange. His favorite color. Carver's favorite color? What was the difference?

"This inn belongs to the Calyndor government. I will get you rooms for tonight. Please wait out here. I don't want you to scare other guests." She smiled politely.

They grouped together outside the door. People walked by, giving them a large berth. Carrion flinched when Clara touched his arm, and she grimaced, "I was just trying to turn you so your back is to the building. People would stare at you less if they couldn't see you were in cuffs."

"Oh." He turned in the direction she indicated.

She smiled up at him, and he could've sworn tears were building behind her eyes. "I used to like the sunsets, right?" He stepped out on the limb.

Her mouth opened, shock filling her eyes. "Yes," she answered.

"Did we," he licked his lips to try and fix their dryness. The walking hadn't been kind to him. "Watch them together?" A partial guess, but her eyes confirmed it the second the words were out of his mouth.

She nodded. "I know I don't remember everything," he whispered. He kept his voice low and was satisfied when she leaned into his space to hear him. He had a chance. "But I remember you. I remember enough. I remember pieces of...us."

She pulled back quickly, and this time there were tears in her eyes. She shook her head as a single tear ran down her cheek. Nate stepped in. "Carver, I think it's probably best if you don't try to dredge up memories with Clara. We're all tired, and the last thing we need is more emotions."

Anger boiled beneath his skin. When he was free from these cuffs, Nate would be his first target. He would snap his neck before taking his head with him. After all, he needed some memento for the king. "I didn't mean any harm," he said calmly, masking all the emotions he had.

"I don't care what you meant. We're here to crash for the night. Tomorrow, you'll be someone else's problem."

Clara turned away from them, and something in his heart twisted with the movement. He did know her. She knew him. He couldn't understand why it was so hard for him to decide how he felt and remember. He wanted to remember her; he wanted to kill her. He didn't know what he wanted. "I know you don't trust me," he had to try again. "But I don't mean any harm." A lie, but it might be worth something. "I've been through hell," again, his appeal for sympathy, "And I just want to be around people I know."

"Really?" Nate questioned. Carrion nodded, hoping he looked sincere. "Okay, Carver." Nate crossed his arms over his chest. "If you can tell me how we know each other before our time with the queen tomorrow, I won't turn you in."

"Deal," Carrion said quickly. It was a shot. All he had to do was remember one memory with Nate. Yet the more he stared at Nate, the clearer it became that he wasn't going to remember anything just from looking.

Nate's lip curled up, "You can't ask Clara, either. You have to figure this one out. Give me some hope that *Carver* is worth redemption."

The words stung even though he didn't believe himself to be Carver. Carrion wasn't looking for redemption. Carrion was looking for revenge. But something was changing the more they called him Carver. He felt torn between the two realities. He was Carrion, but he was Carver too. Each part of him wanted vastly different things. He didn't know how to reconcile the two personalities. He didn't know how to redeem them.

"I'll remember." He assured Nate.

Nate just stared at him, "You better. For her sake, I hope you do." He shook his head, "I won't give her false hope."

"I wouldn't ask you to," he said, convinced that was the Carver response. Carver clearly cared about Clara. He cared about Clara. He wanted Clara dead. Carrion glanced over at Clara, feeling both things at once. He wanted to kill her. He wanted to kiss her. He loved her; he would destroy her to prove himself to King Herring. His gut twisted. This was too much. Something inside him was wrong. Something was split. Why couldn't he push the pieces back together?

Portia stepped back out, "I was only able to get two rooms. I'd suggest men and women split, but I'm not one to tell you what to do with your lives."

"Thank you," Reese said.

Carrion looked at Reese then. Did he know her, too? Was he

supposed to? Reese hadn't interacted with him at all, aside from the group moments and her moments with Clara. Was she somehow integral in this puzzle? Or was she an unimportant piece he didn't need to solve?

His head was starting to pound. He remembered the searing pain from earlier, but thankfully, this wasn't that. This was a dull ache caused by how hard he was trying to rebuild the pieces of his mind.

"We're going to split men and women just like Portia suggested," Nate announced as they followed her inside. He grabbed Carrion's shoulder roughly, and Carrion continued his fantasy about snapping Nate's neck as he was herded inside.

The inn was full of people, and from the smell of things, they were currently serving food. Portia glanced back over them as they followed her up a staircase at the back. The people made no effort not to stare, and Carrion caught many of their glances falling to his bound wrists. He couldn't blame them. It was unusual, the way he was being treated like a prisoner. He hadn't done anything. Yet.

The evening was still young.

55 CLARA

She could feel the exhaustion in her bones. It was the type of weary she pushed herself towards in every training session, plus the stress of the assignment and Carver. Nate was absolutely right. Neither of them could be trusted to make rational decisions around Carver. If Nate had his way, Carver would be killed. If Clara was left to decide, well, she didn't know what she'd do. Set him free? Kiss him and see if it shook something in his mind free? She knocked that thought aside. The exhaustion was making her delusional. There's no way she could kiss Carver. For one, he wouldn't let her. For two, it wasn't rational. She promised she would be on her best behavior.

The inn was clean, thankfully. She ignored the eyes of the patrons, focusing solely on Ryker's back. Reese was directly behind Portia, and they kept up a steady stream of chatter she couldn't make out. Nate had pushed Carver into position directly behind Reese, Ryker was behind them, and Marsh took up the rear behind Clara.

No one else in the group spoke as they walked. The stairs were steep, boxed in with a wall on either side. The railing was long gone, but Clara could still see where the wall had faded from its location.

At the top of the stairs, the hallway split in two directions. She followed the group to the right. Portia stopped suddenly, and Clara barely avoided running into Ryker. Marsh did bump into her. "Sorry," she muttered. "The ceilings here are so weird."

Clara looked up. The ceiling was swirled with every color she could imagine. Stripes, dots, patterns, checkers. Every color and every pattern was represented somewhere. It was a headache. "They are weird," Clara agreed.

Portia unlocked the doors, handing one key to Reese and one to Nate. "We'll be by to pick you up tomorrow at 0800." Portia addressed the group. "Provided the queen finds your intel worth hearing, we will take you before her. Regardless, our guards are going to want the opportunity to examine the material you said you brought." She fixed Carver with a sharp look, "And I'd highly recommend cleaning him up. Calyndor understands the reason for prisoners, but the queen won't want to be reminded of the kind of treatment they received."

With a nod of her head, Portia dismissed herself. Reese entered the room that Portia gave her the key for. Marsh walked past Clara to follow her in. Clara knew she should join them, but her feet felt frozen. Tomorrow, she would lose Carver. Surely, Nate would give her a few moments with him.

"Nate," she said softly when it was only the three of them in the hallway. "Can I come in and help clean Carver's wrists? You heard what Portia said, and I would like the opportunity to..." her voice trailed off. To say goodbye? To prove that he wasn't Carver anymore? To give herself some closure? To try and help him remember one last time?

Nate started shaking his head no, "Please, Nate," Clara murmured. Nate paused.

"Follow Ryker in," he told Carver. Carver's shoulders fell forward.

Clara started to protest, but Nate held up a hand. "Come back in 20 minutes. Let Ryker and me help him shower and get him changed. You can be the one to deal with his wrists." He glanced over his shoulder. "But I need you to promise me something."

Clara's heart rose with hope. She would get her goodbye. "Anything, Nate."

"Promise me you won't tell him anything about his before."

"That's the only chance I have for him to remember anything, for him to be Carver again."

Nate sighed heavily, "He can't inflate your memories and call them his own. Either it comes back to him, or it doesn't. Either you promise me, or I won't let you in."

Clara grit her teeth. She knew it was a long shot to believe that Carver would remember anything tonight. But it was a chance. It was an opportunity, however small it may be. If she didn't agree, she wouldn't get to see him. "Fine. Agreed."

"Good. Now go get cleaned up. Knock twice in 20 minutes, and I'll let you have the time alone with him to clean his wrists. But that is all, Clara. Understood?"

"Understood." She responded. She looked over Nate's shoulder, trying to get another glance at Carver, but she couldn't see him.

56 CLARA

Reese and Marsh let her have the first shower, and Clara took it quickly. As amazing as the hot water felt, she was in the bedroom braiding her hair within five minutes. She dressed in dark pants and a black long-sleeve shirt. Her clean clothing options were limited, but this worked for the moment.

"I think you have to let go of him, Clara. I'm so sorry; I know that sucks." Reese said from the floor. She had plopped down on the floor almost as soon as they entered, and said she wouldn't climb into bed until she was clean, but she was fine with showering last.

The room was small. Two queen beds, with a single nightstand between them. A dingy window let in a minuscule amount of light, but most of the light came from the lightbulb in the ceiling, which flickered occasionally. There was no closet, and the bathroom wasn't anything to boast about. A toilet, shower, and sink. All crammed into the tightest amount of space possible.

Clara squeezed her eyes together, trying to ward off all of the memories she had with him. "It's like," Clara tried to put it into words. "We weren't together, right? He broke up with me. We were supposed to be nothing. But the whole trip we had together was full of tension, and when I saw him kiss Marsh..."

"I forgot about that."

"Yeah, I realized how much I still cared. I couldn't tell him, though, obviously. Then I was making reckless choices, and he saved me. Why did he save me? Why did he subject himself to this?" Tears filled her eyes. "I think he loved me. I'm probably crazy for that. I think I love him."

"You're not crazy, Clara. I think he loved you, too. But Clara, the man in there, isn't Carver." Reese answered.

Marsh opened the bathroom door. Clara turned her back towards her before Marsh could see the tears in her eyes. "Ryker and I were talking about Command's experiments. Specifically, if they could be reversed or undone."

"And?" Clara couldn't help asking. She sorted through her bag just to keep her hands busy.

"Neither of us has heard of it being possible. I'm sorry." Marsh's sympathy was almost more than she could take.

"It's possible," Clara decided. "There has to be someone who can help us. Maybe the queen will have the resources for it."

No one argued, but the silence was telling. She was the only one with hope for Carver, and even her hope was losing ground.

She wiped the remnants of tears from underneath her eyes and took a deep breath before walking out. Two knocks on Nate's door, and he opened it for her. Ryker was already sitting in bed with his eyes closed, and Nate looked like he would be crashing as soon as he had the opportunity.

"He's waiting for you in the bathroom," Nate said. She nodded and walked to the bathroom.

Carver sat on the edge of the tub, his hands still bound behind his back. His hair was wet, droplets of water occasionally falling from the tendrils.

She closed the door behind her quietly, and he looked up. He met her gaze with such ferocity she couldn't breathe for a moment. He looked like Carver.

"Nate said he was letting you help me with my wrists," he stated.

"I can be quite persuasive." She sounded breathless and tried to remind herself to breathe.

Carver stood up. The bathroom was barely big enough for the two of them without bumping into each other. She rummaged under the sink for a washcloth. Once she found one, she ran the water from the sink until it was warm and soaked it. Carver turned his back to her, giving her access to his wrists.

Neither spoke for a long moment as she cleaned away the blood. He didn't complain, even in the areas she had to scrub a little bit harder. His hands were rough and calloused beneath her touch, and again she wondered what Noxvalis could have done to so quickly change the man she loved into someone unrecognizable. Once the blood was clean, she stood back. Tears filled her eyes, and she hurriedly blinked them away as she rinsed the washcloth and washed the watery blood from her own hands.

"Thank you," he said. She startled. He had turned back towards her and was far closer than she expected.

She recovered as quickly as she could. "You're welcome."

She couldn't bring herself to look up at him, not when she could feel his breath on her face. She turned so she was leaning against the counter, giving herself a little more space. "I'm glad I came with you," he whispered. "Even if this is how it ends."

"I don't want this to be the end," she knew her whispered admission could only hurt, but at this point, she wanted to be honest in all the ways she hadn't before. She owed it to the man she loved, and to herself, to be honest. If the queen decided he was a risk, if she took him, if they were all imprisoned tomorrow. So many possibilities for this to go wrong, and almost no chance of this going right.

Finally, she met his eyes. The dark circles she remembered from their first trip were back. The strain of the last few days had left its mark on everyone. He was no longer clean-shaven, a 5 o'clock shadow visible on his jaw. His lips were full and slightly parted. *What would happen if I…*

The thought didn't have a chance to fully form before Carver leaned in and pressed his lips to hers. Her heartbeat raced. This wasn't what she expected. This wasn't supposed to happen. She ignored every one of those thoughts as she kissed him back.

Her hands moved up to the back of his neck, and when he didn't stop kissing her, she intertwined them into his hair. A soft moan escaped the back of her throat. Quiet enough, it wouldn't leave the bathroom. Quiet enough, Nate wouldn't hear them.

Wait.

She pulled away, leaving her hands loosely clasped behind his neck. He leaned over her, his arms still tightly bound behind him. This wasn't right. She bit her lower lip, and his eyes caught onto it.

"This isn't right," she murmured.

He brought his eyes up to hers. "Why not?"

She shook her head. "You don't remember me. This is all a game to you."

"Clara, that isn't true," his voice sounded desperate. Desperate to convince her, but she knew the truth.

"I love you." She told her truth, knowing his would be different. "You don't know who I am, but I love you, Carver. Not Carrion, not this weapon, Noxvalis and Quorath created. I love you. Your soul. The boy I grew up with, the man you became."

His eyes widened, and his lips parted, but she didn't give him a chance to respond. Clara kissed his cheek gently and opened the bathroom door. She looked for Nate, "Thank you." He nodded, and she walked out. She pulled the bedroom door closed behind her, pressing her eyes together tightly.

Waves of emotion crashed over her. Their memories together rushed through her head. He was the love of her life. She saw it now. Every moment she thought he was an asshole, he had only been protecting her. And now, she had to let him protect her one last time. She had to let him go.

57 CARRION

There was no comfortable way to sleep with his hands bound behind his back. Over the past couple of nights, Carrion had found that sleeping on his side was usually the best option. Even like that, his shoulders ached. He was finally reaching the point where his entire upper body was going numb.

Ryker was sound asleep in the other bed, and Nate was lightly snoring beside Carrion. When Clara had kissed him, he felt something change. It was like something new in his brain triggered. Between her and the king? He didn't know anymore. He felt like he knew her. He felt like he was supposed to protect her above all else. He didn't quite understand why he felt that way. The disconnect was still there.

He tried to line up the things he knew for sure. He knew he wasn't from Noxvalis. Not only was that confirmed by the group he was currently with, but it also made all of the guards' snide comments make sense. He knew he had been operated on and changed. However, that didn't tell him whether they had saved his life or done this to him. *Vials...project...*the king's voice rang in his mind. Had the king done this to him? Was he another experiment? Alius had shown him through the labs after each shift.

The biochemistry one was fascinating. Was that where he came from? At the time, looking at the creatures and the tanks, he hadn't thought much of it beyond a morbid curiosity. Was that him now?

Or was it something else entirely?

Had Clara left him, and he changed sides in his anger? Where did his loyalties actually lie? A dull throb started in the back of his skull, but the piercing pain never came. He continued to ponder the details he did remember. Orange and green. Her hands above her head. He had kissed her then, hadn't he? He hadn't pinned her hands in aggression.

Where did Nate fit in? Nate seemed to know him almost as well as Clara did. Although the memories with Clara were starting to filter back in, he didn't have any with Nate yet. He stared at the wall, trying to dredge up a memory. He wanted the opportunity to explore this relationship with Clara before he made his decision. Maybe he would kill her and choose King Herring. But maybe he wouldn't. It needed to be his decision.

He closed his eyes, picturing Clara's face and trying to find more memories. He hoped one of them would lead to Nate, but he had no guarantees. He saw her standing in front of him on a large field with other cadets, maybe? And felt the anger beneath his skin. She wasn't supposed to be here.

He saw himself breaking up with her, the tears in her eyes. It was for her own good. That memory expanded, and he saw himself walking down the hallway. At the end of the hallway, he saw…Nate? Nate clapped him on the shoulder. "It was the right call." He assured Carver.

"Was it?" Carver muttered back.

"She needs to take her own path. You need to be focused. You're doing the right thing for both of you." Carver nodded. "Now, let's get back to training."

Mentor. The word flitted across his mind quickly. Nate was his mentor. He could be free.

"Nate." No response. "Nate," he hissed again. Nate grunted. Carrion continued, "You were my mentor."

Nate sat up in bed next to him. "Why do you say that?"

"After I broke up with Clara, you told me it was the right decision. You helped me push forward in training. You gave me the instruction I needed to survive." Carrion elaborated on the pieces he was pretty sure were true. Between the memories and Nate saying he saved his life. His heart raced. This was his chance.

Nate was silent for a long moment. *He didn't expect me to remember. He's not going to keep his word.* The thought brought more than a little panic. As calm as he had stayed thus far, the cuffs were remarkably uncomfortable, and more than anything, he wanted out of them.

"There's no way Clara could have known that conversation." Nate finally said.

"You told me I had to remember on my own. I did."

Nate exhaled heavily. "I want to release you. I want to believe you. But I know, the Carver I knew, would never do anything to endanger Clara. I'm concerned you're still not that Carver, even with the memories coming back."

"I don't think I'll ever be back to the person I was before," Carrion admitted carefully, "But I don't want to hurt Clara. I want to have the opportunity to figure this out. I think I loved her before all of this, and I don't want to give up on that."

"Hmph," was all Nate responded.

"Are you going to uncuff me?"

"I'll uncuff you in the morning before we go to the queen."

Immediately, Carrion started to protest. Nate interrupted him, "If you can't accept that, I won't uncuff you at all. I don't have to keep my word to you. You're in no position to change anything."

"You act like you have some level of integrity, but you're still a prick."

Nate chuckled beside him. "Go to sleep, Carver. You always did think I was a bit of a prick."

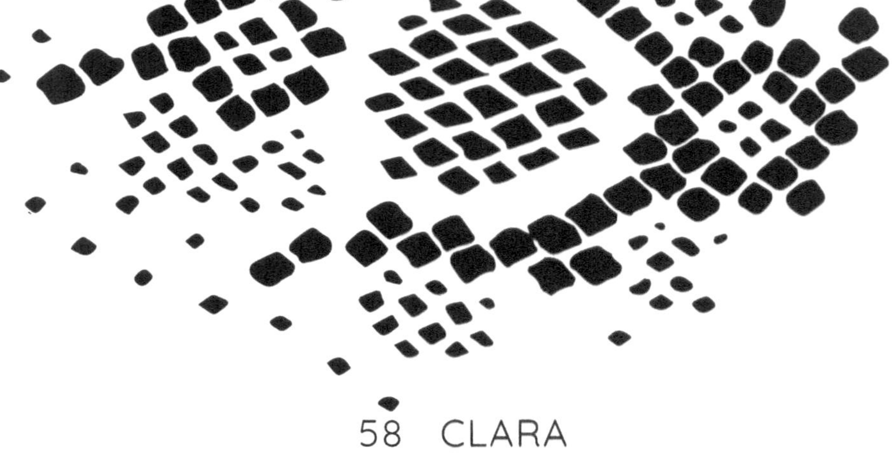

58 CLARA

Clara didn't fall asleep easily that night. Her mind wouldn't let her find rest. She replayed each moment as if she could somehow change it. Kissing him was a bad idea. But even if she could have taken it back, she wasn't sure she would.

It felt like him. All the meaningless flirtation and the extremes he pushed her way felt fake, so she could believe they were fake. Kissing him? That didn't feel fake at all. It felt way too real and was way too much for her to process.

She could still feel the tingle of his lips on hers. She pressed a finger against her lips, willing it to stop the sensation. She needed to sleep. Desperately, she needed sleep. They all needed to be at their best for their audience with the queen in the morning. She rolled over to see if Reese was still awake. They had taken one bed and given Marsh the other.

Reese was completely out. Clara considered waking her up, but eventually turned back to her side and lay there until sleep finally found her.

The next morning passed in a blur. Everyone dressed quickly, and it was clear nerves were high as they prepared to go before the queen.

Even Clara had heard the rumors. While most considered her to be a peaceful ruler, within the armies, soldiers postulated that she was more vicious than that. They said Quorath and Noxvalis wouldn't declare war on her because she'd wipe them out.

Clara didn't know what to believe, but was aware she would find out soon.

"How are you feeling?" Reese nudged Clara's shoulder.

Clara shrugged, "Ready to get this over with? Does that count as a feeling?"

Marsh rolled her eyes, "I think we're all ready to get this over with and figure out what's next. We can't go back, but we have no path forward. Today determines a lot for us."

"Mhm," Clara agreed, knowing today held even more for her. Carver. Today, they would hand Carver over to the queen.

A knock sounded, "Must be Nate," Reese said as she bounced to answer the door.

Clara knew Reese was still hopeful there could be a relationship. For Reese's sake, she hoped Nate was interested in her or stable enough to let Reese down slowly. Clara wasn't convinced he was capable of either.

"Let's go, team," he said with far more enthusiasm than any of them had yesterday.

They filed out, with Clara closing the door behind them and Reese turning back to lock it.

Clara kept her eyes toward the ground until he was next to her. "Sleep okay?" He asked.

Even the simplest question from him made her heart flutter. Yesterday, she told him she loved him. Today, she was turning him over to the queen.

"Fine, you?" She didn't look up at him. She kept her eyes fixed on Nate's back as they started to walk down the hallway.

"You can't even look at me today?" He whispered, sending a shiver down her spine. No, she couldn't look at him. If she did, she would regret what they were going to do today. She had to stay focused. She had to protect her friends, even if that meant protecting them from what he had become.

"Clara," the way he said her name broke through some of her determination. She looked up at him. He smiled.

His arms were at his sides, and he was wearing long sleeves to cover the marks on his wrists. "Um," she tried to take in what she saw. Had Nate let him out? He must have, right? Nate would have noticed Carver wasn't wearing cuffs anymore. She glanced from Carver's wrists to Nate.

"Don't look so concerned. Nate told me if I could remember how I knew him, and prove that I'm actually Carver, he'd take the restraints off." Carver nodded along to his words.

Clara was still at a loss for a response. Did this mean they weren't turning Carver over to the queen? "Um, I'm sure you feel better now that those are off?" Clara cringed at her words, but she couldn't come up with anything better. She was far too thrown off by Carver's lack of restraints.

"I very much do. How would you feel about me holding your hand?" Her heart raced.

I would like that, she thought, but she said, "Let's talk about that later. I don't want there to be any reasons for concern when we go before the queen."

She faced forward, walking quickly to keep up with the group. "Clara? Are you upset that I'm not in cuffs anymore?"

The sadness in his voice pierced her heart. "No, Carver, no. I'm happy that you're remembering things. Genuinely, I'm so glad for that. I just," she paused. She had accepted his fate, accepted her fate. She had accepted she couldn't save him, that they weren't meant to be together. How could she still be torn between the two? How could she protect her heart and make sure she didn't hurt him? Maybe she couldn't. She stepped carefully down the stairs, finishing her thought over her shoulder to Carver. "I just didn't sleep very well, and I'm nervous about taking the radioactive material before the queen. I've heard so many different rumors, I'm not sure what to expect." She whispered the last part as they entered the room.

People still stared at them, but the stares were friendlier than the night before. Clara felt certain it helped that they no longer had a prisoner with them. Hauling prisoners around was generally a sure way to make people very uncomfortable. Portia led them through the streets, and Clara tried to make more of an effort to take in the sights of the city. It was overwhelming. The colors were so bright, the patterns so loud. Everywhere she looked felt like an assault to her eyes, while also being the most magnificent artwork she'd ever seen. She couldn't put it into the correct words.

"I've never seen anything like this," Carver said beside her.

She looked at him, a smile finding its way to her lips as she watched him take in the view. His eyes scanned each building, wide and excited. His mouth was slightly parted as if he was surprised by what he was witnessing. He probably was.

"I can't decide if it's gorgeous or absolutely atrocious," Clara admitted to him.

Carver brought his gaze from the buildings to hers, "Both sound like the right answer."

"Agreed," she laughed.

The morning air was cool, but it was a nice respite after all the time they'd spent in the sun on their journey.

"I remembered something else last night," Carver said quietly.

Clara was scared to ask, "What?"

"I bought a ring for you, didn't I? But I never gave it to you. It was gold with a single diamond in the middle, and two small ones on either side."

She nodded. They both walked in silence. Clara had tried so hard to forget the ring he had. He had even shown it to her. He told her that he would keep it until he graduated from basics, and then he would propose to her. She had been so excited. At the time, she wanted nothing more than to be his wife. She knew she had mentioned the ring to him when they left Noxvalis, but she hadn't given him details.

They walked down side streets and alleys, and every time Clara caught a glimpse of the town square, she thought it looked unreal.

The ribbons and outfits, the colors and music. She would have loved to sit off to the side and people-watch. She felt certain that with the elaborate display of color, the people here would be just as interesting.

59 CARRION

It was far easier than he expected to play the believable role of Carver. They all wanted him to be caring and reminisce to prove he was who they wanted him to be. He told Clara the truth. After he had remembered Nate's role in his life, he started to remember more. The memories had started like a trickle, but by the time he woke up this morning, he felt like he remembered most of Carver's life.

Still, Carver's life felt separate from him. Some of the emotions were there. He wanted to protect Clara, and golly, did he want to touch her again. But he also wanted to make King Herring proud, and he knew the king would not be pleased with his fraternization. It was a very tricky tightrope to walk. How much of Carver could he become to appease those around him, without losing himself in the process? Which one was he really?

Portia led them through the back entrances into the castle. The first hallway they entered appeared to be the servants' quarters, but she brought them through to an elaborate hallway. The floors glistened like gold. The light from multiple stained glass windows coated the floor, and all of it shimmered in every color of the rainbow. He wondered how anyone could focus at all amid so much color.

"Wait here with these guards. I will return when it is time for your entrance." Portia fixed each of them with a stern look. "Be on your best behavior. The queen doesn't usually grant audiences this quickly, but she feels like you wouldn't have come so far if it wasn't important." With a bow of her head, she left them. There were four guards stationed in the hallway around them, and though their gaze was fixed straight ahead, Carrion knew they were focused on their group.

"Why did you leave me in Noxvalis?" Carrion asked Clara.

Clara looked at him with an overwhelming sadness in her eyes. He wanted to reach out and comfort her, but after her earlier comment, he wasn't sure that would be well received.

"I didn't want to leave you. You saved me." Clara whispered.

"How did I save you?"

Clara shook her head, "You don't remember?"

He forced himself to focus on the last memory he had of her. Marsh was in that one. Were they at a bar? It looked like the same bar he had been in with the guards, which would explain why it felt so familiar to him. He felt a sense of panic as he tried to grasp the memory. Something was wrong. Something had happened. Clara had been in danger. Was there anything he could do?

Agonizing pain split his head. He barely heard Portia say, "The queen is ready for you," through the pain.

Clara grasped his arm, "Are you okay? We have to go in."

He straightened, allowing her to lead the way. He flexed his fists. His hands weren't bound anymore. He could complete his assignment. He could fulfill his duty to the king.

60 CLARA

She kept her head high and her posture perfect as they followed Portia into the throne room. She only touched Carver long enough to make sure he was following. Now, her hands were at her sides. Her shoulders were pulled back, and her eyes were focused. She wouldn't miss any details.

They followed Portia into the throne room. After how much color she'd seen, Clara was shocked by the room. Everything was white. Everything. The walls, the ceilings, the floor. Somehow, they were all a perfect white. The carpet under the throne was white, and the throne itself was white. The windows were clear, so no colored light came in. Everything was overwhelmingly sterile.

Clara swallowed hard. Her eyes sought out the queen as they walked. The queen sat casually on her throne, her arms over the armrests on either side. She watched them as they walked through the throne room, her eyes gracing each of them. Her lips were pulled tight.

Her golden hair was curled in perfect ringlets around her face. Clara didn't think she had ever seen someone so perfect. The queen's lips were tinted red, and her eyes sparkled in all the light. She tilted her chin forward just a touch as they entered. She seemed wholly fascinated by their entourage. She was so much younger than Clara expected. How did one so young garner so many rumors and such a reputation?

Portia stopped them and bowed to the queen. They all copied her movement. Ryker clutched his satchel to his side, and Clara really hoped the queen would take the materials off their hands. The last thing their group needed was to remain responsible for radioactive material.

"Please, stand." The queen's voice lilted throughout the room.

"Your Highness, I have brought the group." Portia bowed to the queen once more, then stood off to the side.

"Thank you, Portia." The queen's voice sounded like a melody. "Tell me, why have you come to my kingdom?"

Nate took one step forward from the group, "Your Highness, we are operatives from Quorath. We were sent to Noxvalis to retrieve a radioactive isotope so it couldn't be used against our kingdom. However, we believe that Quorath intends to use it, not destroy it. Additionally, we have reason to believe Quorath would rather see us dead than allow us safe return. We are requesting that you take the radioactive material under your possession, and grant us asylum here."

The queen laughed.

Clara glanced at Marsh and Reese. They both gave the slightest shake of their head. Nate looked over his shoulder at them as if to see if he missed anything. Clara raised a shoulder but dropped it before the queen could notice.

The queen continued laughing for several minutes. "Oh, I'm sorry. You'll have to forgive me." She finally said as she got her breathing under control. "Quorath and Noxvalis have been in an absolutely ridiculous feud for years now. I've been wondering how long it would be until someone finally made it to our door."

They waited for her to continue, but she didn't say anything. Nate motioned to Ryker, who held up the satchel, "We have the radioactive isotope stabilized in this satchel. We'd love to hand it over to you to keep safe. I'm sure you have a much higher capacity for that than we do."

"I'm sure I do," she agreed easily, and Clara started to feel relieved. "But I can't help you."

Clara's eyes widened, and she spoke up without thinking it through, "What? Why not?"

The queen's gaze snapped to hers, "I won't involve myself in this war."

"We're not asking you to involve yourself, Your Highness." Clara tried to course correct her interruption, "We're simply asking you to take this material and allow us to stay. Quorath assumes we're dead. Noxvalis assumes we're back in Quorath. We present no risk to you. No one would assume we came here."

"Why did you come here?"

Nate started to answer, but the queen held up a hand. "I'm asking her."

Clara swallowed hard. "We came here because we're tired of being caught in the middle between two evils. Neither Quorath nor Noxvalis seems to care about the number of lives being lost. They hail progress and scientific innovation, and write past the lives they sacrificed to build it. I'm a soldier at heart. I always thought I was fighting for a good cause. I no longer believe that."

The queen didn't respond for a moment. She just stared at Clara. Clara didn't look away, allowing the queen to stare into her soul as she assessed them. "Fine. I will take the radioactive material." The queen waved her hand, and two guards walked to Ryker and retrieved the satchel. Their footsteps echoed through the room as they walked towards the door with it.

"No!" The animalistic growl in the word reverberated, and ice climbed Clara's spine.

She pivoted to see Carver sprinting across the room at the guards. Two more guards pulled off the walls to stop him. Her heart stopped. What the hell was he doing?

She saw it in his motions. Carver didn't move like that. She covered her mouth with her hand to avoid gaping at him. He shoved through the two guards that tried to stop him, flipping one over his shoulder. The guard landed on the ground with a loud clank.

"Guards, cuff him." The queen said. She watched the scene play out, her expression remaining calm. Clara glanced between the queen, Carrion, and Nate. Nate's mouth was drawn into a tight line, the wrinkles on the corners pulling it even tighter.

Reese fidgeted with her hands in front of her, and Clara just watched it all happen. Carrion took down the first six guards in quick succession. Finally, one landed a blow with a blunt object on the back of Carrion's neck. Clara cringed as the sound echoed. But Carrion barely faltered. He turned, his lips pulled over his teeth in a snarl.

He grabbed the staff the next time the guard tried to hit him and yanked the guard into his chest. He pulled the staff from the guard's grasp and used it to knock the guard out before throwing the staff to the ground and facing the next guard.

Clara heard the sound before she recognized what had happened. They had a similar electric tool to the one Ryker had given them. One of the guards used it on Carrion, and Carrion slumped to the ground.

Clara's heart raced as she looked from Carrion to Nate to the queen. She hoped the queen wouldn't throw them out for this. "Take him to a cell. We'll deal with him later."

Clara wanted to protest, but she couldn't. He'd made his choice. She couldn't do anything about it. Her heart throbbed painfully, but she pushed the sensation away as she turned back to the queen.

The queen tsked at them, "Bringing a Noxvalis weapon into my court was a very poor idea."

The guards converged around them, and Clara could feel her pulse in her neck. "Your Highness, please, let me speak."

The queen's eyes narrowed on her, the calmness replaced with a carefully restrained anger. "You brought a Noxvalis abomination into my court, and you ask for permission to speak? Go right ahead, dear, but be prepared. These may be your last words."

"He was my partner from Quorath. We were sent to Noxvalis. He saved my life on our assignment, and they took him. I don't know what happened to him during that time." Clara reminded herself to breathe. At least the guards had stopped approaching them. "We, the group standing before you, were sent back to Noxvalis to retrieve the radioactive material. During this time, we found Carver. He didn't remember anything. Over the past several days, he's been with us, and he has started to remember his history, to remember us. Forgive us, Your Highness. We thought he was better. Believe me, if we thought he would present a danger to your court, we would not have brought him."

The queen smiled, and there was something feline about it. "You're well spoken for such a young girl. I won't punish you for bringing him. I understand your...sentimentality won over your judgement. However, you must understand I have to keep him now. I can't allow him access to my kingdom. He's a wild card, and not to be trusted."

Clara only nodded. She no longer trusted her voice to speak professionally when her heart was cracking. "Excellent. Additionally, I am going to require each of you to put on one of these anklets. My team is going to assess the material that you brought. You have requested asylum, and it is granted, provided you wear these."

Two of her guards stepped forward, holding out leather straps. Clara took hers, flipping it in her hand to survey it. The leather was flexible and soft with an adjustable lockable clasp. A black box was centered on the leather.

"What are these?" Nate asked.

"These are to ensure you remain in Calyndor and do not get into trouble. Clasp them onto your ankles, and my guards will come around to lock them."

Clara looked to Nate. Were they staying here? Were they willing to hand over a measure of their independence? He knelt to the ground and secured it around his ankle. When he stood, a guard came over and immediately locked it. The queen waited patiently as each of them followed suit.

"Portia will take you to the rooms I have designated for you. I understand you came here looking for asylum, so I assume you do not have much to your name. She will help you get situated. It is my request that you stay here at the palace until we have decided what to do with the radioactive material and you. Feel free to explore the rooms around your suite and the city. There's plenty to look into." The queen stared off into the distance as she finished speaking. No one else spoke up. "Dismissed," she said with a wave of her hand.

She didn't look at them again as they left. Portia met them in the hallway.

"The queen has had rooms established in the east wing for you." They followed her through the brightly colored palace, but Clara barely noticed any of it. Carver was gone. She had accepted he would be gone today, but after this morning, hope had resurrected. Now? She was terrified she would never see him again. She was terrified of what the queen could do to him.

Portia took them to a series of connected rooms. They each had a room with a dresser and a bed, and in the center of the rooms, there was a small living room and kitchen. The hallway to the rest of the palace connected through the living room.

"Please. Settle in. I'll send a servant up with some food." Portia bowed her head and left.

61 CARRION

He was going to fucking kill every single person who was laying a hand on him. His hands were bound again, but not by the same cuffs as before. These were even tighter. Even a fraction of a movement cut rivets in his already raw wrists. He snarled every time a guard stepped too close.

The white coats were back, and they were circling him like vultures. The machines were on, and he was tied to a chair, unable to move. He writhed, banging his head against the back of the seat in an effort to break something. After a few attempts, they restrained his head, and all he could do was snarl and snap. But they were smart enough to avoid his teeth, and that only made his fury rise.

He was so close. So close to retrieving the isotope and getting the hell out of there. But they had him bound in a way he couldn't break. What could he change? How could he break out? Nothing came to mind. He was going to die here.

Panic flooded his veins, and he didn't understand why. He wasn't scared of death; why would he be so scared of this? A needle was injected into his forearm, and though he writhed and growled, the white coat didn't stop.

The world turned hazy before everything faded to black.

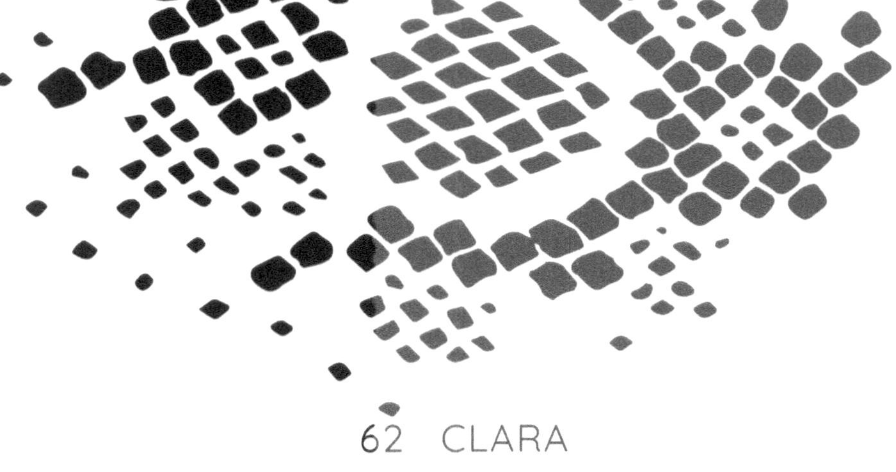

62 CLARA

"You can't rescue Carver again." Nate rubbed the bridge of his nose as they circled the same point they'd been talking around for the past 20 minutes.

"We didn't come all this way just to give up on him. We literally hauled him here. We're so close to being able to save him." Clara protested. Her logic wasn't working anymore. If she were honest, she knew Nate had a point. You couldn't save someone who didn't want to be saved. Carver certainly didn't want to be saved by them.

But there was a moment. A moment she was hanging onto.

"Clara, you need to accept that he played us. We were going to turn him over to the queen anyway. He turned himself in for us. You have nothing to feel guilty for, and nothing to try and fix. You're in the clear. You have to let this go."

Clara flexed and unflexed her hands at her sides, but she managed to avoid pulling her knives. She wanted to, though. She wanted to remind Nate just how powerful and how incredibly reckless she could be. However, recklessness wouldn't help her case here.

"Isn't there anything we can do?" Clara softened her voice as she said the words, hopeful that Nate could come up with a solution she couldn't see.

He shrugged, "It's out of our hands. Pick a room. Get some rest. Pace the floors. I don't really care, but I would like the opportunity to take a few minutes and process what just happened."

"Yeah, that was weird." Reese nudged the leather band on her ankle with the opposite foot. "It feels more like we're prisoners than here under asylum."

"If this is how they treat their prisoners, I would've broken their laws a long time ago." Marsh laughed.

Clara rolled her eyes. "Does no one care that they took Carver?"

Reese paused, taking a moment to actually stare Clara down. "Clara, you're the only one who believes it's still Carver." Her words were spoken softly, but they landed with the force of a runaway train. "We watched him over the last few days. It's not Carver. He's fully Carrion. He was playing you."

Clara glared at Reese, "No, he remembered things."

"No, Clara, he guessed things. You didn't see it because you were too entwined in him."

"He did remember some things," Nate argued, and Clara held her hand out to him as a thank you for proving her point. "But everything he remembered, he used as a weapon. He wanted to earn our trust so we would let him go, and he did just that. It wasn't Carver."

"He remembered me," her voice broke on the last word.

Reese walked across the room towards her until she had Clara wrapped in her arms. Clara buried her face in Reese's shoulder. She was embarrassed by her outburst, but more than that, she was heartbroken. All of her hopes for Carver were crushed, and she could do nothing but accept it.

Reese led her into a room, and she walked with her willingly. There was nothing left for her anymore. Her friends were alive. They retrieved the radioactive material. Her home was safe. Carver was gone.

"I don't want to be here anymore," she murmured to Reese. The reality of those words sank into her soul. It had been a long time coming–this feeling. She'd fought it for longer than she could remember. In every heartbreak, but she'd always found something to keep going for.

Her something to keep going for was gone. There wasn't a war for her to get involved in. Carver didn't exist anymore, and there wasn't an assignment she needed to prove herself on. She didn't need to keep going.

She slumped to the floor, and though Reese tried to adjust her grasp and catch her, Clara slipped right through. She crumpled and let her eyes gaze off in the distance. This was it for her.

"Clara," Reese's voice was firm, "Clara. Don't you dare. Clara, you're here with me. You're still part of this team. I know you're hurt. But we need you. You're my friend. Sit up and act like it."

Clara blinked slowly, hearing the words but unable to process them. She couldn't do anything. She tried to form words of her own, but they wouldn't come out. Reese kept tugging at her hand, trying to pull her off the floor and into the real world.

Finally, Reese gave up and lay on the floor next to Clara. "I know this sucks," she whispered to Clara.

Clara nodded, the tears finally coming. They streamed down her face with abandon. Every emotion she'd ever felt for Carver was released. They didn't stop flowing, and soon her nose was dripping too. And still, Reese stayed. Reese didn't touch her again or try to force her to get up. She just lay there.

Eventually, the light in the room began to fade. The colors dimmed, and finally, Clara felt like she could try to face the world. She owed it to Reese, right? She tried to convince herself. She tried to find some amount of goodness so that her friend didn't have to see her in this position.

"I'm going to take a shower," she told Reese. Her voice grated as it left her throat. It was only then that she realized she hadn't had anything to eat or drink all day. Her head pounded. "First, I think I need water."

Reese nodded and slipped out of her room. Clara braced herself against the bed. "Pull yourself together," she hissed to herself. She hadn't fallen apart like this even after leaving Carver in Noxvalis.

Then, she had an assignment. She had a purpose. She still had something to prove.

It felt like every time she tried to prove herself, she just got herself into trouble and hurt other people.

Reese returned with a glass of water and a piece of bread. Clara tried to smile, but it didn't work. "Dinner is bread?"

"I think it would be good for you to start with. I'm going to close your door while you shower, but don't you dare lock me out."

"You're a good friend, Reese."

Reese nodded, surveying Clara with concern in her eyes. She closed the door behind herself, and Clara almost ended up on the floor again. She told Reese she was going to shower, so she had to shower. She sipped the water and ate a couple bites of bread. It felt heavy in her mouth, like even the effort of chewing was too much for her. She stumbled her way into the bathroom, grabbing the doorframe for support.

It took her a few tries fumbling around to find the light switch, and she closed her eyes tightly when it came on and tried to blind her. She groaned. When her eyes finally adjusted, she saw she didn't just have a shower. She had a bathtub.

She took in the sight greedily. It had been a while since she'd had a bath, and sinking beneath the warm water sounded like an amazing idea.

She ran the water hotter than was comfortable, relishing the feeling of her skin going numb as she sat in the water. She pushed her finger through the water, mesmerized by its movement. She looked around the bathroom, confirming she was in fact alone, and then she submerged.

How long can I stay under? Will my body start to beg for air? Or can I slip away? Drowning was never the way she wanted to go. She knew that even as she forced herself to stay under the water. The water filled every sense she had. Her lungs burned, but she knew she could stay under for longer. How much longer?

She finally forced herself to surface, breathing heavily once her head was above the water. She wouldn't let Reese find her dead body here. She would give up on life at some point in the next few months once there was some space between her and Reese. They'd go their separate ways, Reese would end up with Nate, and Clara would be entirely alone. Then she could end it.

Reese knocked gently, and Clara told her to come in.

Reese pulled a towel from the shelf and laid it on the floor next to the tub before she sat down. "You doing okay?"

Clara just stared at the water. Answering felt like more of a commitment than she had in her.

"He could be okay," Reese tried to assure her.

Clara snapped her eyes to Reese, "I had finally accepted I would never have him. After three years of hating him, loving him, refusing to let him go, I was finally okay. Then this morning, he remembered. I know he remembered. It wasn't just an act. Something happened. He snapped. Now I have to pretend I'm okay with him being gone? While we're here surrounded in opulence, he's suffering!"

Reese didn't respond, just leaned against the tub. Clara sank back into the water, keeping her face above it this time. Killing herself would be stupid. "Do you think I could petition the queen to visit him? Surely, they haven't killed him yet, right?" Logic began to filter back into the dark places in her mind. She couldn't give up yet. There had to be something she could still do.

Her brain spun through the options. What could she do? What could she change? Maybe Nate would have better ideas than she did.

When she approached him again, he didn't give her a chance to ask before he said, "Nope."

"But," he held up a hand and stopped her again.

"We can't save Carver. Our position here is fragile enough as it is. I will not risk our lives for the sake of his, especially, and listen to me, Clara, especially when he's not even Carver!"

She silenced.

Reese squeezed her arm. "Don't you dare retreat again, Clara," Marsh said as she walked past. "We survived. So fucking survive."

63 CLARA

Three days passed with no updates. Clara refused to leave her room until Reese dragged her out on the third day. "There's a woman here to see you. She says she knows you, and I think she may know something about Carver." Reese told her.

Clara blinked hard. Julia? She rushed from the room. Julia was already seated on their couch, but stood when Clara walked in. "Oh, my dear." She gushed, rushing to wrap Clara in her arms. Clara didn't hug her back, too stunned by the interaction. "I can't imagine what you're feeling. Your wonderful husband? And they did this to him?"

Reese shot Clara a questioning look, but didn't say anything. "I'm okay," Clara mouthed at her. Reese nodded and left Clara alone with Julia.

"Have you heard anything about Carver?" Clara managed to say as Julia led her to the couch.

"Mark has inquired after him. He knows that Carver is alive, but we don't know much more than that. Is it true? What happened after we parted ways?"

Clara exhaled heavily. "Do you know anything else about Carver? If he will be kept a prisoner? If they can help him?"

Julia shook her head, concern shining from her eyes. Clara

slumped heavily into the couch. Julia looked at her awkwardly before taking Clara's hand. "I don't know how, but it will be okay."

Clara looked at the ceiling to avoid crying. "We weren't married, you know."

"I know. The queen called Mark in the afternoon after your appearance in court." Julia paused, "He obviously recognized Carver and was inclined to share how we knew you. The queen was hesitant to continue to grant you asylum since you had lied to us, but Mark assured her he felt your lies were only to harm Noxvalis."

Clara nodded in agreement. "Thank you."

"Of course. I don't know that there's much else we can do. Mark attested that Carver was not…what he is when we met the two of you. He was hoping his words would sway the queen towards compassion for Carver."

"Did it?"

Julia smiled softly, "We don't know. Mark has tried to find out what's happening to Carver, but he hasn't told me anything else. I'm sorry, I don't know more."

"I understand. Thank you for coming, and for petitioning the queen on our behalf. I'm very grateful. This is kind of twice now that you've saved us."

"Everyone needs a little saving sometimes," Julia answered. "Mark saved me, too. We feel it's our duty to return the favor to people who need it. However," Julia's voice grew stricter, "Don't lie to us again. We want to be on your side, but we don't appreciate liars."

"Of course, Julia. I'm sorry we had to lie to you in the first place."

Julia's smile returned, "I know this can't be easy for you, and I'm sure you need time. But please know, Mark and I are here for whatever you need. A tour of the city? Done. A place to have dinner with familiar faces? Absolutely. We're here, Clara. Even without Carver, you aren't alone."

Clara sniffed. Julia wrapped her arms around Clara. Clara didn't pull away, and before long, Julia started stroking Clara's hair. Neither of them spoke. Clara couldn't remember the last time she felt that calm.

64 CLARA

Days passed by in a blur, but Clara did her best to focus ahead. She took walks in the city with Reese and tried to smile when Reese pointed out all of the ridiculous outfits and fixtures. She spent each morning outside the courtroom, begging for an audience that was never granted. Julia still hadn't gotten more updates, and Clara's constant presence didn't seem to be effective.

She tried to laugh with Marsh at Nate when Nate ran out of clothes and started wearing the brightly colored ones from the closet. Her laugh fell flat and resulted in a sympathetic smile from Marsh, but at least no one commented.

She sat with Ryker as he explained invention after invention. As uncertain as he had been in coming to Calyndor, he seemed to be fitting in well with all of the opportunities, possibly better than anyone. The queen's scientists were quite interested to hear of his studies regarding the Noxvalis experiments, and he was more than happy to discuss his research.

Nate had begun consulting with the queen's security. They were fascinated to hear Quorath's approach to the war, and seemed to take his advice to heart. He wasn't allowed to participate in anything yet, but the queen allowed him to continue his discussions.

A full week had passed when Reese told her that Nate had officially asked her out. "I didn't expect it to happen this fast, but I guess we're all kind of settling?" She giggled, covering her mouth with her hand, "We're supposed to go out tonight." The smile faded as she looked at Clara.

Clara was sprawled on the couch, pretending to read one of the books she'd taken from the library. She hadn't read the synopsis or asked permission to take it. She'd been stuck on the first page for the past hour as she zoned out. She closed the book, realizing she hadn't actually made it past the dedication.

She forced a bright smile. "I'm so happy for you, Reese!" The words were true, but her positive emotion was fake.

Relief washed over Reese's face. Clara must be getting better at faking. "Okay, good. I wasn't sure if I should tell you or not."

"I'm still your friend, Reese," Clara assured her.

Reese nodded. "Nate also mentioned that the queen would love to have you talk to her soldiers about your experience. He knows you have more practical experience. You killed quite a few guards on your first trip in."

Her first trip in. A melancholy smile found a way to her face. "Did he say when?"

Reese shrugged. "I think it's an open invite. The queen hasn't permitted us to find lodging outside the palace, and I'm not sure any of us are complaining about that."

"Fair enough. I wouldn't mind doing something other than sitting in this room." It wasn't true, but Clara thought it would be encouraging for Reese.

Sure enough, Reese's smile grew. "I think it would be good for you to get involved in something here."

"Agreed," Clara smiled again, and this one felt more real. Her chest still ached, and the world still felt too gray, but she could make it. She could get past this. Right?

"Anywaysss, I need to get ready for tonight," Reese practically squealed. She pulled on Clara's hand, "Aren't you going to come help me?"

Clara was dragged into Reese's room. She sat gently on the edge of the bed as Reese dramatically threw the closet open. "I need to find the outfit that makes him say 'oh my gosh, I have to marry her or I will die slash hate the rest of my miserable existence.'"

Clara laughed, and Reese's smile brightened. "So, something slutty?"

Reese waggled her eyebrows, "Hey, there's so much more to me than that." She pulled out a dress with the sides cut out and a plunging V. "See? This would help show how much more of me there is."

They both laughed, and Clara started to relax as Reese tried on the various outfits. She finally settled on a short maroon dress. Her legs looked fabulous in it, and the sleeves cut off the shoulders, revealing her collar bones and just a tiny bit of cleavage. "You look amazing, Reese. That color is perfect on you."

Reese held out her hand, and Clara took it. "I'm so glad we're friends. And I'm glad you're okay. It's all gonna get better, okay?"

A knock sounded on Reese's door. She grinned, "I bet it's Nate," she practically sang.

"Would you like me to get it? Be your, what would that be, butler?" Reese laughed so hard she snorted, but she agreed.

Clara pulled her shoulders back, fixing an all too serious look on her face, causing Reese to snort again. She opened the door slowly, revealing Nate, "May I help you, sir?"

His eyebrows practically hit his hairline. "Um, I, uh," he stuttered, and Clara thought it was hilarious to see him so flustered.

"He's here for me, butler!" Reese called joyfully behind her. "You can let him in and dismiss yourself."

"As you wish, ma'am." Clara joked back. She nodded to both of them and left them to it.

She decided she needed a walk and started down the hallway to the main palace. "I was just coming to find you," Clara stilled at Portia's voice, but didn't startle.

"I was taking a walk," Clara wasn't sure why she felt the need to explain, but she did.

"The queen asked me to find you." Portia didn't elaborate.

"Did something happen? Is Carver okay?" She asked the question, but she knew they wouldn't give her an answer.

Portia pressed her lips together tightly. "Come with me, please."

Clara's heart raced. Anxiety clamped around her throat, but she followed Portia. She could stay calm and controlled. Portia led her through the halls, and though Clara had a decent idea of the castle's layout, she was beyond lost by the time Portia stopped. She opened the door to a room Clara hadn't been to before. The windows were closed, and the room was lit only by the fire in the fireplace.

The walls were covered in paintings. The furniture was a velvety blue, but looked like it hadn't been used in a long time. "Where are we?"

"I was instructed to leave you here and tell you to step outside on the balcony." Portia nodded her head and closed the door behind her.

Clara didn't move. She continued to glance around the room, waiting for something to jump out. Instinctively, she reached for her knives, but the guards had confiscated those the first day. She hadn't earned the trust necessary to carry weapons here yet.

She kept looking, trying to make sense of this order. The fire crackled, and she spun towards it. No one was there.

Carefully, she approached the doors to the balcony. One of the doors was cracked open, letting a sliver of the dying light in. She stepped to the side, careful to obscure herself from what she would find on the other side.

If this was her execution, she wasn't going down without a fight. She flung the door open, not sure what she expected, but surprised when nothing happened. When she realized nothing was going to come in, she walked out.

The balcony spanned the entire length of the room and was several feet wide. It was surrounded by a fence made of marble pillars. The top of it was about 8 inches of smooth marble. And in the corner furthest from her, there was a man with dirty blond hair leaning against the border and staring into the city.

Her lips parted, but she didn't call out. She had to be dreaming. It was the only explanation. Or it wasn't him. An additional explanation. She dug her thumbnail under the nail of her middle finger, and the stinging sensation proved she wasn't dreaming. Which meant she didn't know who was in front of her.

She approached on careful footsteps until she was within arm's reach. "The city is beautiful." It was his voice.

It felt like her heart stopped beating. Wait, no, she stopped breathing. It took her a second to realize that and remember how to breathe. Her stomach was on the floor. She was certain her jaw had dropped, but she didn't remember closing her mouth. "Carver?" Her voice was barely a whisper, but it was enough.

He turned to face her, a smirk playing across his lips. "It's been a while."

Clara closed her hands into fists, certain this was a trick. "Are you Carver? Or, Carrion?" She hated how uncertain she felt, but she had to know the truth.

He flexed his hands on the ledge. "I'm not entirely sure. Both? I think, maybe. I'm Carver, in that I remember who I am. The queen had her scientists do some kind of detox on my body and brain. I'm not sure how that worked, but I was out for a while." He looked up at her, "When I woke up, I remembered everything. And I'm so sorry." He grit his teeth, pausing as he said that. "I put you through so much, and you were just trying to help."

"I left you. I deserved everything you did to me and more. I deserved to lose you," she confessed.

He smiled ruefully, "You didn't deserve me scheming to kill you." He shook his head, "Anyway, when I woke up, I remembered everything. Every memory with you. I panicked. I thought I had actually killed you for a little bit. It took time for me to calm down and be able to actually process where I was and what had happened." He stared off at the city again, "So, I am Carver." Clara couldn't help but feel like he was trying to convince himself. "Yet I'm also Carrion. I can feel it inside, now. There's these instincts that I didn't have before. And my body. They changed me physically."

"I know," she whispered.

"I'm not sure what they did. I was unconscious for everything that's been done to me." He closed his eyes tightly, "I can only imagine how that's affected my mind. I'm both. Carver and Carrion."

They descended into silence. She didn't know what she was supposed to say. Her emotions were flip-flopping. She wanted to grab him and remind him how much she loved him. But was that the right move? What if he didn't still love her? What if he needed time before he was ready?

She would give him anything he wanted. She was just happy he was alive. She took a couple of deep breaths, trying to ground herself in this moment. He was alive.

65 CARVER

What he told her was a summary. He didn't talk about the hours that he was awake for. The detoxing process was insanely invasive and painful. Today was the first day he could talk normally. The last couple, his voice had been too hoarse from the screaming.

He'd thought about her a lot. As the detox took effect, he'd pictured her face when he needed a reason to get through it. He had a million things he wanted to say to her. But he didn't know what she would say back. Was she ready for him to tell the truth?

Everything from the past few weeks, the time he was Carrion, felt like a blur. Had she told him that she loved him and meant it? Or was it an attempt to bring him back to himself? What was she actually feeling?

Right now, it felt like there was ice between them, and one wrong move would drown them both.

"Clara, I–" he started to say, just as she started to say, "Carver–" they both cut off and chuckled nervously.

He turned away from the railing, leaning his back against it so he could look at her. The sun was setting behind her, making her glow. He smiled, and she smiled back. "You go first," she offered.

He forced himself to keep his eyes on her. "The only part I haven't sorted in my mind is everything that happened while I was Carrion. I don't fully remember what I said or did, and I don't know how much of it I meant vs how much of it was to get what I wanted from you." He stopped for a moment, but she didn't interrupt. She was so beautiful. He prayed to anyone that would listen that he wouldn't lose her. Not after all of this.

He inhaled deeply. "That's besides the point. Clara, I messed up." Her eyes widened. "I never should have broken up with you all those years ago. You're not weak. You're the strongest woman I know. I would be so proud to be your man." He took another breath. "I understand if that ship has sailed and you want nothing to do with me, but I love you. I love you, Clara. I love you so much. I don't want to lose you."

His eyes scanned hers, and he noted the slight drop of her jaw. "Carver, I," she shook her head, looking away from him.

His heart plummeted. Oh. "Oh, I mean," he began, trying to cover how much the rejection hurt.

She rushed towards him, throwing her arms around him. He relaxed into her embrace, holding her close. *I guess this is goodbye.* She pulled back from him, but he let his hands linger on her waist. If he was losing her, he wanted to hold on for as long as she could.

She looked up at him, and moved her hands from his shoulders to the sides of his face. She cupped his face, staring deeply into his eyes. He shifted, feeling all the emotions he'd ever had for her at once. He was truly and deeply in love with this woman. He would do anything to prove it.

"Carver, I love you too. I've done a lot of shitty things I hope you can forgive. But I want you too." She glanced down as if she was shy.

He took his right hand and tilted her chin up. "Good." He whispered, "Darling."

She smiled, and he took his opportunity.

He pressed his lips to hers, and when she kissed him back, he gently parted her lips with his tongue. She leaned into him, and he wrapped his arms around her back, pulling her flush against him, letting her feel just how much he wanted her. She kissed him just as hard, slipping her tongue into his mouth in return. She groaned against his lips, and it was all he could do to pull away and look at her.

Her cheeks were flushed, her eyes sparkling in the little light that remained. "Are you sure you want this?" He asked against her lips. He couldn't stand to pull away more than that.

"Yes," she whispered back, kissing him again and capturing his lower lip with her teeth. This time it was his turn to groan.

They stayed on the balcony until the sun fully set and the night air thoroughly chilled them. Then they moved to the floor in front of the fireplace.

Clara lay her head in Carver's lap, and he stroked her hair, so scared that this was only a moment in time. How long until it burst, and he didn't have her anymore?

He reached into his pocket and pulled out the gold necklace. He dangled it in front of her. "Would you accept this necklace from me?"

She reached her fingers up, taking the necklace from him carefully. "I love you," she whispered. "Put it on me?"

She sat up, and he traced his fingers over her neck as he clasped the necklace. She shivered. "I love you too."

She leaned back into him, and he wrapped his arms around her tightly. If he had it his way, he'd never let her go again.

"Was it worth it?" He asked softly as they stared at the flames.

"Was what worth it?"

"The cost we paid to be here. To have this. Was it worth the years spent apart and the mistakes we made?"

She didn't answer for so long he thought she wasn't going to. He did his best to relax, even without her answer. Finally, she said, "Yes. Everything worth having has a high price. I wouldn't want to go through it all again, but I would if that was the cost of attainment. The price of us."

EPILOGUE

Eventually, the queen trusted them enough to allow them to live outside of the castle. She even helped them find jobs and truly integrate into society. As much as they urged her to take the war with Noxvalis and Quorath seriously and intervene, she said it wasn't yet in her best interest, but she would take it under consideration.

Clara was surprised by how quickly their life and routine started to feel normal. She spent her mornings working in the local library and her afternoons training the guards. While the queen wasn't ready to involve herself in war, she wasn't averse to preparing for it. The guards had spent far too long without strict instruction, and Clara thrived on being in charge.

Carver dropped out of warfare altogether and decided to write a book. Clara had stolen a couple of his journal entries, and that was all it took for her to encourage him to pursue writing, so he did.

Every morning when he woke up, he expected to see his bed empty. But every morning, she was there. He kept waiting for it to feel normal, but so far it hadn't. In fact, every day seemed to bring a new surprise. He'd even managed to find a ring to replace the one he'd left behind in Quorath. He couldn't believe how much joy it brought him to see it sparkle on Clara's finger.

Nate proposed to Reese after only a few months in the city. She was desperate to start a family, and while he was hesitant, everyone knew he would give in to her.

Ryker was officially hired to work for the queen's science department. The advances they had made to combat Noxvalis were impressive but outdated, and he was determined to get them up to speed.

No one was 100% sure what Marsh did anymore, but she seemed happy. Carver and Clara saw her every couple of weeks, and Clara was pretty sure Marsh and Ryker were together, but neither of them would confirm it.

A year passed as they adjusted to "normal" life, and still Clara felt on edge. She wasn't sure what was going to come next, but she was prepared. She had Carver, and that was all she needed to take on the future.

ACKNOWLEDGMENTS

Wow. Writing this book took more than I thought it would. I can genuinely say I wouldn't have made it to the end if my husband hadn't pushed me here. Ben, thank you for standing by my side, encouraging me, and taking on my responsibilities so I had the time to write. I am forever grateful for you, and excited I get to call you my husband!

To my friends. Thank you for listening to me talk about this book for months, and for being the first to order and support me. I am grateful for all of you!

ABOUT THE AUTHOR

Alex Lane started writing at 11 and is beyond thrilled to have published two books. She loves all things fantasy, romance, sci-fi, and dystopian. For more information, and to keep up with coming releases follow her on social media (@alexlanecreative) or visit her website:

www.alexlanecreative.com

Sign up for her newsletter to receive bonus content from the Rules Duology!